Bitter Bayou

KAILEE SAUNDERS

This book contains on-page intimate scenes and is intended for mature audiences only. For more details on the content warnings for this novel, please visit: www.kaileesaunders.com/bitter-bayou

For Grandma Edie.
You put that first romance novel in my hands and started
a fire nobody could extinguish.
Love you always.

One

His evening began with three stolen cigarettes and ended with a body in the duck pond.

As the sun sank behind the trees and speckled the patio in leafy shadow, Cade Thurstan made his move. Ducking low, he weaved across the crowded concrete slab. Adults, decked in sparkling gowns and silk cummerbunds, didn't notice his slight frame hunched near their waists. Whether due to his stealth skills, the dim string lights, or the copious amount of champagne flooding their bloodstreams, Cade wasn't sure. But it didn't matter. He seized the opportunity and snuck through the mansion's back door.

Inside, he veered toward the kitchen. Servers supported silver trays on their shoulders while chefs buzzed from fridge to oven, pantry to countertop. Dish clatter and endless chatter made it hard to think.

Seeking solace, he slid onto the lowest shelf of the steel island, plucked the walkie-talkie from his belt and whispered, "In position. Target in sight, over."

His cousin's voice broke the static. "Acknowledged. You're clear to head in, Agent. We'll reconvene at, um ..."

He rolled his eyes. "Nineteen hundred."

"Nineteen hundred, right. Good luck, Agent. Over and out."

Cade huffed. James Bond never dealt with such incompetence.

Clipping the walkie on his waistband, he moved behind a potato sac and observed his target.

A chubby man loomed over a quadrant of saucepans, drizzling oil into each. As if on cue, the liquid spattered, dotting grease on the man's chef jacket and sending him in search of a rag. A perfect distraction. Cade darted to the coat rack, and removed a pack of cigarettes from one of the pockets. He grabbed three of them, then returned the box.

Just in the nick of time.

"Evening, Cade," the chef called, lumbering across the tile.

"Hi." Though this man had worked in the mansion for many years, Cade didn't know his name. His family employed several people to tend to the chores—cooking, gardening, cleaning—and it was too difficult to memorize all the names. He did, however, know two things about the man: he enjoyed his smoke breaks and usually left his jacket unattended.

"You enjoying the party?" the chef asked.

"Yep. Sure are lots of people here." He toyed with the cigarettes in his back pocket, and glanced at the exit.

"Your mom's a popular woman. You hoping for a peek at the birthday cake? Because I'll let you know now, Renee told me not to let you anywhere near it."

"Darn." He snapped his fingers, reversed. "Guess that plan failed. Have fun at the party, bye!" Before the chef probed further, Cade whisked from the kitchen and rejoined the patio festivities.

The guests were dancing now—a tradition once the sun dipped. He shimmied along the wall, wrinkling his nose at the perfume and cologne hanging pungent in the air. He really shouldn't complain about the scents; a few more hours and this whole area would reek of body odor. Nothing could withstand Louisiana's summer heat. Even the black tupelos framing the yard ached for a cooling breeze. Wiping his tux sleeve over his forehead, he continued toward the meeting spot at the base of the willow tree.

Except his cousins weren't waiting for him.

Scanning the crowd, he searched for their brunet heads. They'd cemented the plan hours prior: Cade would steal the cigarettes while they found a lighter, then they'd all meet back here. He'd been assigned the more difficult task, so where were Lawrence and Greg?

He found his answer beside the DJ table where their butler, Peter, was dragging his cousins across the patio. The dummies got caught.

"Kincade Thurstan"—Peter dropped the boys' forearms and motioned for them to stand beside Cade—"you want to tell me why I caught these two pick-pocketing this?" In his hand, he held a scarlet-red lighter.

Cade glared at his cousins and plastered an innocent smile. "We wanted to light a fire and make s'mores."

"S'mores, huh?" Peter crossed his arms. "Give them here."

"Give what?"

"The cigarettes, Cade."

"You tattled?"

At Cade's evil eye, Greg shuffled behind his older brother. Though, with his flicking gaze, Lawrence didn't look too brave himself.

"I didn't want to get in trouble," Greg squeaked.

"And he was blabbing before I could stop him!"

"That's enough, all of you." Peter stuck out his hand. "Come on, Cade. Give them here."

Slumping his shoulders, he dug out the cigarettes and passed them over. "So unfair."

Peter pointed at Lawrence and Greg. "You two, scoot. I'd like to talk to Cade alone." Once the cousins were out of earshot, he sighed. "What's this all about? You've never stolen before."

"Why're you blaming me? Lawrence could've masterminded everything."

"I figure the oldest is the one calling the shots. Am I wrong?"

He kicked a tree root. "No."

"So, out with it. What's going on?"

"I wanted to try smoking."

"Why?"

He shrugged.

"If you won't tell me, maybe you'll tell your mom."

"No!" His head shot up, and he snatched Peter's sleeve. "Please don't tell Mom. I don't want to wreck her birthday."

Peter looked down. Mom always said he had alligator eyes, a fact which never made sense to Cade considering their butler wasn't at all vicious. Quite the opposite, actually. Peter has stepped in when Cade's father had died, playing catch and attending baseball games. He was practically family.

But that didn't stop him from being strict. "Tell me why you're stealing, and I'll think about not telling Renee."

"'Cause they all smoke them," Cade said, gesturing to the throng of people dancing to some hip-hop song. "Smoking's real adult, just like wine and taxes. And I want to be an adult."

Peter shook his head, smiling. "You've got a few years for that yet."

"I don't want a few years. I want to work at TIG just like Mom and Auntie."

Thurstan Industrial Group, TIG for short, was one of America's largest manufacturing companies, and the source of their wealth. His mother worked there, grandparents too. A tradition which, at age twelve and three quarters, he yearned to continue.

Peter ruffled Cade's blond hair. "You'll get there. Think of it this way: you'll be an adult, working and sweating away at the company for at least thirty years, but you only have six more to be a kid. Why not enjoy them?"

"Easy for you to say. You're already old."

"What a compliment." He put a fist over his chest, simulating a stab to the heart, and Cade giggled.

"All these people are here to celebrate Mom's birthday and everything she's done." Scanning the partygoers, he sighed. "You think I'll be that successful when I'm older?"

"I know you will."

"Really? You mean it?"

"Sure I do." Peter smiled. "You convinced your cousins to steal a lighter in front of five hundred people. With those persuasion skills, you'll have no problem being an executive. Now, rumor has it they're bringing out dessert soon. How about making sure we're the first ones in line?" At Cade's nod of approval, they headed back to the party.

His mom, a vision of sleek blonde curls and red lipstick, waved and walked over to them. She slicked a hand over his hair, the comforting way mothers do, and he leaned into her gown. "You having a good time, sweetheart?"

"Yep. We're looking for the cake."

"I got vanilla, especially for you." She grinned and pecked his forehead. To Peter, she said, "Thank you for watching the boys."

"My pleasure." Peter motioned to the DJ, who beckoned Mom to the stage. "Looks like they're calling up the guest of honor."

In awe, Cade watched his mother thank the guests for their birthday wishes and charity contributions. She'd requested donations rather than gifts because she prided herself on public service and giving back to the community.

Good woman.

He heard those words frequently throughout the evening, from the district attorney, the state governor, and a handful of others he didn't know.

Hours passed, and his eyelids started to weigh more than the dessert in his tummy. At midnight, Cade glanced at his watch. Not some Velcro-banded one either; this watch was silver and heavy and very grown-up. Everybody said so.

He'd enjoy his final years of childhood, just as Peter said, then he'd join his mother in the executive suite of TIG. As the oldest, running the company was his destiny. And boy, was he excited.

For now, he was old enough to realize when it was time for bed. He didn't need to be tucked in—they'd stopped doing that a long time ago—but, because he wanted to wish her happy birthday one more time, tonight he searched for his mother.

Music poured from speakers as the crowd, thinner now, picked at the dessert platters and polished off the remaining alcohol. He spotted his grandparents by the buffet table, his aunt and cousins on the dance floor, and Peter sweeping up a broken champagne flute. But where was Mom?

Cade tugged on his aunt's sleeve. "Have you seen Mom anywhere?"

She tapped her lip. "Last I heard, she was going for a walk. Is everything all right?"

"Yes." To reassure her, he grinned. "Just wanted to say goodnight."

"Speaking of which"—she glanced at his cousins, both high on sugar and dancing like maniacs—"should probably get them to bed soon. You want help looking for Renee first?"

"I can go by myself."

Like a proper adult.

Cade wasn't afraid to leave the safety of the patio lights. Felt no unease as he ventured beyond their manicured lawn and into the wetlands framing their acreage. He knew the way; Mom had taken him on walks around the property several times. Though, never at night.

A breeze hissed through the trees, tickling the hairs on his neck. He unclipped his bowtie and took a shaky breath. This was the way they usually walked—he was sure of it. He recognized the citrusy aroma and the mush of the ground. "M-Mom?"

Nothing. The crickets didn't call, the katydids didn't sing. Cade swallowed and continued walking.

He wasn't allowed out this far, where the dirt turned to mud and the woodland creatures to swamp creatures. He glanced over his shoulder. Had she returned to the house? No. Auntie would've shared where he'd gone, and Mom would've come searching for him. She didn't like him being out after dark. Especially alone.

Something urged him forward. Like a rope encircling his waist, it pulled him farther and farther into the darkness. The tree canopy thickened, and he stuck his hands out, feeling his way through the dangles of moss. Careful steps, Cade reminded himself, don't need to scrape a knee or stub a toe and be lost in the bayou all night.

A scream splintered the branches. High-pitched, terrified.

Mom. Oh God, could it be?

He tore deeper into the brush, pulse clobbering his ears and nightmares polluting his mind. Was she out here? Was she in trouble? He yelped as another shriek sliced through the trees. This time, it was accompanied by flapping wings.

"Bats." Saying the word aloud did nothing to lengthen his breaths or calm his heart. "Just bats, hunting the night bugs, making it all quiet."

Sound, logical. But he didn't want sound and logical; he wanted his mom. Cade called for her, and finally, something called back.

A deep, guttural grunt.

Following the sound, he emerged near the pond edging their property, and what floated in the water brought him to his knees.

Mom. Face down. Her gown lapping with the waves.

Cade screamed.

"Help! Somebody help!" He raced into the pond, tugging and yanking, trying to drag her to shore. His feet slipped on the sediment, and liquid filled his nostrils and stung his eyeballs. Panicked, he thrust upward and hacked out water. The mud was too slick, Mom too heavy. He couldn't save her, couldn't help her. He kicked and kicked, clinging to her head, trying to keep her chin above water. Flashlights wagged in the darkness, and voices shouted his name. He opened his mouth to cry out, but the pond water silenced him.

Mom didn't struggle or open her eyes. Her hair was matted to her cheeks, her body limp and sodden.

That last image of Mom branded his brain, flashing like a psychedelic picture show as an ambulance barreled onto the property and loaded her up. His aunt and grandmother hopped into the patient compartment while Peter held his hand, repeating how she'd be okay, how nothing would keep Renee away from her child.

Nothing—except death.

Pepaw broke the news hours later: accidental drowning.

"Liar!" Cade shook his head, tears spouting down his cheeks. "Stop lying."

"Cade, baby, listen to me." Memaw stroked his bangs off his forehead and cupped his cheeks, but he wasn't in the mood to be coddled.

He scrambled to where Pepaw was staring out the window with bloodshot eyes. "She's coming home. You'll see." He bumbled with his grandfather's dress shirt, clutching its hem. "The doctors will fix her. They just need more time, more money, and she'll heal up real good. You'll see."

Pepaw turned away, rubbing his eyelids with thumb and forefinger, his shoulders shuddering. Cade froze. Was he crying? Impossible. Pepaw didn't cry. Unless …

"No." Cade's limbs hardened to granite, and his oxygen evaporated. Wheezing, he stumbled forward, blinded by a tide of tears. Dead? How could she be dead? He buckled to the floor. "Mom wouldn't leave me. She wouldn't."

"For heaven's sakes, help the boy!" Pepaw thrust from the windowsill, scraping his fingers through his hair.

Memaw collapsed and bundled Cade into her arms. Pressed her lips to his curls, rocked him. "I know, darling, I know. Let it out. You let it all out now." She began humming a lullaby, but the sound brought no comfort. Nothing would. Ever again.

"Where are you going, Ian?" Memaw asked.

Cade looked up. His cousins were huddled on the couch, sniffling and wiping their weepy eyes. Auntie sat beside them with her arms locked around her knees, her pupils large and unfocused. Peter stood behind them all, supplying the tissues.

Pepaw placed his hand on the room's archway. "The office."

"Now?" Memaw's voice cracked.

"Preparations need to be made. Stockholders contacted, succession plans redrawn."

"No. You can't. Not after we just lost—"

"I need to be alone, Perla."

Cade burrowed deeper into her neck, and Memaw tightened her arms around him, her glare searing her husband.

"I'll be back soon. Comfort the child."

Child. The word had him wailing again. No child could endure this raw agony and survive. He was officially an adult. His wish, granted.

The sadness stayed with him through the wake and the funeral. Lingered behind his eyes for every forced smile, every "thank you for coming" he whispered in the receiving line.

Years passed, and his devastation waned. He learned to nullify the nightmares, to smile at old memories and cherish the good times. His mother was at peace, her drowning an accident.

And for two long decades, Cade believed that lie.

Two

Twenty Years Later

Maren Sharpe had a superpower. She couldn't shape-shift, teleport, or move objects with her mind. No, her ability was far less useful. Monday to Friday, during business hours, she could tell time with her nose.

Herbed cream cheese and strong coffee signaled half-past nine—her manager's arrival time. Isaac Primrose shouldered into the building carrying a slathered everything bagel and a piping Starbucks cup. He headed straight for his office, acknowledging nobody.

Maren spent the next few hours sorting through emails, and grimaced when scents of banana and peanut butter wafted toward her cubicle. In the kitchen, a blender screeched as Primrose traded his caffeine for an afternoon protein shake. Nobody dared inform him of the receptionist's peanut allergy; he wouldn't care.

When a sweaty stench permeated the walls, she smiled. She looked forward to her boss's workouts because sweat meant it was a quarter to five. Almost time to leave.

Fifteen minutes later, Primrose's secretary tapped on her partition. "Mr. Primrose would like to speak to you."

She groaned inwardly. "Five o'clock on a Friday? Can't be good news, can it?"

The secretary offered a sympathetic smile. "I read Friday afternoon is the best time for promotions."

"Where'd you read that?"

"Some magazine," she said, waving dismissively. "Anyway, he's in his office whenever you're ready."

Maren gathered her things, sighing at the holes on the bottom of her backpack. Hopefully, the fabric would hold until payday. After tucking her laptop into the front pocket, she squared her shoulders and headed down the hallway. Gray cubicles lined the walls, and desks were cluttered with bobbleheads, snow globes, and other knick-knacks that failed to improve her mood.

"Mr. Primrose?" She rapped on the doorframe. "You wanted to see me?"

"Sit."

His office resembled an unwashed community center. Smelled like one too. Neon-green weights rested in the corner, still shiny with palm sweat, and glossy exercise magazines littered the otherwise empty bookshelves. She wrinkled her nose, sank into the peeling leather chair, and spackled a smile.

Perched in his plush throne, Primrose waited for her to settle. "I read your latest manuscript."

"And?" She leaned forward. "What'd you think?"

"It's terrible."

Her shoulders sagged.

Primrose slapped down her manuscript, and slid it across the desk like a soiled napkin. Maren thumbed through the biography. Months of drafting and revision, all contained within these four hundred pages.

And he inked up her words like they were nothing.

Gritting her molars, she returned the manuscript. "With all due respect, this is my usual quality. You've never had a problem with my work before."

"No doubt you're talented. You were my top employee, even. For a while." He scratched his ear, and white flakes fluttered onto his blue tracksuit. Swatting them away, he continued, "But the world's changing, and Primrose Publishing needs to change with it. Nobody wants to read fluffy biographies anymore."

"What do they want to read?"

"Drama." Primrose tapped his tablet and scrolled through various articles. "Our customers spend hours perusing social media, seeing stories about happy families. Who wants to read that in a biography too?"

"I do. I pride myself on working closely with my clients and creating something we're all happy with." She cringed at the screen. "These are nothing more than paparazzi puff pieces. I write facts, Mr. Primrose, not fiction."

"I'm not asking you to lie. The opposite, actually: I'd like you to spend *more* time with them. Dig deeper into their histories and see what skeletons are hiding in their walk-in closets."

Her eyes widened.

Most of her clients were celebrities, politicians, or other public figures; undoubtedly, they harbored secrets. Expose those to the world? No. She worked as a biographer solely for the money, and even she wouldn't stoop that low to garner sales.

"I can't. My clients trust me, and I won't backstab them."

"Fair enough. You have ethics, that's admirable. I would encourage you to think on it though." He smirked. "Because, thing is, the universities let out soon. For months I've had fresh grads knocking down my door, begging for a position in publishing. They're eager." His finger popped up. "Cheap." Another finger. "And malleable."

Three fingers. Three reasons she was replaceable.

"You can't just give them my job. I've worked here for seven years."

He shrugged. "New York's an at-will state. Doesn't really matter how long you've worked here."

"I still have rights. If you're firing me to hire some young graduate, I'll argue you discriminated based on my age. That's illegal."

"Will you be able to afford the lawsuit?"

Maren shoved her fists beneath her thighs and blew a breath. Was there a choice? He was asking her to choose between money and morals—and she needed the money.

Her expression must have displayed her defeat because Primrose, with his wretched smile, leaned back and rested an ankle on his knee. "Now, I understand you have an upcoming project."

"Yes. The Thurstan family."

He whistled. "Now that's a name. Southern money, business empire. Catch one of them in an affair or money laundering scheme and our books will fly off the shelves."

"Just so we're clear, I won't lie about anything."

"Not expecting you to."

"I'll press harder during interviews, maybe snoop a bit. That's it."

"Music to my ears." He rose, planting his hands on the desk. "But, just so *we're* clear, I am expecting you to find something. One tiny scandal: that's not too much, is it?"

"No." Maren glanced at the clock. "If that's everything, I'd better be going. My sister's expecting me."

"Run along. And Maren?"

She stopped on the threshold and turned around.

"Keep me posted while you're in Louisiana, hm?"

With a nod, she strode from the office and flew down the stairs. Alone in the lobby, she cussed and kicked the door. Taking out her anger on inanimate objects didn't solve her problem but damn, it felt good.

Pedestrians choked the sidewalk and towers jutted through the clouds. Throwing her elbows, Maren took her place amongst the perspiring commuters. At the crosswalk, she billowed her blouse. Sweaty. Uncomfortable. She despised summers in New York City.

She stepped off the curb as the walk signal chimed, and her head ripped left at the sound of a blaring horn. A taxi was barreling toward her, and at the last second, she dove out of the way. A bunch of voices spoke to her as the car fishtailed to a stop.

"Holy shit, are you okay?"

"That was close!"

Maren wiped the blood from her elbow and dusted the gravel off her knees, swearing when she noticed the rip in her nylons. Her last pair, ruined.

"What the hell are you doing, girl?" the taxi driver yelled.

"Me?" She scoffed, pointing at the traffic light. "I had the right of way, asshole. Slow down! This isn't a racetrack."

The man sneered at her before speeding down the street, and she glared after him. Maybe it wasn't just the season she hated, maybe it was the whole goddamn city.

FREE FROM HEAT-CRAZED NEW Yorkers, Maren wrestled open the door to her building. The elevator didn't work, so she took the stairs, careful not to step in mold or get a splinter from the banisters. Her mother used to pester their landlord about doing some renovations, but that old crone didn't want to spend a dime on this place. Still, the apartment had some positives: cheap rent—for the city—and climbing six flights of stairs every day eliminated the need for a gym membership.

Maren toed off her ballet flats and tossed them in the entranceway closet. "Min, you home?"

"Kitchen!"

She crossed the threadbare carpet, inhaling deeply. Sauteed garlic and tomato: her first pleasant scent of the day. "Smells good. What're we having?"

"Spaghetti. I'm really letting the spices get fragrant. You want a taste?"

"Sure." She dropped her backpack on a barstool, and smiled at her little sister who resembled an animated princess with that apron cinched around her waist.

Minowa scooped some tomatoes from the pot, a blonde ponytail bobbing at her crown and moisture glistening on her nape. She twirled from the oven, and the spoon clattered on the counter. "What happened? You look awful."

"I ... tripped on the way home."

"Tripped?" She retrieved the spoon, dropped it in the sink, and crossed to where Maren was slumped on a chair. "Must've been one heck of a fall because you look like somebody just shot your puppy."

"It's a similar feeling. Did you clean today?" The carpet was covered in vacuum treads, and the couch appeared fluffy and inviting. A total façade—the stuffing would separate as soon as your butt hit the cushions, and it'd feel more like a hammock than a sofa. She glanced at the freshly dusted picture frames. Paintings of exotic beaches and colorful fruit hung alongside the snapshots from Maren's college ceremony and Minowa's high school graduation. Happy images, none of which included their mother.

"Uh-huh. I had some time between classes this afternoon so I popped home and—hey, stop changing the subject. Wait there."

While her sister rummaged through a bathroom cupboard, Maren scrubbed her hands over her face. Monotonous job, overbearing boss, grueling commute. Definitely not the lifestyle she'd pictured having at thirty-one. But at least she had one thing going for her: an unbreakable bond with her little sister. Single with two kids to raise, their mother had worked three jobs to keep food on the table. So, for an enormous chunk of childhood, Maren had been left to care for Minowa and decades later, she was still the rock.

But cracks were starting to show.

Minowa returned with an ointment tube in hand, and squeezed a dollop onto Maren's scratched elbow. "You should be more careful. Who knows what kinds of diseases are on those sidewalks?"

"Yes, ma'am."

"There. Right as rain." She stood up and gripped her hips. "What else is bothering you?"

"How do you know there's something else?"

"Gut feeling. Crap." Frowning, Minowa rounded the counter and scraped the burned bits from the saucepan. With a twist of her wrist, she opened a jar of store-brand pasta sauce and dumped it in. "That'll do. Now, tell me what's wrong—and don't you dare say nothing."

Maren never complained about work at home. If her sister knew the issues, she'd demand Maren's resignation and begin strategizing how to ease their financial troubles. They could apply for loans, find rich men. Or Minowa could postpone her pre-law studies to find work. That had never been an option.

Until now.

How much longer could she endure this routine? How many more years could she tolerate a manager who had no sense of workplace etiquette or human decency? With her sister working, Maren could conduct a proper job search, and find something more stimulating. Minowa was smart; she'd be able to juggle a part-time job with her college studies. This could work. She'd tell Primrose to shove his precious Louisiana assignment and find happiness again. All she had to do was talk to her sister.

"I've just been having some issues at work, that's all," Maren said.

"Oh?" Minowa tasted the spaghetti sauce and smiled.

"My boss pulled me into his office today and ..." She trailed off, staring at the envelope sitting beside the dish rack. "What's that?"

"Open it."

Curious, Maren read the letter. Gasped. "Is this real?"

"No, dummy. I faked an acceptance letter." Minowa's eyes sparkled. "Of course it's real. I'm going to NYU!"

She leaped forward and trapped her sister in a hug, catching a mouthful of hair as they laughed and swayed. "Congratulations, Min. You've worked so hard for this."

Law school. Unreal.

"We both have." Minowa pulled back, her cheeks balling. "I hope this won't be a problem. I've applied for dozens of scholarships, but money might still be tight."

"You don't need to worry about that. God, I'm so proud of you." Maren stared down. Like a cedar next to bonsai, she towered over her sister. And height wasn't the only thing differentiating them. Maren was brunette while Minowa had a halo of bright blonde. But eye color, that they shared: a marriage of brown and gold. Minowa's eyes shone when she was happy—a sight that never failed to warm Maren's heart. She'd spent hours in front of the bassinet, giving tickles and raspberries, squealing when her little sister bared a toothless grin. Even then, she knew she'd do anything for that baby. With law school no longer a pipe dream, could Maren disappoint her now? Could she finally prioritize her own needs?

She shelved those questions for the time being. Right now, their shabby kitchen bore all the happiness of a delivery room. And nothing, not staggering life decisions or spewing stovetop sauce, would quell that joy.

THEY LOUNGED ON THE couch with brimming stomachs, listening to the mumble of the television and the whir of the traffic below the window.

"What was it you wanted to say earlier?" Minowa asked. "We sort of lost track in the hubbub."

Maren tapped her lip. Say nothing, and she'd have to deal with Primrose's bullshit for another four years, the rancid smells and tightrope walking, the ethical pressures and veiled threats. Say something, and she'd be sacrificing Minowa's dream.

The decision came easily.

"Oh that? It was no big deal. I just wanted you to know I'm heading to Louisiana next weekend."

A month down south wouldn't be so bad. Who didn't enjoy unforgivable humidity and ravenous mosquitos? She propped her feet up and closed her eyes. Weather and insects be damned. Her sister was headed to law school, and she'd do whatever it took to help get her there.

Three

THE COUNTRY SONG BLARING on the radio said the devil lived in Georgia, but Maren knew better. He had to live in Louisiana because it was hot as hell.

She shifted in the passenger seat, gathering her hair in an elastic. The driver mumbled and jabbed one of the dashboard buttons. Icy air pumped from the vents. She inched back, letting the coolness wash over her.

"First time down South?" Peter asked.

She turned toward the man. "Is it that obvious?"

When she'd learned the Thurstans' butler would be retrieving her from the airport, images of gray, frail men had popped into her brain. However, with a full head of jet-black hair, Peter was late fifties at most.

Wrinkles touched his dark eyes as he smiled. "Your clothes give you away."

"My clothes?"

"You dress heavy." He gestured to her shorts. "All that denim will kill you in summertime."

"I'm starting to realize." She tried to move her thighs, but sweat glued them to the leather. "Were you born here?"

"Born and raised. Moved to New Orleans for a spell when I was young, but we wound up back in Penngrove soon enough."

As if on cue, a metal sign welcomed them to the town of Penngrove.

"What's the area like?"

A toddler ran down the sidewalk, her pigtails flapping. No pedestrians trampled her, and no bikes rang to pass. She could've gone for miles unimpeded, but an ice cream cart had her skidding to a stop.

"Safe, quiet." Peter eased off the accelerator. "Pretty close-knit."

"Sounds lovely." They rolled by bustling shops and greasy-spoon diners. At the end of the block, an abandoned building caught her eye. "Are businesses doing well?"

"Most. They're not millionaires, but they make a living." He followed her gaze, frowned. "'Course, some business owners just give up and move on."

Soon, the views traded brick and mortar for flora and fauna. Despite the endless mud and blackened cypresses, the land pulsated with life. Dangling Spanish mosses dotted the bayous, and birds sung in the branches.

They turned onto a smooth driveway, and followed the topiary bushes to the fence which guarded the property like a mountain range of intricate wrought iron.

Closer and closer, they inched. Harder and harder, her heart hammered.

They'd arrived.

Peter fiddled with a device clipped to his belt, and the gate crept open. A family crest was centered on the fence rails, snakes slithering through thorny roses. Maren swallowed. Did snakes symbolize kindness?

This was no time to be intimidated. She had a job to do.

She wiped her palms on her shorts, and opened the notes app on her phone. "How long have you worked for the Thurstans?"

"Let me see now." He stroked his chin. "Forty years? Yeah, that sounds about right. Forty years."

She gaped. "Forty years? You must've been a teenager when you started."

"You flatter me." He chuckled as they approached a tunnel of live oaks. "I met Desdemona when we were kids. After my parents died, her family let me live here, gave me a job, and I've been working for them ever since."

"Do they treat you well?"

Sure seemed like it. Shiny cufflinks kept his sleeves neat, and a silver watch looped his wrist. Even his cologne smelled expensive.

"Yes, ma'am. They're good folks. Reckon they employ more than half the town too."

"It's a big operation they're running. What about household staff? I'd love to get acquainted with names before we arrive, if that's okay."

"That's an easy one." He tapped the brakes as the driveway curved. "It's just me."

"What? Thurstan Hall's square footage is ..." Maren switched apps, scanning her research from the past week. "Nearly thirty thousand. That's a lot to maintain for one person."

"I've been at this a long time, learned how to cope."

"Cleaning, cooking, landscaping: that's all you?"

"Not landscaping. Chores inside the house are my responsibility. Contractors take care of the lawn and the gardens."

She scratched her temple. "Why wouldn't Ms. Thurstan hire more help?"

Strange oversight. Thurstan Industrial Group's CEO seemed organized and efficient. The company regularly outperformed competitors and raised employee salaries, and quarter over quarter, market analysts were left baffled by the company's earnings reports. Their press releases were timely, their products top quality. Why would a woman that thorough only have one person maintaining her estate?

He jutted his chin forward. "You can ask her yourself soon."

Maren followed his gaze, and her breath hitched.

Surrounded by lush shrubbery and burly willows, Thurstan Hall stood undaunted. It was a Greek-Revival style home complete with marble pillars and muntin windows. Apart from the window shutters and front door, the house was a pristine white. The SUV rounded the fountain and stopped near the porch steps. She craned her neck, unable to pry her eyes from the house.

She was staying here for a month. The thought was equally terrifying as thrilling.

Peter opened the passenger door, and she stepped out. Holy humidity. Was the air always this wet?

He lugged her suitcase from the trunk, and she reached for the handle. Peter stopped her. "Please, let me."

"Thank you," Maren said, following him to the porch. "How big is the property?"

"Too big. Acreage is roughly two hundred thousand."

"Don't think I'll apply to be your gardener anytime soon. Too much lawn to mow."

"Guess I'll throw out your resume then." He unlocked the door, and she stepped inside.

White tiles, pierced with veins of obsidian, coated the floor. Her stained sneakers looked ludicrous atop the fine marble. Ahead, dual staircases joined at the top to create a half-moon. Who knew a foyer could be so beautiful?

High heels clicked, and Peter looked upward as a woman appeared on the second floor. She glided her manicured nails down the banisters, the chandelier spotlighting her descent. Watching her, Maren added another item to the list of things she knew about Desdemona Thurstan: the woman adored a grand entrance.

Glossy lips opened, revealing a sparkling smile. "Ms. Sharpe! It's lovely to meet you."

"Likewise, Ms. Thurstan."

"Please. Don't bother with formalities." Desdemona shook her hand. "Around here, I'm Mona."

"Then I'm Maren. Your home is breathtaking."

"Mama insisted on these renovations." She glanced at the ceiling, and drew a quick cross on her chest. "They're far too extravagant for my taste."

Odd. Everything about Desdemona screamed extravagant. From the gold bangles swaying on her wrist to the red-bottom shoes on her feet, the woman looked ready for tea at the royal palace.

"You'll have full rein during your stay, so feel free to explore. Peter"—Desdemona batted her Nordic-blue eyes—"could you accompany Maren to her bedroom?"

"Be happy to."

"Wonderful. Maren, I'm not sure what your process is, but please ask Peter any questions you may have. And the boys too." Desdemona strode past them, her perfume wafting. She peeked through an archway, and her fingers curled. Turning to Peter, she asked, "Where are the boys?"

"Not sure, I didn't see their ca—"

The front door crashed open, and Maren spun around as a man strode inside. He was young—late twenties, maybe—with beaver-brown hair slicked back from his forehead, and a tie pulled loose over his blue dress shirt.

"No, you listen. If this deal falls through, I'll come up to Baton Rouge and stick your—" The man froze, nearly colliding with a red-faced Desdemona. He pocketed the phone and glanced at Maren. "Shit, was this today? I'm sorry, Ma."

Desdemona put her fists on her hips and muttered, "Maren. This is my son, Lawrence."

"Pleasure." He sent her a friendly wave. "We're excited you're here. I read the book you wrote for the governor. Great work."

Maren stiffened. "You read my book?"

"Sure. We all did."

Lawrence's words lingered as she headed upstairs. Guilt manifested, an indigestible pit in her stomach. Clients didn't read her books: they were too busy, too important. Their assistants would study the pages and recommend her, or they'd trust a friend's referral. This client—this family—read her books. They trusted her to show their best side, to write quality like she'd done countless times before. Instead, she planned to expose their darkest secrets.

She planned to betray them.

Four

HOW LONG DID IT take to strangle someone with a shoelace?

Glancing under the desk, Cade frowned and cursed himself for selecting slip-ons this morning. With no means of escape, he leaned back and accepted his fate: death by boredom.

"... and then Lola on the factory floor said this shirt is ugly. Can you believe it? This shirt." The employee pointed at the vomit-yellow fabric. "We've got a hostile work environment down there. Will you help me out, Mr. Thurstan?"

First name basis was typically fine with Cade, but after listening to this guy drone on for twenty minutes, he saw no reason to prolong the conversation.

"Listen ..." He rose, trying to remember the man's name. "Chief, how about you just don't wear the shirt anymore?"

"I'm a free American, and I've got every right to wear this shirt."

"Then you must agree that she has every right to insult it."

The employee scowled, and Cade held his breath. Get out, get out, get out. The words repeated until the man nodded and left his office. Thank goodness.

Directing employee relations had sounded like a good idea six months ago. Fresh from a failed medical prac-tice, Cade had reluctantly returned to the family business. Unable to heal patients' ailments, he'd figured healing employee relationships would provide the purpose he craved.

He'd never been so wrong.

"Another satisfied employee?" Smirking, his cousin leaned against the doorframe. Six years his junior, Greg was the baby of the family. He'd joined the company after graduating college and quickly became a well-respected authority in the Marketing Department. He loved his job, and it showed.

"Yeah." Cade motioned to the closing elevator. "That hero felt victimized because somebody insulted his shirt."

Greg scoffed and sank into a teal tub chair. "A shirt today. What was it yesterday? An offensive humming?"

"About right. Thirsty?" Rustling through his bottom drawer, Cade snagged the bottle of cognac. As was Friday tradition, he filled two snifters and slid one across the desk. They raised glasses, the clink of crystal like a victory bell. Another workweek defeated.

About damn time.

Cade stretched, resting his long legs on the desk as the liquid sizzled down his throat. "Your brother isn't joining us?"

"Guess not. I figured he was here already since he wasn't in his office."

Strange. Lawrence typically had two fingers guzzled by now.

"More for us then." He polished off his drink and poured another swig. Lifting the bottle, he offered Greg a refill.

"I'm okay, man." His cousin traced the cup's rim, watching him drink the alcohol. "How're you doing these days? You've been through a lot with the job change and everything."

Not this again. Cade eyed his wristwatch. After only a few sips, concern would flood Greg's eyes, and he'd start saying stupid shit like "what's going on with you, man?" or "I'm here if you need to talk, man".

He didn't want to talk; he wanted to drink the week away with a friend. Did Greg even know the meaning of the word anymore? It seemed, in his dictionary, friend and therapist had identical definitions. Cade didn't need a shrink to deal with what had happened. He'd killed a girl, lost his business—and he was over it.

If only his family would get the message.

Conversations with his cousins used to be filled with taunts and jests, but now their words were stiff and deliberate. Did they think him too fragile to goof around with? Auntie had always gushed to everyone about her nephew, the physician. Where pride had once colored her eyes, pity remained. Peter had been his cheerleader. He'd spent months restoring a building for Cade's practice, painting the walls and installing the windows, always ready to offer a helping hand or a phrase of encouragement. But when they'd boarded up those windows last year, he hadn't said a word.

"I'm fine." Cade capped the bottle and retrieved his briefcase. He couldn't enjoy himself with Greg counting drinks. "Think I'll head out. Can you lock up?"

"Whatever you need."

He stabbed the elevator's down arrow, and his heart slammed his stomach when he glanced at his phone. Five missed calls from Desdemona.

"Greg! Grab your phone." Alarm must have blasted on Cade's face because his cousin practically dove for the device. "Mona called me five times. No messages. You got anything?"

His cousin strode over while checking his screen. "Shit. That biographer arrived today. Ma's pissed we're not there."

He rolled his eyes. "Hell, I thought it was something important."

"It is." Greg snatched his forearm as the door dinged. "This book will do great things for us."

"I'm sure it will," he said, shaking from his cousin's grasp and stepping into the elevator. "For you."

Windshields beaconed in the sunshine, and moisture sparkled on the pavement. Cade shielded his eyes and marched toward his car, stopping in front of the adjacent space. Scary to see this one empty. Thurstan Industrial's vice president rarely left before sunset—he was half vampire bat. Tonight, however, Lawrence wasn't barricaded in his office or flying around searching for blood. He'd probably blown off drinks to welcome the biographer. Golden boy wouldn't miss that.

White-knuckling the steering wheel, Cade sped from the lot. Thurstan Hall was his refuge, a place to hide from his mistakes. He didn't want strangers prowling the hallways and pestering him with questions, monitoring him under a microscope. He wasn't an amoeba for God's sake. Despite his concerns, Desdemona had remained adamant: a biography would help business by making their family relatable to everyday folk. To improve their public image, they had to expose their private lives—and that was downright infuriating.

Driving simmered him down. He raced the wind, music blaring and fingers drumming. Approaching the fork, Cade tapped his brakes. The quickest route home was to drive down Main Street. He tensed his jaw. No, can't do it. Not today. Passing that abandoned building on the edge of town filled him with too many emotions, and he didn't need to be angry right now. After all, he still had to meet the precious biographer.

DESDEMONA WAITED ON THE porch as Cade parked the car. He climbed out, and she stomped across the driveway, her heels clicking.

"Kincade Thurstan!" she shouted, her voice teeming with heat. "Does the word punctuality mean anything to you?"

"Yes, ma'am." He squeezed past her and snagged his briefcase from the backseat. "It means staying on top of your periods and commas, right?"

"Very amusing. You should think less about making jokes and more about not disappointing me." Skin bunched around her eyes, and she covered her mouth. "That came out wrong, you never disappoint me, I'm so proud of—"

"I know, Auntie." Because she still looked mortified, he kissed her cheek.

Sighing, she stepped back. "Maren has arrived safely. I wish you would've been here."

"Sorry about that." Cade inched toward the house, and she strode to keep up. "But hey, one out of three ain't bad. At least Lawrence showed up."

"Fashionably late, I'm afraid."

"Lawrence? Late?" He whistled. "That's one for the books."

"Oh, stop it." Her laughter made his chest ache.

Memories of his mother were grayed and faded like photographs stored in the attic. Desdemona's laughter dusted off those images and for a few seconds, Mom was back. She was taking him to the park and pushing him on the swing, buying him ice cream and wiping the sprinkles from his cheeks. This joyous sound was a time machine that transported him back to happier days.

If only his aunt laughed more often.

Peter greeted him at the door, taking his briefcase, patting his shoulder, asking how his day went. Too positive. Too frantic. Just like Greg's therapist routine. After Mom passed, it'd taken his family two years to treat him normally. He sighed inwardly, returning Peter and Desdemona's sailboat grins.

A year and a half to go.

"Is Maren satisfied with the room?" she asked Peter.

Cade kicked off his shoes and placed them in the storage chest, the only brown item to survive his late grandmother's renovations.

Peter nodded. "Her eyes almost fell from the sockets. It's plenty bigger than what she's used to."

His aunt clapped like a delighted seal. "And is supper being prepared?"

"Yes, ma'am. First course is cooking."

"Terrific. Last thing we need is her going hungry on our watch." Desdemona span, her skirt flaring at the hem. "Cade, please go introduce yourself and invite her down for dinner. Apologize for your tardiness, too."

He nodded. No use in delaying the inevitable.

The front door opened as Cade went upstairs, and Greg's voice carried through the foyer. A second later, Desdemona was reprimanding him. His aunt's temper was about as big as her heart. Luckily, she only unleashed it on those deserving of her wrath.

A blast of air conditioning welcomed Cade to the second floor. He rubbed the goosebumps on his arms, and stepped into his bedroom, smiling as plastic and chrome transformed into oak and maple. He rooted through his dresser, savoring the smell of varnish. Had circumstances been different, he would've ended up in the mountains. Spent his days chopping lumber, alone and unbothered. Pulling on a t-shirt, he trudged to the opposite wing.

A door creaked open, then closed. Another opened, closed.

He flattened against the wall and, shrouded by a houseplant, watched the woman—Maren—search the guest suites. She released a frustrated groan. Had she lost her room? He couldn't blame her: the mansion possessed an ungodly number.

After shutting another door, she slumped. Even with hunched shoulders, she stood well above the door's midpoint. Taller, and younger, than he'd expected. Her arm jiggled as she scooped the hair from her face. Her body struck a sweet spot between overweight and slender. No doubt she was attractive. Cute, even.

But honey badgers were also cute—didn't mean he wanted one in his house.

With a growing suspicion she wasn't lost, Cade exited his hiding spot. Let this hellish month begin.

Five

Buckingham Palace has fewer rooms, Maren thought as she pushed her hair away from her face. She'd looked behind every one of these damn doors, and found nothing but silk sheets and fluffed pillows. What a waste of time. She moved to the left, examining the pictures in the hall-way. Love radiated from the image of a woman throwing a child in the air.

A pin pricked Maren's heart.

Would her mother have played like that if she'd worked two jobs instead of three? Would she have spun them, tickled them, delighted them if there'd been enough money, enough time? Probably not. Rebecca Sharpe had displayed her true colors when she'd abandoned her daughters four years ago. One taste of money and she was off to travel the world, leaving Maren to pick up the slack.

"You lost?"

Yelping, she whirled around to see a pair of blue eyes bearing down on her. It seemed that striking color was hereditary in this family. Catching her breath, she pointed a thumb over her shoulder. "No, I'm fine. Just checking out the pictures."

"Had to explore every room for that, did you?"

Caught. On the first damn day. Great job, supersleuth.

Maren looked at the floor. Snooping wasn't her forte, and why should it be? She wasn't a detective. Didn't know

the first thing about espionage. She was a penniless biographer with an unhealthy addiction to people-pleasing,
and this assignment was way outside of her wheelhouse.
But it had to be done; Minowa's future depended on it.

Maren lifted her chin, locking stares with the man. This
was her Bond villain, and she would destroy him. Luckily,
she came prepared. She channeled her research, recalling
faces and names. His body was heavier, his hair longer,
and there was something new in his eyes too. Sadness?
Whatever. She still recognized him as ...

"Kincade, right?" She thrust her hand forward. "Maren
Sharpe. It's lovely to meet you."

"Likewise." Judging by his venomed voice and vice-grip
shake, that was a lie. But she wasn't worried about his
distaste for her; if his online presence was any indication,
Kincade Thurstan wasn't a prominent player in this family.

"Dinner's ready. Come down when you can." He tapped
on the second-last door. "And this is your room. Steer
clear of the other ones unless you want problems."

She glared after him. Why the fuss over a couple of
empty guest rooms? Was Kincade Thurstan just a man who
prioritized privacy, or did he have something to hide?

MAREN COULDN'T DECIDE WHICH stunned her more: the dinner or the dining table. She sat down, ogling the table's
center where a river of lava rock split the pine, its jagged
edges sparkling beneath the pot lights. Only a family of this
caliber could splurge on such elegant furniture.

"Maren?" A man plopped down across from her. "Greg.
Nice to meet you."

"You too." She smiled at the marketing mogul. Him, she recognized immediately. Greg was the charming face of Thurstan Industrial Group. The man whose dimples made statues swoon. The peacock.

"Finally, you've met all my boys." Desdemona passed around a basket of dinner rolls, and Maren plucked one out. Yum. It'd been ages since she'd eaten homemade bread.

"I look forward to getting to know them more." From the corner of her eye, she spotted Kincade eating dinner at the end of the table. Six seats away from them. "It must've been difficult raising three kids on your own. You've done a great job."

Desdemona dipped into her mashed potatoes. "I certainly can't take all the credit. A team rallied around me after my husband passed." Maren had read about the car crash that happened twenty-five years ago. At first, she'd thought the victim blood related, but further digging revealed the man had adopted the Thurstan name after marrying Desdemona. "Mama was my rock, always ready to help on my bad days. Even Peter stepped up."

"Renee too," Greg said.

Maren leaned forward. "Renee?"

An unknown name. Nothing online mentioned anything about a Renee.

Desdemona dropped her fork, and Lawrence palmed his face. Metal scraped against porcelain as Kincade cut into his steak. Maren frowned at their taut faces. It was as if they'd been playing musical chairs, and the song had just stopped.

Greg glanced around. "What?"

Lawrence glared at his little brother.

"My apologies, Maren." Desdemona unclenched her fingers, and the cloth napkin fell to the table. "Renee was my sister."

"Was?"

"I'm afraid so." Desdemona stared at the plate. "She died when Cade was young."

"I'm sorry." Looking at Kincade, Maren felt a tinge of pity. Her relationship with Rebecca was strained, but she couldn't imagine how painful it would've been to lose her mother during childhood. "What about your father?"

Kincade kept his head down, apparently ignoring her question.

"He left when Cade was a baby," Desdemona answered, stabbing into her asparagus.

"That's terrible. How did Renee pass, if you don't mind my asking?"

"Why don't we find something happier to talk about?" Lawrence asked, pushing away his meal. "Like what do you have in store for us this month, Maren?"

"Nothing too strenuous." She nodded as Peter collected the soiled dishes. "I'd like to sit down with each of you for an interview."

"An interview?" Greg snorted. "Sure sounds strenuous."

Lawrence crossed his arms. "You give thousands of product presentations every year, and you're afraid of a one-on-one?"

"Those are rehearsed. This is improv."

"You should grow some—"

"Boys, please." Desdemona narrowed her eyes. "We'll help however we can, Maren."

"I appreciate that. I'd also love to see the property if it's okay."

"It's more than okay. In fact, we'll give you a tour. Perhaps—"

"I'll do it." Kincade smiled, a cat unlocking the birdcage. "Be happy to."

Maren stared straight back. "Thank you."

"Anybody ready for dessert?" Peter asked, his arms racked with plates of chocolate cheesecake. At this rate, she'd waddle back to New York.

A round of coffee finished off the night. Maren typically didn't drink caffeine this late, but she didn't want to sit empty-handed as the conversation turned corporate. Peter passed around the coffee mugs, and to Kincade, he gave a glass of reddish liquid.

"The contract is settled then?" Desdemona asked, her tone leeched of humor.

"I hope so." Lawrence raked his hand through his hair, but the gel kept it static. "I spent an hour talking with Dave. I think he's on board."

Greg returned with two laptops. "Can we start on promotional materials?"

Kincade spoke only when asked about his department: Human Resources. A surprising role for someone with the charisma of a rattlesnake.

Maren slid out her phone and typed notes; she'd need some normalcy in her book to pad the life-shattering gossip. "The Imperial March" blared from her lap, and she quickly silenced the ringtone. "My boss. Sorry."

She excused herself, zipped into the foyer, and slipped on her shoes. Couldn't risk anyone eavesdropping on her call.

Outside, the country air was anything but peaceful. Water splashed in the fountain, and crickets chirped in the trees. Bullfrogs croaked, which sounded more like light saber battles than mating rituals.

Maren walked to the porch swing, and the cushion coughed under her weight, shooting up a musty smell.

Should she feel depressed it reminded her of home? With her head back and her eyes closed, she basked in the night's rhythm. The volume of it surprised her. So too did the Thurstans' kindness. From the matriarch to the butler, their enthusiasm could've suited a presidential visit. Kincade, however, chose the opposite tactic.

She couldn't blame the man. She hadn't exactly made an impeccable first impression. Tomorrow she'd rectify that. Kincade could provide information on his mother, so it'd be helpful to be on his good side. A Thurstan death, hidden from the world. Had to be a story there. She could—and would—ask Desdemona about Renee, but being so high profile, the woman might not disclose much. The nephew, the cousin, the outcast: Kincade might be persuaded into divulging his family's past. Though, getting him to open up would definitely require some elbow grease.

Speaking of grease, she called her boss, and Primrose answered on the second ring.

"Screening my calls, are we?"

"Is it screening if I call you back five minutes later?"

Something crunched in her ear. Chips? "How's Louisiana?"

"Wet. Hot." Two words she never thought she'd say to this man. "But the family's lovely. Most of them, anyway."

"And?" The slurp of a beverage made her wince. "Anything we can use?"

Was he serious? She'd arrived six hours ago. "Nothing concrete, no. There's a death I'd like to dig into. Might be something there. Might not."

"Whose death?"

"Renee Thurstan."

Aluminum crinkled on the line in what sounded like Primrose discarding his snack bag. She moved the phone away as he swirled saliva.

"There is no Renee Thurstan."

"I didn't recognize the name either. But she's real—or was real. She died a long time ago."

"How long ago?"

"Twenty, twenty-five years." Her guess seemed realistic considering Kincade's age. Thirties. Maybe forties. "I'll confirm later. Don't want to come on too strong."

"Just remember you're there to work, not make friends. Get me something good."

She stood up, and rested her elbows on the porch railing. "Aren't you worried about defamation?"

He cackled. "Defamation? Please. You don't succeed as long as I have and not know how to avoid nonsense lawsuits. In fact, we get sued because of something you write, I'll give you a raise."

After bidding farewell to Primrose, Maren hurried upstairs. The flight, and that conversation with her boss, made her feel unclean.

Silky linens dressed her bed, and the ensuite bathroom provided an array of sulfate-free hair care. Atop the vanity, bound in twine, two lavender bar soaps awaited usage. Excessive—regular Dove suited her just fine—but she appreciated the effort. She snagged one and stepped into the shower.

Under the stream, she plotted. She'd tour the property with Kincade tomorrow. Bat her lashes, butter him up, poke and prod until she discovered the circumstances of Renee's passing.

And ignore how much she hated herself for it.

CADE GAWKED AT HIS cousin.

"You're just being paranoid," Lawrence said. With his educational background, Lawrence was used to being the smartest man in the room. In this one, he was the dumbest.

"Paranoia is when you don't have proof. I *saw* her searching the bedrooms. I'm not suggesting we kick her out." Although he adored the idea. "I'm only saying to keep an eye on her."

"Even if she was searching the guest rooms," Greg began, "what harm could she do?"

Scratch that. Greg was the dumbest.

"Your room isn't far away. Is it not weird, a stranger rooting through your things?"

"So long as it's not my browser history."

Cade whipped his napkin across the dining table, aiming for his cousin's dopey smirk, but Greg easily dodged the attack; he'd always had the reflexes of a peregrine falcon.

"Have to do better than that, old-timer," he said.

Cade blew air from his nose, amused, and sipped his cognac—a drink nobody questioned in front of Maren. One positive to her visit, anyway.

He turned to his aunt who was tapping away on her keyboard. "What about you? You're good with this?"

"If that's her process, so be it. Maren came highly recommended. You should read her stuff. She does good work. Besides, you've got a lock on your door. Use it."

"Jesus Ch—" Desdemona severed him with a glare, and Cade cleared his throat. "Sorry, Auntie. My lock is broken. Besides, I shouldn't have to lock anything in my own home."

She patted his cheek. "I know you're having a hard time with this, but it's done. She's here and I'm not sending her away. Just think of all the positive publicity this book will give us."

With the conversation going nowhere, he joined his cousins in gathering around Desdemona's computer. The document overflowed with business jargon, and Lawrence cited the details. Half listening, Cade rested his chin in his palm, mulling over their biographer. His suspicions about Maren weren't unfounded. She'd been frazzled upstairs, nervous—but not over meeting him. No, she wasn't the type to get nervous around wealthy people.

She was up to something, and he intended to find out what.

Six

A WARM BREEZE LAPPED Cade's face, filling his nostrils with the dank stench of midmorning. Sunshine boiled the acreage into a stew of brown and green while mud—not hot enough to solidify—caked the soles of his rubber boots. Maren lagged behind him, the ground suckling at her shoes.

"Dammit." She placed both hands behind her knee and yanked. Nothing moved. Huffing, she tried again. "Come on, you stupid thing."

The corner of his lip twitched.

She'd come ill-equipped for southern weather. Her sleeves were too long, her shorts too heavy—denim in this humidity, really?—and those little sneakers were no match for this terrain. He owned an extra pair of boots, looked right at them while he was readying for this trek. Though twice her size, they'd have prevented her current predicament. If he'd offered them. Which he didn't.

He wanted her uncomfortable. Hopefully then, she'd turn tail and head home.

"You go on ahead." She panted. "I'll catch up with you in a sec."

"I'm good. Wouldn't want you getting lost again, would we?"

"I'd like to apologize for that." She flipped her head and sent him a smile. "I didn't intend to get off on a bad foot with you."

"You didn't intend to get caught, you mean." He shifted his weight, and the mud gargled around his heels. But unlike her, he knew how to escape.

"Caught doing what, exactly?" She looked down again, squirming and wiggling, making slow progress.

"Searching."

"Searching empty rooms?"

"You didn't know they were empty."

Whether she'd ignored him or hadn't heard him, Cade wasn't sure. Maren stayed silent and tugged on her leg. Finally, the ground released her with a bubbling gasp. Her feet slurped against the slickness, her arms flailing as she tried to regain her balance. He lunged and snatched her hand before she plummeted into the dirt.

He wanted her uncomfortable, not utterly humiliated.

Like partners in a log roll competition, they clung to each other until she'd stabilized herself.

She made a sound, an adorable half laugh, half snort. "Thank you."

"No worries. Try walking in my footprints. We'll reach the path soon."

He parted the willow branches while she sloshed in his trail. Soon, the pebbles would bite into her ankles, and the sogginess would blister her heels. She'd be begging to leave by lunch.

Maren fell in step with him as they reached the concrete. "Something solid. Finally."

"M'hm." He fished his sunglasses from his pocket, slipped them on his nose, and scanned the route ahead. Cloudless, treeless. Defenseless. Maybe she could handle blistering feet. What about blistering heat?

"Are you this short with everyone, or is it just me?" she asked, moisture beading on her forehead.

"Right now? Just you."

"Which means you've had others before on this ... brooding shit list of yours."

"Brooding shit list." He scratched his chin. "Is that what it is?"

"Seemed fitting to me. Are those greenhouses?"

He squinted at the huts in the distance. "If it looks like a duck and swims like a duck—"

"Alright, wisenheimer. You've made your point."

Sunlight reflected off the glass, blinding them as they passed. The woman tending the flowers waved her soiled gardening glove, and Cade returned the greeting with a nod, trying to press onward. Failed. Maren sauntered over to Harmony Coulter. Kneading the kink in his neck, he followed.

Huddled between cypress trees and spider lilies, the greenhouses soured the landscape. These eyesores had ignited Desdemona's philanthropist streak. She'd chattered nonstop about how Penngrove needed a city garden. Then, made it happen. Trusted community members received a key to their mansion's gates and could enter as they pleased. With that successful project, his aunt's charitable initiatives had snowballed. Hospital foundations, animal sanctuaries, and homeless shelters had all benefited from her generosity. He'd rallied around his aunt, attending ribbon cuttings and supporting her every endeavor.

But he couldn't support hiring Maren. He didn't want her harassing the townsfolk for information about his family because, in his gut, he knew it wasn't just information she was looking for. Secrets, that's what she wanted. Why else would she peek behind those bedroom doors? She wanted the skeletons, and that scared the hell out of him.

Maren pocketed her phone. "Thank you for your time, Harmony."

"You're welcome, cher," Harmony said, her voice as sweet as the cookies served in her bakery. Years of running a business had creased her face and purpled the shadows under her eyes, but she still stole breaths. "Mornin' Cade. How you holding up?"

"Morning, ma'am. I'm good." He spotted the sympathy in her eyes and knew to change the subject. The Coulters were old friends; if given the chance, she'd happily soothe Cade's sorrows. "How's Bryan?"

"Busy as ever. Hardly see him most days."

"Well, you cook up some beignets and I'm sure he'll come crawling on hands and knees."

Nobody could resist Harmony's baked goods, not even the deputy sheriff.

She laughed, her straw hat flopping. Turning to Maren, she asked, "You ever have a beignet, cher?"

"Never."

"No beignets?" Harmony wrinkled her nose and wagged her shears. "That's why you'll never catch me living in one of them big cities. New York. Puh. Even if they had 'em, they wouldn't taste right. Only place to get real Southern cooking is in the South."

She wasn't lying. He'd visited New York City a few times and hated every minute of it. Big, loud, and unfriendly. Why would anyone subject themselves to that?

Harmony's eyes glinted. "I've got an idea! Maren's never had Southern cooking or seen our town, so"—she focused on Cade—"why don't you bring her down tomorrow? Around noon? Get her a Po'boy at LaSalle's and stop by our place for a few beignets. I'll whip 'em up fresh."

"Oh, I don't think—"

"I'd love to!" Maren pounced on the idea like a malnourished feline.

"It's settled then," Harmony said, the finality of her tone smothering his instinct to argue. "Don't be late now. They taste best warm." She collected her beach bucket of dirty tools and strode off through the trees.

"She's delightful," Maren said.

"There's lots of good people in this town."

"I'm excited to meet them."

"Bet you are." Cade seethed as they backtracked to the pathway.

"She said you guys don't grow anything in those greenhouses. Is that true?"

"We're not a farming family."

"Still. You could've hired people to grow food, but you didn't. You give that space to the community, free of charge, and don't benefit at all."

"Is that foreign to you, rich people helping the less fortunate?"

"Frankly, yes. I've been in this business a while, studied lots of wealthy people. It's rare they help anyone, let alone without some kickback."

"How long you been doing this?" He didn't care, but he wanted to steer the topic away from the motives behind his aunt's philanthropy. These days, he figured Desdemona helped the community for publicity rather than charity.

"Seven years."

"Long time. What do you enjoy most?"

"The people. It's intriguing to see how the other half, well, the other five percent live."

"Who've you written about? Anyone I'd know?"

"Depends. Do you rub elbows with politicians and bratty socialites?"

"Regularly."

"Stupid question." She rattled off some names and asked, "You know any of them?"

"All of them."

Having a powerful last name meant he conversed with many people, but it didn't mean he enjoyed it. Greedy, conceited, haughty: the traits his peers shared didn't flatter. Most inherited their wealth rather than accrued it. Being born wealthy required no skill, yet they lived, snub-nosed and sure of themselves, as if they'd achieved something amazing rather than just lucking out in the genetic draw. Cade had been the same way until his mom died.

She'd loved Penngrove and had spent hours mingling with locals, helping when needed. So when her life was cut short, he'd stepped up in her place. Opening his practice had never been about money—working at a hospital paid more; it was about giving back to the community and making his mother proud. And for a while, he'd believed he had. Then he killed someone, shut down his practice, and withdrew from society.

Yeah, she probably wasn't proud anymore.

"You didn't read my books?" Maren asked.

"What?" He massaged his neck again, the tightness refusing to dissipate.

"My books. Lawrence and Desdemona read them, so I thought maybe you did too."

"Do you think we read together? Like some Thurstan family book club?"

She lifted a shoulder. "It wouldn't surprise me; you seem close."

Against his better judgment, Cade smiled. "Not that close. Anyway, I wouldn't call myself much of a reader."

"What would you call yourself? Any hobbies?"

He pointed toward a clearing in the trees. "Head over there."

"Is that a cemetery?"

"Yeah." The mausoleums came as a welcome distraction; the last thing he wanted to do was play the get-to-know-you game with this woman.

Maren opened the rickety gate and gestured to the concrete huts. "No graves?"

"The dirt is too soft to bury anything. Crypts work better."

"Interesting."

He followed her down the cobblestone path, watching as she dusted off the nameplates. She used gentle caresses, the kind reserved for injured pets or newborn babies, and at the end of the walkway, she stilled. The final tomb wasn't crafted from plain old cement; it was made of fine marble and surrounded by magnolias.

"This is hers, isn't it? Your mother's."

"Yeah."

She moved slowly, as if walking on fresh ice. "Twenty years ago. How old were you when you lost her?"

"Twelve."

She wrapped her arms around her stomach. "That must've been difficult."

"Gets easier with time."

"But it never stops hurting."

"No." The sun spotlighted her legs. Long and muscular, they'd prove useful when he chased her out of his house. "You have any family?"

"A younger sister. We live together."

"Dad? Mom?"

"Dad ran off when I was seven. Probably drank himself to death by now." She rose, dusting off her butt. "And mom ran off when I was twenty-seven. Might be dead, might be alive. Who knows?" She turned away, her posture stiff.

Something must've happened with her mother, but he didn't ask what. It was none of his business.

She glanced at him on the way out. "Thanks for showing me around. I know you're not my biggest fan after yesterday."

"Mona wants you here, and I trust her judgment." He blocked her path. "But another incident like yesterday and you're out. I don't let anyone hurt my family."

"Me neither." She returned his hard stare and exited the cemetery. "Besides, I was only doing my job last night. Thurstan Hall is part of your heritage. Not including it in your biography would be a huge misstep. I needed to see the layout, the structure."

Credit where it was due. She was a damn fine liar.

"Well, next time you want to see any of our structures," he began, not even trying to disguise the vitriol in his tone, "make sure you let me know."

Her eyes flicked over his body, and her cheeks turned a soft pink. If any other woman had given him that look, Cade would've considered it a sign of attraction. But in this instance, it was a taunt, like an enemy kingdom laying down their arms before charging into his barracks and killing everyone inside. That's what Maren Sharpe was: the enemy. And it would do him good to remember that.

"Got it," she said. "So are we good now?"

"We're good."

"Wonderful." She shot a breath toward the sky. "Also, don't worry about babysitting me tomorrow. I'm fine visiting Penngrove alone."

"I'm afraid I can't let you do that."

Her head snapped upright. "You can't?"

"No, ma'am. I take my job as tour guide very seriously." He met her gaze. Smirked. "So for the entirety of your visit, you won't go anywhere by yourself."

"Oh, you don't have to do that."

"But I insist."

Her eyes narrowed. "You're too kind."

"Aren't I?" He grinned and circled a finger over his eyes and chin. "Get used to this face, lady, because you're going to be seeing a lot of it."

What was it people said about flies and vinegar? His vinegared approach wasn't working; Maren was still cheerful and energized, a lot stubborner than he'd predicted.

Time to change tactics.

Seven

Maren waited in the guest hallway, trying to ignore the painful throbbing of her lower half. Socks clung to her ankles like slime-laden seaweed, and blisters bubbled on her heels. She needed to clean her face and wash her hair and bandage her feet. But still, she waited.

Finally, a door clicked. Kincade's door.

Content he wouldn't hear, she surrendered to agony. Her legs noodled, and she crumpled downward, the tiles sizzling against her cheeks. Sweat leaked from her pores, vanishing into the creases of her lips.

When Kincade had flipped out his sunglasses, she'd realized what was happening. He was trying to break her, to make her so uncomfortable she would run back to New York. Foolish man. He could drown her in mud, bake her in heat, and scrutinize her every move, but she wasn't going anywhere.

Grunting like an aroused boar, she crawled to her room. Her phone buzzed in her pocket, and she dragged herself onto the bed and accepted the video call.

"Hi, Maren! How's Penngrove?" Minowa's voice was like the ding of an airplane after a dreadfully long flight.

Eyes closed, she melted into the duvet and mumbled inaudibly.

"That good, huh?" A book spine cracked, and her sister coughed.

Maren lifted her head. "You at the library?"

"Yup."

"Did you bring your pills?"

Maren had returned home once to find dozens of dusty books scattered on their living room floor. Minowa had sat in the middle of them, studying for her exam with a sniffling nose and watery eyes. They'd walked to the clinic where the doctor had diagnosed her with a dust mite allergy. Just one of the countless instances where Maren had stepped into the motherly role.

"Sure did," Minowa said, shaking the medication.

"Good. How're you doing there by yourself?"

Adaptable, spunky, Minowa could take care of herself. But she also possessed the naivety of being in her early twenties. Eager to prove herself, to find her place, but still carrying a childlike wonder that disappointment hadn't yet dulled. Minowa believed good things happened to good people and everything happened for a reason.

One day, she'd learn. One day, someone would shatter her optimism, break her faith. But, unlike the way it'd been for Maren, that someone wouldn't be family.

"I'm totally fine. Just miss you. Forget that though, I wanna hear about your trip. Tell me everything."

From bumpy coach flight to agonizing property tour, Maren recounted the events of the last twenty-four hours. By the time she'd finished, the scorching pain in her feet had morphed into an irritating sting.

"Wow. The house sounds amazing. Can you show me your bedroom?"

Maren moved the camera. "I'd show you the outside, but my feet are on fire. Try searching for pictures."

"On it." Her nails clacked on a keyboard. "Holy crap."

"Right?"

"It's beautiful. Hey, this must be them."

She padded to the bathroom and set her phone on the counter. After dampening a tissue, she sat on the toilet seat and wiped her heels.

"Damn. I was hoping they'd be ugly."

She laughed. "Why?"

"I just hate when the family is rich and good-looking, y'know?"

"Life's an unfair bitch."

"Is this Kincade?" Minowa asked, adjusting the phone and pointing at the man behind Desdemona.

"You got it."

"There aren't many pictures of him."

"I noticed that too. Most of the online pictures are from business articles, and I don't think he's super involved with the company." She opened the cupboard and found a box of bandages. Brand-new and brand-name: this family truly provided everything.

"Why not?"

"He doesn't seem interested in TIG. Barely talked about it at dinner last night. His whole branch of the family is a mystery." Maren glanced at the soaker tub. Four massaging jets and large enough to bathe an elephant. Tempting.

"His whole branch?"

"Yeah. He's actually Desdemona's nephew. His mom died when he was little."

"Oh no. How?"

"I don't know. Nobody talks about it, and I can't find any obituary."

"Weird. Especially for such a high-profile family."

"My thoughts exactly. I'm going to dig more and see what turns up."

"Check if there's a newspaper in town. I'm sure their archives would be filled with info."

"Good idea." Maren returned to the bedroom and switched the video call to audio. She couldn't handle another minute in these sweaty clothes. She unbuttoned her shorts and stripped them off. "But I doubt Penngrove has a newspaper. There's maybe a thousand people here."

"Stranger things have happened. I know you're busy, so I won't keep you any longer. But I wanted to tell you ..." She exhaled slowly. "Mom called."

Maren stopped undressing. Wearing her rolled shirt like a necklace, she tightened her grip on the phone. "She called you? When?"

"Yesterday."

Because her legs threatened to buckle, Maren sank to the bed. She rested her forehead on her hand, forcing in steady breaths. "Why is she calling now, after all this time?"

"She wants to come over."

"Sh-she's in New York?"

"Yeah. I told her you weren't home, but she might pop by anyway."

"Pop by." Heat worse than any Louisiana sun raged through her. "Unbelievable. Un-fucking-believable. She leaves to gallivant the globe with a man we've never even met—doesn't visit, doesn't call—and shows up years later hoping to *pop by?*"

"I know you don't love the idea but—"

"Love it?" She threw back her head in forced laughter. "Why wouldn't I love it? I love working my ass off to support us while she's lounging around in Mexico or Portugal or wherever the hell she's been. What kind of mother doesn't call to see if her daughters are okay?"

A beat passed. "Aren't we okay?"

"Oh, of course we are," she reassured, softening her tone. This wasn't Minowa's fault, and getting upset with her solved nothing.

"You said she could go."

"I know." For a week or two. She never agreed to Rebecca leaving for four years. Never agreed to put her own life on hold so they'd have food on the table.

Despite her sixty-hour workweek, Rebecca had always been there for the big moments. Christmas morning and Thanksgiving dinner, choir concerts and science fairs. In those precious few hours, Maren didn't have to be the mother. She adored her sister but had also yearned for freedom, to abandon the city and find her own way, to stay out all night without worrying about what Minowa would eat for breakfast.

Once she'd graduated college, Maren thought that time had finally arrived. She'd become a historian, chase her dream. Then Rebecca had announced she was taking a little trip. She hadn't been worried at first. Stay at Primrose Publishing and postpone her job search for a while, no big deal. But the weeks kept passing, turning into months and years, and that betrayal had burrowed deep. Rebecca couldn't just come back and fix everything. The wounds had long healed over.

"Would you at least consider seeing her?" Minowa asked. "There's a lot we should talk about."

"No. You can see her if you want, but count me out."

Maren ended the call, and her phone clanked on the nightstand. Did Rebecca have no shame? Why show up now and pretend everything was okay? And why did Minowa want to see her after everything she'd done?

Enough.

She couldn't focus on family right now: she had an interview to do. After a quick shower, she crossed to the opposite wing and knocked on the first door. "Is this still a good time?"

"Absolutely." Desdemona capped her marker. "I've just finished. Please, have a seat."

A quaint space. Light gleamed through the windows, feeding the forest of houseplants. Squinting, Maren sank into an armchair. Her vision adjusted, but she rubbed her eyes anyway. This didn't look right. No bookshelves or framed degrees—and no desk. She had met many CEOs over the years, and though their personalities varied widely—caring, indifferent, egotistical—one factor had always remained the same: a mammoth desk. It was present in all their spaces. Work office, home office, didn't matter.

So why didn't Desdemona have one?

"I adored days like this when I was a girl. Didn't pay any mind to sunburns or sweat." Desdemona's eyes twinkled as she adjusted the drapes. "Did you and Cade get on okay?"

"We did. Do you always work Sundays?"

"I avoid it, much as I can. Daddy always said: 'Work hard, pray harder.'" Laughing, she plopped down across from Maren. "Of course, who's the first one with his boots on when factory work goes wrong?"

"I've read a lot about Ian. Were you guys close?"

"Reasonably. It's been hard running TIG without him."

"For what it's worth, I don't think anyone's noticed. You've increased profits and worker satisfaction, expanded into international markets. It's all very impressive."

"Thank you." She squeezed Maren's forearm. "I know we've done well, and I'm grateful for it. I ... well, I miss him. That's all."

"I'm sorry. It's hard not having parents around." Her eyes wandered to the paintings on the wall. Six of them, nailed neatly. "That's him on the end, isn't it?"

"Yes, it is."

Maren stood for a closer look. Sculpted jaw, straight nose. His grandsons had inherited everything but the curled mustache. Her gaze latched onto the artist's signature. "You did these?"

She nodded.

"Wow. Do you paint often?"

"No." Desdemona glanced away, fidgeting with the ring on her finger. "Not anymore, at least."

"That's a shame. These are fantastic."

Perla Thurstan hung second from the end, her sweet smile directed at the frames next to hers. Lawrence and Greg, solemn and silly, and Kincade with his unruly curls. Peter was staring back from the last frame as if watching over the entire family. But no Renee. Even here, in this intimate place, Desdemona didn't commemorate her sister. Weird. If Minowa passed away, Maren would plaster pictures of her sister all over the house. She'd make wallpaper from their memories. Didn't Renee deserve the same courtesy?

"I noticed your sister isn't here," Maren said. "Could you tell me about her?"

"I don't like talking about her." Desdemona waved as if clearing smoke.

"Nobody does. Almost like once she died, her existence was erased."

"I don't blame my family for wanting to forget."

"I'll need to know for the biography. How she died, and—"

"No."

"Sorry?"

Desdemona flattened the creases on her skirt. "I don't want you writing about her death."

She raised her chin. "What about defining qualities? Was she smart, sassy, goofy? Surely, you'd like to include *something* about her."

"Why did I hire you, Maren?"

The question paused her. She opened her mouth, closed it. "I'm experienced, reputable. And I write good books."

"Partly," Desdemona said. "I spoke to your previous clients and one thing stuck out to me. Do you know what that is?"

"I don't."

"You kept things light. Wrote what they told you to, didn't pry. They trusted you in their homes, so I'm trusting you in mine." She trapped Maren in a steely stare. "My sister is not a light subject. Do you understand what I'm telling you?"

"I understand."

"Wonderful." She clapped and hopped to her feet. "Now, if you'll please excuse me. I have something to take care of."

In the hallway, Maren stared at the door. How could Desdemona dismiss her sister so easily? She was cold. Indifferent. Did grief drive her actions—or guilt?

She descended the staircase and found Greg lounging on a velvet chaise with his nose tucked in a novel. Shorts and t-shirt, brown hair messily styled: he was the picture of a lazy Sunday afternoon.

Flashing a camera-loving grin, he tented the book on his chest. "Hey, welcome back. You enjoy the tour?"

"Very much. The property is breathtaking. Not sure I'd ever visit town if I lived here."

"It's a never-ending battle, believe me. Luckily, Penngrove's not half bad. Makes leaving a lot easier. You seen it yet?"

Settling on the couch next to him, she shook her head. Crystal vases glittered on the mantle, and the floors appeared to have been scoured on hand and knee. Even the hearth, which should've been laced with ash or soot, shone with a dull brilliance. Her sister had a dust allergy, and even her apartment wasn't this clean.

"Shame," Greg said. "Whenever you feel like going, grab Peter. He'd love to take you."

"Actually, Kincade's taking me tomorrow."

"He is?" Greg sat up. "Voluntarily?"

"Not exactly. Harmony Coulter pushed him into it."

"Sounds like her."

"You seem surprised Kincade would come. Any particular reason?"

"He just doesn't like going into town anymore, that's all."

"Why?"

"Uh ..." Greg's jaw slid back and forth. "You hungry? Kitchen is always fully stocked. Did Cade show you where it is?"

"No. I haven't seen much of the house. Would you mind showing me?"

"I'd be happy to."

He slid a bookmark into his novel and laid it on the table. In the kitchen, he pointed out the teas and coffees and demonstrated how to use the espresso machine. Gestured to where, if she had a craving, the snacks and sodas were stored. She snagged a piece of licorice, and followed him into a hallway where the doors looked like they'd been created for basketball players. A treadmill thumped nearby as he showed her the cinema, conservatory, and wine cellar.

"The gym is in there, and this"—he gestured to the last door—"is the library. Some Austen and Steinbeck, but it's mostly old photo albums and stuff."

"Mind if I peek inside?"

"By all means. I've got an unfinished chapter calling my name but you need anything, you know where to find me."

The library's cleanliness shouldn't have surprised her, nor should its selection of books cozied together with color-coordinated spines. Still, she took a minute to admire the room, inhaling the scent of aged paper.

With a scan of the shelves, she spotted a scrapbook toting Kincade's name. On the cover, his date of birth was written in glitter. A year older than her, she mused, not that it mattered. Maren flipped it open.

Yellow glue clung to images of a woman holding a chipmunk-cheeked infant. This had to be Renee—Kincade inherited that blonde hair. She browsed through the rest of the pictures, taking in the macaroni lions and backyard mud pies. He beamed alongside his projects, his smile missing two front teeth. Cute kid. Cute man, too. A smidge too sarcastic for her taste, but she could appreciate his aesthetics.

Maren returned the scrapbook to the shelf, and removed another with Renee's name. The birthdate stilled her: it was identical to the death date etched on her crypt. She shuddered. To lose a mother, a child, a sister, on the same day you celebrated their birth must've been unbearable. And here she was, dredging up that pain, making them relive those memories.

She locked away those thoughts. Her reason for investigating the Thurstans was sound: to keep her job and protect her sister from disappointment. She repeated that over and over as she fingered through the pages of Renee's scrapbook. Finding nothing useful, she slumped against the chairback. Renee stared up at her, wearing a swimsuit and gripping a gold trophy.

Maren grazed the photo. "What happened to you?"

Eight

CADE EASED OFF THE accelerator as they approached Main Street. Brick buildings lined the bustling sidewalks in a pattern of red, gray, and brown. People held dripping water bottles to their foreheads, flocking to the sanctuary of the awnings. The car windows were closed, yet he could still smell the dampness in the air.

Maren sat in the passenger seat, her gaze fastened to the windshield. "I've never visited a town this small before."

"Not missing much. New York City is probably far more exciting." He flipped his indicator and slowed at the first of Penngrove's trio of stoplights.

"The city's got perks, sure: anonymity, job opportunities. But there's no sense of community like this." She twisted to face him. "You ever visited New York?"

Making his turn, Cade headed for the neon sign of LaSalle's Place. "Yeah. New York, L.A., Chicago. All the big ones."

"And you've always lived here?"

"Never felt right anywhere else." He'd attended medical school in Maryland. Enjoyed the people, the atmosphere, and the December snowfall. But Penngrove would always be home, like it had been for every Thurstan in recent memory.

As they rolled into the diner's last available parking space, her head tilted. "Is it always this busy?"

"Usually. LaSalle's makes the best po'boys on this side of Baton Rouge. Plus, the place is locally owned. That matters around here."

"Not a McDonald's kind of town?"

"No, ma'am. Chains don't want to come here given the low population, and we don't want them anyhow since they take business away. It's human nature to opt for something familiar. A tourist sees a chain restaurant and eight times out of ten, that's where their money goes."

"Can't really blame them." She climbed out of the car. "You've got some weird names for food down here. What even is a po'boy?"

"A Louisiana staple. Isn't this the kind of thing you re-search before hopping on a plane to write a book?" He'd woken this morning intending to sweeten up to Maren, but he was only so strong. Couldn't resist a bit of teasing.

She slammed the door, harder than required, and saun-tered past. "I research my clients, yes. Not so much the state they live in."

Following her, he smirked. In a pink spit of a sundress, the woman screamed tourist. One strong breeze would send that skirt flying to her ears. Which, he decided, ad-miring the curves of her calves, wouldn't be such a bad thing. Her sandals teetered on the gravel. City shoes made for city pavement. And those city shoes showed off a pair of bandaged heels.

His grin widened.

"Be right with ya, sugar," Rhonda May, LaSalle's wife and longest-serving employee, shouted from behind the counter. She hustled orders out, yelling for her husband to hurry the cooking.

"Place is popping," Maren said, almost inaudible against the jukebox pumping out oldies. With checkered floors and booth seats the color and texture of a rooster's comb, LaSalle's Place was a time capsule.

In signature teal uniform, a blonde waitress beelined toward them. Must be a newcomer; Cade didn't recognize the woman. "Afternoon! I cleared a table near the window. Head on back. I'll follow with menus."

Maren led the way, shuffling through the herd of servers and flying-handed bar top patrons. Good reflexes. Probably from years of living in a sardine can city.

The table shined with vinegary cleaner. Cade thanked the waitress and set the menu aside. The diner looked vintage American, but burgers and fries weren't found here. LaSalle's served only southern eats.

She read the menu and scrunched her brows. "A sandwich? All this hype over a sandwich?"

"Louisianans aren't high maintenance. Give us a bun and fried shrimp, and we're happier than a dead pig in the sunshine."

She blinked. "Is that happy?"

"Thought I saw a handsome Thurstan wander in." Rhonda May lumbered to the table with a face-splitting grin, and squeezed his shoulder. "How you been, sugar? Haven't seen you in town of late."

"Been fine, Rhonda May. How're you and—"

"And you must be Maren Sharpe." In typical fashion, Rhonda May couldn't wait to get on with it. "Happy to have ya. So drinks? Eats? What're we having?"

"I guess I'll try one of these po' boys. As for drinks, any favorite I should try?"

Rhonda May licked the plum lipstick off her teeth. "Ginger sweet tea. People guzzle it down like water around here. You want that po' boy dressed?"

"You want lettuce, tomato, pickle, and mayo?" He clarified when she hesitated.

"Oh. No tomato, please."

He handed over the peeling menus. "Same for me, but tomatoes are fine."

With a nod, Rhonda May walked away as new diners arrived, tinkling the bell above the entrance.

Counting on his fingers, Cade said, "Weather, cuisine, slang. You researched none of those before coming?"

"I can learn everything as I go. Exhibit A." She hooked a thumb in her spaghetti strap and gave it a yank. "I wore cotton today."

"Yeah. The mosquitos will love that exposed skin too."

"One step at a time, Kincade."

"Kincade, huh?" Arm sprawled atop the backrest, he stretched. "Am I in trouble or something?"

"I wasn't sure if you wanted me calling you Cade."

"Go ahead. Nobody uses Kincade."

"Then why's it your name?"

"Tradition. Thurstan boys are always given strong names. Kincade, Gregory, Lawrence. I like the informality of a nickname. Feels more friendly, approachable."

She rubbed her chin. "And here I thought rich people came with the elitist attitudes by default."

"I'm full of surprises."

"What about Lawrence? He doesn't subscribe to the whole approachable and friendly thing?"

"One of the many things we don't agree on."

The beverages arrived, condensation dripping from the clear plastic cups. He stole a glance at her while they sipped. Pink gloss shimmered on her lips and mascara stiffened her lashes, but the makeup failed to conceal her under-eye bags. Sleep deprivation? Stress? He could relate.

"It's good." She unpuckered from the straw, and tapped her finger on the tabletop. "Ask me something about your family." When he angled his head, she added, "I want to restore your faith in me. It's not my job to know this state, but it is my job to know the Thurstans."

"You've been here like two days. What could you possibly know about us?"

"Try me."

He looked down his nose at her. "Fine. When did we start the company?"

"1850, but"—she flashed her palm as he moved to correct her—"that was just the fertilizer company. In 1920, you rebranded to include other products."

"That's a pretty easy one. Simple internet search. What colors are on the family crest?"

"Green, red, and yellow. Do you want to know the animal too? Because that's a snake—or serpent, depending on which you prefer."

"Where did we emigrate from?"

"You've lived in America for generations, but if you want to get technical ..." She gulped her drink and wiped her mouth with the back of her hand. "The origins of your last name come from either England or Norway. But I don't think even you know the correct answer."

Damn. She was good.

He shrugged in defeat. "Why visit us if you know everything already?"

"I have some questions still."

She was baiting him. If he bit, she'd ask her questions, and he'd find out what she was after. Or she'd ask a question he didn't want to answer, and it'd be like dumping blood into a shark tank. She'd smell the fear, the weakness. And follow it. Should he take the risk?

A man sat on a barstool, spanking his near-empty ketchup bottle while Irma Thomas belted through the staticky speakers. The environment hummed with her jazzy notes and the spitting of a deep fryer.

"What questions?" Cade asked.

Maren wasn't stupid; she'd get answers with or without him. At least this way, he'd know what interested her.

She stopped stabbing her ice cubes. "How did your mother die?"

"Here we are!" Rhonda May set two red baskets on the table and wiped her hands on her apron. "You need anything else, holler."

With her eyes trained on him, Maren made no moves to eat.

"It's not some colossal tale. She drowned when I was a kid."

"Drowned?" Lines creased her forehead, and she pursed her lips. "In the ocean somewhere? Deep water?"

"No. We have a duck pond at the back of the property. She was drunk, slipped in."

"You talk about it so casually."

He picked up the sandwich from its bed of checkered tissue, shrugged. "It was a long time ago. No point in dwelling on stuff you can't change. She died, and life goes on."

"Then why is her death so hush-hush?"

"Are you talking about the other night? I wouldn't call that hush-hush. I'd call it knowing what appropriate dinner topics are. Death not being one of them."

She popped a battered shrimp in her mouth, chewing slowly, carefully. Her shoulders slackened in what looked like she was melting from the flavor, and she snatched another.

"Tastes better with the entire ensemble."

Nodding, Maren followed his lead and devoured the meal. She ran her fingertip over the tissue paper, cleaning off the dripped mayo. This woman ranked low on Cade's list of people he liked being around, but watching her enjoy a po' boy so thoroughly boosted her score—slightly.

She leaned back, resting a hand on her abdomen.

"Hope you saved room for beignets. I'm sure Harmony expects you to eat a bushel's worth." He checked his watch, noting it was twenty minutes until noon. Excellent. He'd hate to disappoint Harmony by being late.

"Don't worry. I always save room for sweets. Bathroom?" As she slid from the booth, he pointed to the corner.

Instead of watching her walk away, which he cursed himself for wanting to do, Cade scooted to the counter where Rhonda May handed him the debit machine. A paper taped above its screen read NO TAP, scrawled in yellow highlighter.

"So how you been, really?" Rhonda May rested on her elbows, keeping her voice low. "I didn't wanna ask in front of Maren 'cause I wasn't sure if you'd told her about your place shutting down."

He smiled as he pushed the faded buttons. If only everyone in town could mirror her discretion. "It's been difficult, but I think I've reached the other side."

"Cade, baby." Her hand, cracked from years of kitchen work, grasped his. "Nobody blames you for what happened to that girl. You know that, don't you?"

"I know, Rhonda May. Thank you."

"Glad to hear it. You ever wanna pass a good time, you know where we are." She ripped the receipt and handed it over. "You've got a pretty thing waiting over by the jukebox. Get on out of here now."

Cade steered away from the counter and found Maren by the door. "Ready?"

"Yes, sir. How much do I owe you for lunch?"

"Nothing. Call it a peace offering."

Thick as honey, the air stuck to them as they walked to Coulter Bakery. He would've offered to drive, but the building that had housed Thurstan Family Medical neighbored the bakery and was easily identifiable from the car. The sidewalk, however, put them at a steep angle. So, unless she planned on running into the middle of the street, she wouldn't identify his old building. Still too close for comfort, but there was no avoiding it. Harmony wanted them to visit, and he'd do anything for that sugar plum of a woman.

"Did you visit town a lot as a kid?"

He ushered her beneath the awnings because, unlike the baskets of swamp azaleas swinging from the streetlamps, he didn't enjoy baking in the sunshine. "Mom and Mona dragged us along sometimes."

One minute and they'd reach it. No prickly welcome mat with a tacky phrase. No sales racks lining the sidewalk. A cold, empty storefront blackened from where his last name had once hung.

"And what kind of trouble did you get into?"

His throat bobbed, and the countdown began in his mind.

Three.

"We were perfect, little gentlemen. Catching frogs and not putting them in purses."

Two.

"Buying bags of candy and not eating it all in one sitting."

One.

"We were just three good kids with time to waste and allowance to burn."

She gawked at him.

Why was she staring? Were his anxious rants that intriguing? There was only one thing to do in this situation. Ramble on.

"You might be surprised to know—"

"Hold on." She strode to the metal box labeled the *Penngrove Gazette* and flipped through an issue. Right outside his old building. He tapped a curled knuckle against his lips and looked upward. He hadn't been on speaking terms with God since his mother died but desperate times, right?

Hey, Jesus. Could really use an earthquake right now, or a parade of ice cream trucks, or a damn hurricane warning. Anything to distract this woman, please.

Nothing. Cade scowled at the sky.

See, this is why people don't believe in you.

His stomach churned as Maren peered between the cracks in the window boards. The boards he'd nailed there. His secret was about to be exposed. She'd grin, her pupils turning to dollar signs as she plotted out her next story. In newspapers, TV shows, and published books, the world would learn how Cade Thurstan—a member of the business empire—had been forced to liquidate his practice.

Worse, they'd find out why.

He should've fought harder, should've declined Harmony's invitation and booted every tire at the mansion so nobody could drive Maren to town. He should've—

"Was this a newspaper publisher?"

"What?" He'd barely heard her over the heart drumming a rock concert in his ears.

She squinted at the sunlight. "I didn't know Penngrove had a newspaper. Was it here? Did it shut down?"

"No." He blinked as his adrenaline drained. "This was a law office or something. The newspaper's back that way." Beckoning her forward, he said, "We'd better get to Harmony's. She'll skin us if we're late."

"Could we go to the newspaper place after?"

"Sure."

He wasn't sure why she wanted to see a print shop so badly, and frankly, he didn't care. He'd pay for an all-inclusive trip to Bora Bora right now if it meant she'd vacate this area.

Hinges squawked as Cade opened the door to the bakery, and a cornucopia of smells wafted out: powdered sugar, fresh bread, warm apples. The smell was so sweet and comforting it loosened the knots in his back. Maren snuck beneath his arm, and he followed her inside, eager for a treat to restore the energy his adrenaline rush had zapped away.

Harmony beamed behind the bakery case with a dusting of flour gracing her cheeks. "Right on time. Hope you brought an appetite."

People occupied the tables near the window, and chatter filled the air. Harmony's graying ponytail fell over her shoulder when she bent, reaching over the pralines and slices of pecan pie. She tonged four beignets and placed them in a paper bag. He reached for his wallet.

"Don't go pulling that out," she said, handing the bag to Maren. "Can't a woman provide some free treats to her favorite customer?"

"There's no—"

"Don't you go arguing." She shook the tongs at him. "Take the beignets and be happy with what you get."

He smiled. In his hiatus from Penngrove, the diner had hired a new server and the hanging baskets had rotated their blooms, but Harmony had stayed the same, so generous and persistent. But so was he.

Cade removed a twenty and stuffed it in the tip jar. At Harmony's scowl, he shrugged. "What? Can't a man tip his favorite baker?"

"Stubborn as a mule, this one." She glanced at Maren. "See if you can take him down a couple pegs while you're here, cher."

She laughed. "I'll do my best. Thanks for these."

"Always. We've got napkins over there. Forks too, if you're needing one."

On the corner table, he set two plates and a handful of napkins. Maren slid the beignets from the bag and sat down.

Taking a bite, she looked around. "Harmony runs this place by herself?"

"Mostly. She owns it with her husband, but you won't see Bryan behind the counter; he's the deputy sheriff."

"Seems like everyone's connected somehow."

"Roots span back generations around here. People grow up together, graduate together. We may live separately, but we're one big familial community."

"Lucky. Relationships like that make me want to leave the city."

He dabbed powdered sugar from his lips. "Why don't you?"

"There are ... obligations I can't get away from." She propped an elbow on the table and gazed out the window. What caused that twinkle in her eye? Wonder? Longing? He hadn't expected that from a city girl. Also hadn't expected his disdain for the woman to simmer into curiosity.

A curiosity he could not—and would not—indulge. It was none of his business what her obligations were. None of his concern why she was on the outs with her mother or why she put up with a boss who had earned a Darth Vader ringtone. But still, he felt a pull toward the woman. She shared his humor, shot back his sarcasm, challenged him in a way no one had in a long time.

A façade, had to be. She was trying to win him over, to lower his guard. And if Maren thought parading around with a mesmerizing smile and double-take sundress was going to break his resolve, she wasn't as smart as he thought.

Because when the niceties stopped, it would leave one truth. She was here to do a job—unearth his past, expose his secrets, hurt his family.

And nobody hurt his family.

Nine

WHEN PEOPLE HAD TOLD her Southern cuisine trumped all other foods, Maren had scoffed at their idiocy. Now, sucking the remnants of sugar off her fingers, she felt like the idiot. Surrounded by a buttery bun, the seafood in her Cajun shrimp sandwich had been perfectly seasoned with garlic and paprika. The beignet, with its mountain of icing sugar, had sweetened her tongue, and reminded her of when Rebecca would bring back leftover donuts from work.

Even better, she'd discovered this tiny town had a newspaper. Everything had blurred when she'd spotted the gazette rack. Finding the newspaper archive could break open this investigation; it'd be a treasure trove of information about Penngrove, the Thurstans, and Renee's death.

Drowning.

Something didn't feel right about that. Hadn't she seen pictures of Renee in her swimsuit holding the first-place trophy? How does someone with such ability drown in a backyard pond?

In the parking lot of the *Penngrove Gazette*, she unbuckled her seat belt. "You can wait here if you'd like."

"Nah," Cade said. "I've come with you this far."

She nodded, exited the sedan, and climbed the stairs. The building mimicked the rest of the town with its flaked redbrick and expansive front windows, though the barrels of white snapdragons near the door upped its curb appeal.

"You're Maren, aren't you?" the secretary asked, his voice booming like a volcano eruption. The reception area wasn't very big; the welcome desk sat on one side, and two armchairs sat on the other, separated by a coffee table struggling to support a mound of magazines.

"That's right. And you are?" The carpet scrunched under her sandals.

"Waldo Samson. Afternoon, Cade." He tapped the bill of his cap. On the dome, embroidered in red and white, were the words Ragin' Cajuns. Maren knew college football was popular down here, but like New York's northern neighbors, she preferred hockey.

Waldo scratched his nose, which was pickled by acne scars. "Is there something I could do for y'all?"

She layered her arms on the desk and stifled a grimace. The cloud of body spray had failed to mask his unshowered musk. "I'm in town to document the Thurstan family. May I access your archives? I'd love to get an idea of their history with the community."

"We're not really s'posed to let anyone down there." He looked at Cade, a mischievous grin crawling across his lips. "But I could be convinced to break the rules."

She twisted to see Cade's fiery glare pinning the man.

"I got this weird crick in my arm, see?" He rotated his wrist. "I can't get out to my doctor for a few weeks, and I'm worried it might be something serious. So, if you'd—"

"How about we don't discuss your bodily issues in front of the lady? Let's get Maren set up with her articles, then we'll talk."

Waldo pointed at him. "Holding you to that."

Had she just witnessed small town blackmail? Strange, but Maren decided not to dwell on it. There were more exciting things to think about.

Waldo led her down a long corridor. Nailed to the walls, black-and-white images depicted the heritage of the town's newspaper, their dates spanning back roughly a hundred years. It wasn't a question anymore: this place must have information on Renee.

"Make yourself at home," he said, shoving open a dent-ed, metal door. "Boxes are all labeled. Take as long as you'd like, but make sure you're putting stuff back where you found it."

She palmed the wall and flipped a light switch, the flu-orescent tubes hissing as they flickered to life. A library of rusted shelves spanned from wall to wall, stacked to the rafters with bulky plastic bins. A musty smell choked her as she descended the stairs, examining the date ranges on the shelves before skirting into an aisle. Hopefully, whatever liquid was causing the stench and the rust hadn't spoiled her papers. She dusted a container and squinted at the label. Not this one. She delved deeper into the aisle, but the dates were only becoming harder to distinguish. With a grunt, she pulled out a bin. Had to start somewhere.

The creak of a door perked her ears.

"You're just in time!" She pried open the lid and divvied the papers into piles. If Cade insisted on coming along, she'd work him.

The lights buzzed. A clock ticked.

She glanced over her shoulder, but it was impossible to see the staircase from where she was. Surely Cade and Waldo would've acknowledged her by now, right? The room was old and packed to the gizzard; no wonder it creaked.

Dismissing the noise, she coaxed open the newsprint with a gentle finger. Any harder and the yellowing paper might disintegrate. She scanned the pages and, finding nothing, placed the newspaper aside. That pattern continued, and her stomach stirred from the lack of results. There had to be something helpful in here. She snatched another container, and anticipation flooded through her veins as she neared the date of Renee's death. May, June, July. September. Narrowing her eyes, she checked again. Was this a joke? The month of August, the month of the drowning, was missing.

Trying to calm her paranoia, Maren brainstormed reasonable explanations. Could it be in another bin? No, because July and September were correctly filed. This was the only logical place it could be.

Had someone borrowed the issues and forgotten to return them? She checked the log sheet taped to the lid, but this bin hadn't been disturbed in years. The town newspaper had no record of her death. What reason was there to hide it, unless ...

Unless they didn't want anyone investigating.

The temperature plummeted, and her insides trembled. Scorpions. They were all over her, scurrying up her ribs and into her hair. She itched frantically and whipped around. Did that paper just move? Was there someone here? She gripped the shelf as her heart galloped into her throat. Air. Need air. She was in a windowless basement, and visiting an unfamiliar family in a strange town. No wonder her imagination was going crazy. That's all it was, her imagination. She'd feel awfully silly once she found out the explanation for these weird coincidences.

Reaching the foot of the stairs, she froze. Noises. Behind her, near the far wall, they were swift and muffled, but they definitely weren't imaginary.

Footsteps.

"Cade? Waldo?" Nobody answered, and sweat dripped like ice water on her spine. Someone was sneaking around down here as her questions deepened around Renee's death. Was it a coincidence? Or design?

Needing answers, Maren tiptoed left. The blinking fluorescents cast an eerie shadow as she crept to the end of the room, watching for movement between the plastic bins. Everything appeared normal, but she hadn't heard the door open which meant they must still be here. Hiding, waiting. Watching.

She reached the corner and glanced behind her. No movement. No sound aside from the pulse battering her eardrums. Expelling a few rapid breaths, she lurched into the open corridor at the rear of the basement. The floors squeaked, and shoes slapped.

"Hey!" Maren yelled, flying past the shelves.

Natural light poured onto the ceiling, and a door slammed. She swore, hurrying toward the sound. She stopped at the emergency exit and when no alarm sounded, peeked outside.

The alleyway wound against a backdrop of leafy green. A puffy-cheeked squirrel snacked by the dumpster, scurrying as she leaned from the threshold. Nothing else stirred, but she wasn't fooled by the innocent looking atmosphere. Someone had been here. Someone who didn't wish to be identified.

A hand grabbed her shoulder.

She reeled, colliding with a muscular chest.

"Hey, whoa, it's me!"

"Shit, Cade." She shoveled the hair from her eyes. "Don't creep up on me like that."

He flashed his palms, and Maren shut the door, bracing herself for the adrenaline hangover. Her arms were heavy, and her head felt like an abused blender. Looking up, she caught his gaze. And her chest thudded.

Cade stood close—with another layer of mascara, her lashes would've grazed his chin—and a curl bobbed inches from his arched brow. It unnerved her, the concern in his eyes. She'd become so used to his scowls and glares that she almost missed them.

"Why're you hanging out in an emergency exit?" he asked.

"Maybe I like the view." She side-stepped and crossed her arms. "Were you upstairs until now?"

"I was."

"And Waldo was with you the entire time?"

"Yeah, he wanted money for a doctor's appointment. What's going on?"

"Nothing. I'm just seeing things." Before he could inquire further, she asked, "Did you read newspapers as a kid?"

"This a riddle?"

"It's a genuine question." She smiled, and they returned to the aisle cluttered with lidless bins.

"Then no. What kid does?"

"I did." Maren winced.

Sharing childhood memories would be a mistake. She already felt dirty for betraying this family; befriending them first would only make it worse. But without trust, Cade refused to divulge information, and if these piles of yellowing newsprint proved anything, it was that investigating alone was going nowhere. She needed him, which meant it was time to get personal.

"Minowa and I were alone a lot when we were growing up, and we didn't have any electronics, so we read newspapers, magazines, anything we could get our hands on really."

Following her lead, he returned the stacks of newspaper to their bins. "Minowa. That your sister?"

She nodded.

"You like her?"

"Most of the time."

"That's good."

"I think so." She had to keep going, couldn't let him shut down the conversation. "We live together—did I say that already?"

"You did. Apartment?"

"Yeah. It's nothing fancy though. One bedroom, a kitchen, a bathroom. The bare essentials."

"One bedroom?" He paused and loaded a bin onto the shelf. "Cozy."

"What about you? You live with family too. Except with a lot more bedrooms."

"And a home gym, and a library."

"No owlery though."

Cade laughed. Nothing uproarious, just a deep chuckle in the throat—but it was a lovely sound. "You got me there. I'll issue a work order immediately."

"I'd hope so." She traced the lid of the bin sitting in her lap. "Are you close with your family?"

"Yes, ma'am."

"And your mom? Were you close with her?"

"As close as a kid can be to their mom." He leaned against the shelf, his legs crossed at the ankle. "What's up?"

"Did people like her?"

"Sure. You going to tell me what you're getting at?"

"I'm trying to figure out why there are no reports of her death. Or her existence at all for that matter."

A tube light dimmed, darkening his face. "What're you talking about?"

"Sit down, I'll show you. I was looking for records of Renee's death—and before you say it, I think it is my business." Maren pointed at him as his eyes narrowed. "She's part of your family, part of you, and she deserves to be in this book. Now, flip through the papers and hand me the stack from the August she passed."

His glower shifted to the container as he rifled through the issues. Stopped. "Where'd you put them?"

"They were missing when I got here."

He held her gaze, saying nothing.

"It's not only this either, Cade. Like I said, I'm good at my job. I research my clients extensively, and I arrived here thinking you were Desdemona's son. There's nothing about Renee online. No pictures, no articles, nothing."

"To be fair, how much is there online? We're a fertilizer family."

"You're not just a fertilizer family—you're a *rich* family full of handsome bachelors. The internet eats that up. Hell, I found a quiz asking which Thurstan brother I was."

"Really?" He stroked his chin. "Who'd you get?"

"I didn't complete it."

Cade squinted at her. "You're lying. Tell me."

She pursed her lips to prevent a smile. "Lawrence."

"Oof. The worst. Makes sense though. You're both pains in my ass."

"Ha ha." After a minute, she asked, "So none of this strikes you as odd?"

"Not really. We could clear this up in two seconds by asking Waldo where the issues are."

"Not yet. I'd like to know who's involved first."

"You're making assumptions. Could just be a flood that ruined those newspapers."

"Maybe. But I'd still like to look into it."

"Knock yourself out."

"Seriously? What happened to the whole 'stay out of my business' act you've been putting on?"

He shrugged. "Even if I told you to leave this alone, you wouldn't listen. At least this way, I can say I gave permission. That'll keep my pride intact."

"Oh, the last thing I'd want to do is damage your pride."

"Bullshit." He flashed a stellar smile, and in that moment, Maren realized the internet had it wrong: Cade's dimples far outshone Greg's.

BY THE TIME THEY'D arrived home, her phone showed four voicemails from Primrose.

Cade stopped near the trunk. "You okay?"

"Yeah." She eyed the empty driveway. "Where is everyone?"

"Out and about. Best way to spend sunny days. You up for a walk?"

"Really?"

"Yeah, why not? I could use the fresh air."

"Okay, sure. But can you wait a bit? I have to call my boss."

"You guys don't get along, I take it." Keys jingled, and he pushed open the front door.

"Not exactly. We've got different values."

"Why don't—" A cellphone rang, and Cade sent her an apologetic look before reaching into his pocket. "I have to take this, but I'll come grab you later."

While he settled in the parlor, Maren climbed the stairs and paused at the landing. She knew why Primrose was reaching out, and she couldn't very well call him back with nothing to offer. She needed something, anything to tide him over. To the right, laid potential secrets, and to the left, guest rooms.

She glanced backward, and forced her thickening throat to swallow before sidling to the right. There wasn't much time. She'd just repaired the trust between herself and Cade. The last thing she needed was to be caught snooping around again. He'd given permission for her to delve into his mother's death not raid his family's quarters.

She twisted the first knob. Unlocked. Wonderful. Smiling like a honeybee infiltrating the florist's greenhouse, Maren crept inside. Unlike the rest of the manor, this room was filled with mismatched wood.

She hurried to the dresser and yanked the top handle. Belts and boxers, underwear and socks. She hated herself for invading their privacy this way, but what other choice did she have? Minowa would attend law school, unconcerned with funding. That was her priority, and she refused to acknowledge the guilt residing in her stomach—hell, it'd already purchased a mortgage and moved the kids in.

The dresser was useless, so she switched to the desk. The drawers stored pens, tape, and scrap paper, all organized meticulously. Nothing screamed illicit affair or insider trading. With a huff, she pulled open the last drawer, and found a silver frame holding a matted degree. At the top, John Hopkins University was written in black cursive. She read the rest of the document: this degree certifies the recipient below as a ... medical doctor? She looked at the name, and the frame nearly slipped from her fingers.

Cade Thurstan.

What?

Maren stuffed the frame back in the drawer and fled from the bedroom. It took ages to become a doctor. Why spend years grinding for a medical degree only to wind up in human resources? Had he lost interest in his medical career, or was there something more sinister at play? She didn't have any answers, but she had enough to satisfy Primrose. Maren sat on the edge of her bed, and shook her head as the line rang. Unbelievable. Cade, a doctor.

What made him stop practicing?

Ten

THE HORDES CAME AT night. Under a veil of dusk, cicadas chanted on the cypress trunks, and mosquitos hovered over the bayous like a buzzing oil spill. Above it all, the katydids shouted for an encore while nibbling on the leaves of sugar maples.

Listening to the serenade, Cade smiled. A peaceful end to a good day. Maren hadn't learned his secret. Better yet, she pursued a dead lead. Mom's death, really? There was no juicy story there, but he'd gladly let Maren waste her time.

"Here," he said, handing her a bottle of bug spray and jerking his chin toward the gum boots. "They're too big for you, but they're better than nothing."

"Thank you." Maren stooped to spray her legs, and his eyes wandered to her ass. It wasn't bad, slightly rounded with a hypnotizing jiggle, an ass he could sink his teeth into. Her thighs were tempting too, lean and long. He liked tall women and damn, if he wasn't growing a measly bit fond of this one.

Reeking of kerosene, she plodded toward him. "Can you show me the back of the property today?"

"You sure? There's no path back there, and the terrain's terrible."

She twirled her boots. "You prepared me well."

Moss and tree bark scented the air as they tromped past the house, using their phones to light a path. A light breeze rustled the treetops, and the sticky mud popped against their boots like suction cups.

She glanced around. "I can't believe this is all yours."

"I don't think of it as 'mine'. It's hard to own land like this. Always alive, always changing. We maintain the front of the house, but this ... this we leave wild."

"You're an enigma."

"How do you figure?"

"I can't picture other clients preserving the land this way. They'd sell it for development like that." She snapped her fingers.

"As you said, the house, the land, it's all part of the family. Our first factory was built here."

"Really?"

He nodded. "It's gone now though."

"You're lucky. I can't imagine being able to walk the land my ancestors walked."

Distance dimmed the mansion lights. In the blackness, he couldn't pinpoint exactly where they were, but he had an inkling. A few more minutes and they'd hit the pond his mother drowned in. Knowing Maren, she'd ask to see it eventually. Might as well get it over with. Adjusting course, he said, "Tell me more about your family. You don't talk about your parents much."

"There's not much to tell. My father left shortly after Min was born. He was never around anyway. The only thing I remember about him is his cigarettes. The man smoked like a forest fire."

"Great mental image." He grinned. "And your mother?"

"We're not super close. She worked a lot when I was young, and now she's traipsing the globe with some fat cat who wipes his ass with hundred-dollar bills."

He studied her profile as she stared at the ground. Narrow-eyed. Frowning. A heavy subject, this. Probably better to keep things light. "In his defense, Benjamin Franklin wipes better than any store brand."

"Yeah?"

"Ben's perfect for the job too. Those pursed lips, that disappointed scowl. He knows exactly what's going down, and he really ain't happy about cleaning your shit."

Laughter brimmed, loud and unrestrained, the kind you craved after a long, stressful day.

Cade smiled.

She'd grown up hard. One-bedroom apartment, newspapers for fun. Not homelessness, but to a man who grew up in a twenty-thousand square-foot estate, it was close. Admirable, to provide for herself and her sister. To sacrifice her own needs—the soles of her sneakers flapped in the wind, for Christ's sakes—and remain positive was an impressive feat.

Maren released a contented sigh. "Under that cold exterior, we've found some humor. Never would've guessed."

"Don't go telling anyone. I've got a reputation to uphold, you know."

"It'll be our secret."

As they crested the ridge, she gasped. The bayou flowed lazily beneath a buttered moon, creating pockets of ponds along its length. Frogs perched on a calico of lily pads, readying their tongues to taste the glinting fireflies. The mallards weren't so lively; they nestled along the bank, their eyes closed and their beaks tucked beneath their wings.

"This is breathtaking. Look!" She crouched and pointed. "Ahh. So cute."

"M'hm." His gaze traced her ponytail and slipped down the arch of her back.

"Did you come here a lot when you were young?"

Focus. He gave his head a good shake. "Rarely."

"Really? Seems like a great place to catch those frogs you loved gifting to the townsfolk."

"No, this ... this is where Mom drowned."

She stiffened and stood upright. "And here I am spouting on about how beautiful it is. I'm sorry."

"All good."

She inched closer to him, and the breeze caught her hair, twirling scents of bug spray and vanilla. "Can you tell me what happened?"

Staring into the trickling black, he began, "It was her birthday, and the house was packed. I didn't know ninety percent of the people, so I played with my cousins. We were just having fun, everyone was. Mom had that kind of warmth. She brought people together."

Cade breathed deeply. He didn't recount the story often—preferring to remember the good times—but when he did, the memories hit hard. She touched his arm, and he nodded, letting her know he was okay.

Her hand didn't move.

"I wanted to wish her happy birthday again before bed, so I came looking for her. Mona said she went for a walk, and I got this sick feeling in my stomach. It was as if my body knew something had happened." He shut his eyes. "I found her floating here."

"You're ... you're the one who found her?"

"Yeah."

Her thumb moved, brushed his inner elbow. "That must've been devastating."

"It was. No child should see their parent that way—hell, no adult should see their parent that way."

"No, they shouldn't." She dropped her hand and flicked glances at him. Rocked on her heels. "How deep do you think it is?"

"I'm not sure. Probably not very deep."

"I didn't know we could drown in such shallow water."

"We can drown in a tablespoon of water."

She grabbed a stick, and dipped it into the pond. "I can feel the bottom. It's a couple feet down, if that." She pulled the stick out and narrowed her eyes, as if examining the wet tip.

"The sediment's slippery, so it's hard to maintain your footing. It's like constantly having the rug pulled out from under you."

"Why would she get in anyway? The water's disgusting."

"Pepaw said she was drunk."

Her gaze clipped to something in the distance. A strong tail chopped the surf, thrusting through the liquid as if jet-propelled.

"Gators," he said.

"I forgot you had those here." She backstepped. "But it strengthens my argument. Why swim in alligator-infested water? Don't you have a pool?"

"No. Memaw didn't like the smell of chlorine." He shook his head at her skeptical expression. "Mama's death was an accident, Maren. There's no mystery to solve here."

She gave a curt nod. "How'd you end up in human resources?"

What a random question. Eying her suspiciously, he said, "I like helping people."

"Don't take this the wrong way, but you don't seem like a people person."

"Don't take this the wrong way, but you don't know me."

"You won't let me get to know you." She tipped her chin upward, and strands of hair blustered across her cheeks, touching those dainty lips. She stood close. Too close, but he couldn't bring himself to care. His resolve weakened with each breath warming his jaw. Shouldn't do this, shouldn't want her.

"I could be persuaded," he said.

"Could you?"

"Yeah."

She blinked up at him, those hazel irises sparkling. "And how would I do that?"

"You want me to show you?"

Her chest rose with a breath, and his gut stirred, the final knot of restraint weakening. She dropped her eyes to his lips, and the rope snapped. He dipped his head and captured her mouth.

The kiss was careful, like a pair of gazelles nosing their first snowfall. He cradled her head, his fingertips brushing the underside of her ponytail. Her hands flattened on his chest and slid upward, finding a home on the back of his neck. He lost himself in the taste of her, a sweet orange popsicle. His brain berated him; it knew making out with this woman would only complicate things, but when her lips parted, he shut out those objecting internal voices. The only thing that mattered was touching her, getting closer to her.

With the tip of his tongue, he explored the unfamiliar, tasting every delicious indent on her lips, sweeping inside. Her mouth was soft and receptive. But then, he'd expected that—why had he expected that? A soft sound escaped her throat, and Cade eased away, admiring how the firefly light danced in her eyes. Looking at her, he felt his heart take a tumble.

What the hell?

He wrenched away from her and took a deep breath, a difficult task since he'd apparently swallowed Saturn.

Maren stared at the grass, appearing slightly dazed as if she'd stood up too fast. "Never done that before."

"Could've fooled me."

"Well, I've done *that* before." She tucked her hair behind both ears. "Just never with a client."

"Sampling southern comfort food, making out with clients. You're really broadening your horizons down here."

"Look at me go." She fidgeted with her blouse buttons on their way back to the house, and as they neared the porch steps, she caught his arm. "I'd like to keep that kiss between us. It wasn't exactly professional."

"I get it. You don't have to worry. Night, Maren."

"Good night."

She disappeared upstairs, and Cade retired to the living room. On the couch, he fished for his phone, intending to scroll mindlessly. Instead, the device stayed on his chest while he stared at the ceiling.

He'd kissed her, had enjoyed kissing her. She called it unprofessional, but he called it batshit crazy, downright moronic. Yet he couldn't stop thinking about the tickle of her breath and the scent of her perfume. He wanted more. Shit, why did he want more?

"Did I wake you?" Lawrence asked, setting his laptop on the coffee table and plopping onto an angled chaise.

"Nah. Where've you been?"

"Fighting fires." From finger to striped sock, he stretched and relaxed into the fabric. "You remember the supplier deal from a couple weeks ago?"

"That company in Baton Rouge?"

"Yes. They wanted to pull out of the deal. Months of work, gone."

"But you swooped in and saved it at the last minute?"

He closed his eyes and smiled. "Damn right I did."

"Typical."

"Don't be grumpy. It's not my fault you joined a boring department."

"Hey, I solve the employee's mundane problems. I'm vital to the organization."

His cousin's eye popped open, and they roared in laughter. Bullshit. Cade's job was such bullshit.

"Speaking of boring and mundane," Lawrence began, bracing on his elbows, "how're the biography interviews going?"

"They're going okay. She's determined, I'll give her that."

"I hate to say I told you s—"

"No, you don't."

"You're right, I don't. I told you this would be easy. A brief visit, a few questions, and a shwack load of good publicity for the company. Total win-win."

"When are you sitting down with her?"

"Tomorrow. The woman lives in the house, yet she emails to get a time set up. Can you believe that?"

"Nothing wrong with being organized."

"Emailing someone you could walk downstairs and talk to borders on obsessively organized."

"You're lounging around the house in a dress shirt and tie. Who's obsessive?"

"Touché." Lawrence made a beckoning gesture. "So give me more details. What questions should I prepare for?"

"Like I said, obsessive." Cade chuckled softly and sobered before he said, "She might ask you about Mom."

His ankle stopped bobbing. "Why?"

"She thinks the drowning seems suspicious. Trying to stir up drama if you ask me."

"She wouldn't even know about Renee if Greg had kept his fat mouth shut," Lawrence muttered, rubbing his eyebrow.

"Doesn't matter."

"Yes, it does." He whipped his hand down. "Why is she looking into Renee anyway? Ma said it was off-limits."

Cade crooked his neck. "She did? Why?"

"She hates talking about Renee. You know that."

"It's been decades," he said cautiously.

"Not to Ma. For her, it's always yesterday."

"So what's her plan? Take every picture down and pretend she has no siblings? This is a perfect excuse for her to finally deal with the past. Renee's my mother, and you don't see me cowering."

"It's not the same. You had Renee for twelve years. Ma had her for thirty."

He jerked his head. "Are you serious?"

"I'm only saying—"

"You don't get to say anything. The fuck do you know about grief?"

"Hey. I lost someone too."

"Not the way I did," Cade said quietly. "Your mom's still here."

"Bullshit. Ma treats you like one of her own."

"You think that's the same?"

"No." Lawrence uncurled his fingers. "No, it's not. Sorry, man. I just hate seeing Ma upset."

"Me too, but I'm keeping an eye on Maren. She won't be hurting anyone, don't worry."

"Well, good." His cousin leaned back. "How're you feeling about everything? Has Maren found out about ...?"

"No. And we're going to keep it that way."

Lawrence rolled his eyes.

Cade had agreed to hire a biographer under the condition his family swore not to reveal his medical background. Lawrence had argued disclosing that information would only bring good things. A Thurstan offering affordable patient care? It was the perfect philanthropist story to exploit.

Lawrence opened his laptop. "I still think she should know. Ma's got the charity angle covered and if we could say you offered discounted medical services then—"

"I'm not discussing this with you again," he snapped. "Share what you will about the business or your personal life or even Mom. But keep me out of it."

"Aye, aye, Captain."

Bidding him goodnight, Cade exited the parlor.

Lawrence had helped to grow TIG exponentially over the years. Hobbies, relationships: he'd sacrificed everything for the company, and would do anything to protect Desdemona from heartache. If Maren brought up Mom tomorrow, Lawrence would change the topic, give her something juicier to gnaw on.

Would that something be the secrets of Cade's past?

Eleven

LAWRENCE THURSTAN WAS A show pony.

He strutted into his workspace with his shoulders back and shuffled the folders on his desk. His hands were scoured, his fingernails squarely trimmed. Every movement seemed orchestrated, every breath rehearsed. Even his hair looked as fake as a Broadway wig.

Maren glanced around the office. Built-in bookshelves dominated the two walls, displaying a wealth of business texts, and a Stanford University degree hung behind a hulking computer desk. On its front corners sat two potted succulents. Thurstan Industrial's future CEO: well-groomed, business savvy, environmentally conscious. He played the part well.

But no businessman was perfect.

"My apologies for this," Lawrence said, shoving his papers into a drawer. "My secretary should've checked with me before sending you in."

"I don't mind. It gave me a chance to get comfortable."

"Well, I won't keep you waiting any longer." He laced his hands on the desk. "Fire away. What questions do you have?"

She launched into the general inquiries: how he liked his childhood, his involvement in the business, his educational background.

"... so Ma fostered a love of learning and encouraged us to pursue higher education. I received many employment offers during my post-grad, but TIG is where I belong."

She frowned. As second in command, Lawrence was a busy man, much too busy to prepare for their meeting—or so she'd thought. He'd prepped answers, and that was a problem. She wanted slipups and mistakes, wanted other leads to chase. Perhaps if she pushed him to reveal Cade's medical background, he might scramble and share other classified information. Worth a shot, anyway.

"Did Greg also attend Stanford?" she asked.

He nodded.

"And Cade?"

"Hopkins."

"Why the different schools?"

"Cade graduated high school earlier than us. He chose the best university at that time."

"I didn't know John Hopkins had a business school."

"Then you learned something new today." Lawrence rolled his neck and smiled.

He'd bested her at direct questions. Time to lob a few roundabouts.

Maren relaxed, mirroring his posture. "You've got a nice office. Great view."

Birds zipped past pillowy clouds, and the sun bathed the treetops in a yellow glow. No parking lots, no skyscrapers. Just nature and wildlife enjoying another scorcher.

"Thank you. I had to turn my desk around to stop from staring outside."

"Smart move. So tell me, why are you the one sitting in this office? Why isn't Greg becoming CEO?"

"It's typically given to the oldest. Plus, you've met Greg. He's not what I'd call executive material."

"Oh?"

"He doesn't like confrontation. Too empathetic to run a billion-dollar empire. If it were up to my brother, we'd be giving handouts to every Tom, Dick, and Sally who requested one." He pointed at her. "That's off the record."

"Certainly." She wasn't interested in brotherly rivals anyway; she needed something far more scandalous. "If CEO is always given to the oldest, why isn't Cade here?"

"I didn't say always, I said typically." Lawrence tugged on the collar of his dress shirt. "Cade didn't want it."

Maren leaned forward. "Why not?"

"I don't know."

"You never asked?"

"No."

"Cade gave up all this"—she gestured around—"to run Human Resources? Strange."

"No, it's not. Everyone's happy. I like my job, and he likes his." He averted his gaze. Excellent. Her fish was yanking the line. Now, to reel him in.

"Except he doesn't." Sweat dribbled down his temple, and Maren smiled. "Come on, Lawrence. I saw him the other night. That's not somebody who loves HR. Did you force him into that department?"

"No."

"Did he disgrace himself and lose his candidacy for CEO?"

"No." His throat bobbed. "Nothing like that."

"Did he fail—"

"No!" He flattened his hands on the desk and flew upward. "Can you just drop it? Cade isn't hiding anything. Besides, this isn't the first time a younger sibling was named CEO."

"What?" She froze, and Lawrence slapped his forehead. "Who else was there?"

"Not important. Are we done?"

"Who was it?"

He clicked his intercom. "Vanessa, could you please escort Ms. Sharpe—"

"Renee." The name dribbled from her mouth as she pushed her hair back. Holy shit, holy shit. "It was Renee, wasn't it?"

His jaw sharpened, his glare blistering her like a blue flame. No need to oxidize it with more questions: she had her answer.

"Thank you for meeting me," Maren said, quickly gathering her things and bolting into the hall. Her gaze traced over wooden floors to where Desdemona's name shined on a silver doorplate. Shivers crept over her skin. She didn't have much before: shallow water, missing newspapers, an estate devoid of staff. But this? Renee was set to inherit one of America's biggest conglomerates. This wasn't just new information—it was a billion-dollar motive.

But Maren needed more. Primrose was content with the tip about Cade's medical career, but it wasn't big enough to satiate him. Just an appetizer, and to keep her job, she needed an entrée. Soon.

Spinning on her heel, she hurried to Cade's office and knocked on the door.

"Come in." He was sitting at his desk massaging the sides of his head, but as soon as his eyes met hers, his scowl softened. "How'd it go with Lawrence?"

"Fine." She didn't sit down. Didn't enter the room. "I need a ride."

"Where?"

"Penngrove. I'm finding those missing newspapers."

THE WINDOWS RATTLED AS she barged inside of the *Penngrove Gazette.*

Waldo, who'd been slouched over reading his phone, snapped upright. He wore no hat today, showing off a black helmet of hair. "Maren, Cade. Great to see you again."

"You too." She splayed her hands on the counter. "I have some questions."

"What's up?"

"Are people allowed to borrow issues from downstairs?"

"This ain't a library."

"Did any floods damage the newspapers? You had to throw some out, maybe?"

"No way. You've seen it. Place is a fortress."

She pursed her lips. "So, if a month was missing, there'd be no explanation for that?"

"None that I can figure."

"I came here the other day looking for the publications from when Renee Thurstan died, but they were all gone."

"Really?" Waldo's brows shot up. "That's news to me."

"You work here every day. How does something go missing on your watch?"

"You accusing me of something?"

"No, I'm just trying to understand what happened."

"Like I said, I didn't know they was missing."

"But you do know something," Cade said.

"What is this?" Waldo crossed his arms. "I do you a courtesy, let y'all into the basement, and you come in here saying I'm doing a poor job?"

"Neither of us said that," Maren replied, sweetening her tone. "I'd really like to know how Penngrove rallied when the Thurstans went through crisis, that's all. Does anyone else have access to the basement?"

He tapped his fingernail on the wood. Stopped. "Actually, yeah. The sheriff has a key. Needed somebody trustworthy to hold the spare."

"When did you give it to him?" she asked.

"While ago. If he's been downstairs, there's good reason for it."

They thanked Waldo before leaving, and on the sidewalk, Cade snagged her wrist. "There's something you're not telling me. Like why you're so hell-bent on believing somebody else is involved in this. Before we go any further, I need to know everything."

She couldn't tell him about the archive visitor. Weakened by the moment and the sadness in his eyes, she'd kissed him last night. No way around that. But there weren't any fireflies romancing this scene, and he hadn't shared any tragic stories. She was clear-headed now, and until she found out what, if anything, was going on with Renee's strange death, she couldn't trust anyone.

"It's a gut feeling."

"Don't do that." His grip tightened on her wrist. "Don't you bullshit me."

"I'm not bullshitting anyone." She shook him off. "I noticed some discrepancies in Renee's accident, that's all."

"Discrepancies? Suddenly you're a detective because some newspapers go missing and a stick doesn't pass your dip test?"

"Go wait in the car if you're going to be an ass."

"I'm not waiting in the car. Something is going on, and I'm only asking you to trust me enough to share what that is."

"Trust you?" Her expression pinched. "What reason have you given me to trust you? Jesus, you've been gunning for me to leave ever since I got here."

"Didn't seem to be an issue last night."

"Just because I kissed you doesn't mean I trust you. It was a momentary lapse in judgment and, believe me, won't ever happen again."

"Bummer. I quite enjoyed it myself." He stared at her. Hard. "Anyway, bickering gets us nowhere. You don't want my help, fine. But the sheriff is a busy man, so if you want to talk with him, I want to know why."

"I don't need your permission."

He shrugged. "True. But, if you haven't noticed, I carry a lot of influence in this town. Influence which could prove beneficial to you in the future."

Valid point. Perhaps having Cade on her side wouldn't be such a bad thing. If it turned out something nefarious happened to Renee and a member of law enforcement was involved, she'd need a powerful ally. Plus, if she disclosed her information and he tried to block her from discovering the truth, she could turn attention to his medical background. She won either way.

Maren crossed her arms. "Fine. I'll tell you. Tag along—if you must—but I don't want your opinion. It'll just waste time. Deal?" He nodded, and she said, "I was looking through scrapbooks the other day and saw a picture of your mom. She was an excellent swimmer, earned trophies and everything. You said the pond was slippery, but you were twelve. A thirty-year-old woman, extremely comfortable in the water, wouldn't have any problem."

Cade remained silent, his eyes never leaving hers.

"There's something else too," she said quietly. "There was somebody in the basement with me yesterday."

"What? Who?"

"I'm not sure. They ran away once I noticed them." She drummed her fingers on her thigh. "It can't all be coincidence, can it? Not that I'm asking for an opinion, mind you."

"You weave an intriguing story, but speculating gets us nowhere. Come on, let's go talk to Sheriff Harlowe."

Soon, she'd have answers. She only hoped they were the ones she was looking for.

Twelve

WALKING TO THE STATION, Cade updated her on Sheriff Harlowe's and Deputy Coulter's backgrounds. Eighteen years prior, Reggie Harlowe had left New Orleans and replaced Penngrove's former sheriff. He hadn't been around when Renee died, however, Deputy Bryan Coulter had been a young officer when she'd passed away. He'd lived in Penngrove all of his life, and the citizens respected him.

The Penngrove Sheriff's Office was the last building on the block. It was a simple structure with a pair of bright blue mailboxes flanking its front steps, and the interior was a long rectangle of scuffed hardwood and tile. A man waved from across the room. Balding with eyes like an exhausted Saint Bernard, he lumbered toward them.

"Cade, my boy," the man said, slapping Cade's shoulder affectionately.

"Nice to see you, Sheriff."

"It's been Harlowe for years, you know that." He glanced at Maren, smiled. "And you must be the biographer."

"That's me." She accepted the handshake, and his skin felt like a cheese grater against hers.

"What can I help you with?"

Maren set her shoulders and summoned a professional tone. "Do you have a key for the *Penngrove Gazette's* basement? Waldo Samson recalled giving you one."

"We've got a few keys downstairs. He locked out or something?"

"No, nothing like that." She smiled to ease the worry creasing his forehead. "Does anyone else have access to the key?"

"My officers do, and my deputy."

"Any civilians?"

He shook his head. "What's this about?"

"I noticed the archive's door was ajar when I visited, that's all." She probably shouldn't lie to law enforcement, but what other choice was there? She didn't know who was involved in this, and until she did, Maren had to be careful.

Cade nodded. "That's right. Waldo mentioned you had a key and wanted us to remind you to close the door properly."

Well, well, well, he didn't expose her lie. Good to know he had her back—for now, anyway.

Harlowe scratched his stubble. "I'll remind the team to be more careful. Anything else?"

Might as well try her luck. "Yes, actually. What do you know about Renee Thurstan?"

"Jeez. Haven't heard that name in a while."

"Cade said you weren't around when she drowned?"

"The investigation was before my time. I've heard a lot about her though." Glancing at Cade, he said gently, "She was a kind woman."

"Would you mind if we discussed the case?" Maren asked.

"Be happy to." Oh, how she loved Southern hospitality. "Far as I recall, there wasn't much of a case. The file's pretty skinny."

"I'd love to review it anyway. I'll be writing an In Memoriam page and want to make sure I get the details correct."

"We really shouldn't be sharing files with civilians, but ..." He tilted his head back and forth. "What the heck. Take a seat and I'll see about finding it."

Maren spun at the tinkle of a bell. A man sporting an oatmeal-colored dress shirt and a pair of olive slacks stood at the entrance. His black hair was thinning at the temples, and the gold star pinned to his chest glinted under the lights.

Cade nodded. "Hey, Bryan."

"Heard murmurs you two were in town." He smiled at her. "Deputy Bryan Coulter. Happy to meet you, ma'am."

"Likewise." She escaped his clammy handshake. "I met your wife the other day. Lovely woman."

"She told me. Best be careful or she'll be packing you a pound's worth of sugary treats to take home."

"I wouldn't say no."

"Neither can I," he said, patting his belly. "You two just looking around or was there something I could help with?"

"Harlowe's taking care of it. He's downstairs grabbing the file on Mom's investigation."

"Oh? What for?"

"I'm including a piece about Renee in their biography," Maren explained, "and I wanted some first-hand accounts of what went on that night."

"Well, why don't we wait in my office? I'm hankering for a smoke and don't want any looky-loos tattling to the wife. Can I get you anything? Water, coffee?"

"I'm good," they said in unison, and rounded the reception desk. Portraits lined the narrow staircase, a memorial to past sheriffs.

"This is it," Bryan announced, opening the door on the landing and ushering them inside.

She sat near the window overlooking the rocky parking lot, and wrinkled her nose at the strong smell of tobacco.

Various knick-knacks cluttered Bryan's desk and in the middle, like a sacred ornament, sat a full ashtray.

"You're all I've heard about these last couple days." Leaning back in the leather swivel chair, Bryan wrestled a cigarette box from his pocket.

She smiled. "News travels fast. I hope I don't disappoint."

"Travels in tidal waves." He hacked out a chuckle, waving a finger toward Cade. "Add in our resident millionaires, and the gossip turns into a monsoon. They treatin' you well at the mansion?"

"Yes, thank you. While we're waiting for the file, do you mind if I ask some questions?" When he shook his head, she asked, "Did you know Renee well?"

"In a town this size, you know everyone well. Renee and I actually went to high school together, though, she was a couple years younger than me."

"Did you attend the party the night she died?"

"Sure, I think everyone did. Was a happy affair before it all went to hell."

"Were you there when they discovered her body?"

"No, ma'am. Harmony and I left around eleven, and we were in bed when I got the call. The team and I rushed over, saw Renee being loaded into the ambulance. I helped interview some people from the party, but otherwise wasn't involved much in the investigation." He blew a puff of smoke ceilingward. "She was one in a million. I wish I could've done more."

"You did all you could," Cade said, trading a smile with Bryan.

Hopefully, his fondness for the Coulters wouldn't influence his objectivity. There were only a few people who could've entered the archives—assuming Harlowe was telling the truth—and Bryan was among them. Once she identified the person, she'd need to figure out why they'd been there, and every neuron in her body said the reason wasn't innocent.

Harlowe stopped in the doorway, carrying a purple folder. "Whoops, sorry for interrupting. Didn't realize you were back, Bryan."

"Not a problem. You find Renee's file?"

"Sure did."

"Mind if I peek at it? Might refresh my memory."

"You bet." Harlowe headed for the desk. "You wouldn't believe the mess down there. Usually, I send Bryan down for the files. Young legs on him. Well, younger than me anyway. We really oughta hire an intern to—" His shoe caught on a chair leg, and both hands shot out to grab the desk. The file tented on the floor, spitting its contents in every direction. "Shoot."

"Don't worry, I got them," she told him, leaning down.

"Thanks, Maren. I got no business bending. My back ain't what it used to be."

"Getting butterfingers in your old age?" Cade asked.

Maren tuned out their conversation as she swept the papers into a pile. One header read "Coroner's Report" typed in her favorite font, and her mouth went dry. The information contained within those pages would deter- mine the course of her future. If it revealed evidence of foul play, she'd have the bombshell for Primrose and if not, she'd be forced to investigate Cade's past. With a deep breath, she handed the file to Bryan.

Harlowe hovered near the wall, razzing Cade and rem- iniscing about people she didn't know. Meanwhile, Bryan kept his eyes focused on her—narrowed eyes, at that.

Was he ... angry?

"Wouldn't you agree, Maren?" Cade's voice yanked her back to reality, and she cocked her head.

"Sorry?"

"I was just telling the sheriff how you'll probably know more about my family than I do once this is over."

"Yeah, probably." She turned back toward Bryan. "Are you reacquainted with the case yet, Deputy?"

He nodded. "Here. Have a look through and let me know if you've got any more questions."

Cade slid closer as she opened the file. Crime-scene photos showed the pond lightened by streaks of sunrise, but nothing caught her eye in the images so she flipped to the witness statements. They all corroborated Cade's story, detailing Renee's midnight disappearance.

A drawer squeaked and a lock twisted, but Maren was so focused on the coroner's report she barely registered the sounds. The document confirmed the cause of death as drowning. There had been no strange marks on her body, no defensive wounds, and no signs of foul play.

She drooped against the chairback. Cade had been right; there wasn't any mystery here. What an idiot she was for thinking otherwise. Renee probably passed out and couldn't swim. As for the archives visitor ... she must've imagined it.

Cade smiled, and her trachea turned to charcoal. No more playful heckling. She had to find out what happened in his past and reveal it to the world. Just thinking about it made her stomach hurt.

Maren stared longingly at the papers. If only they'd shown something different. If only they'd verified—wait. This wasn't right. The one she'd seen earlier had been typed in Cambria, but this was Times New Roman. Two reports?

She felt like a figure skater who'd just nailed the double axel. Sweet relief. Figuring the other report was in the back somewhere, Maren rustled through the remaining pages. And found nothing. Impossible. She'd definitely seen the other report. The pages must've stuck together, the staples entangled. She sorted through the papers again, and her heart dropped. The other report was gone.

"Everything okay?" Cade asked.

"Uh-huh." She bit her lip and glanced at Bryan. "You're certain this is everything?"

"Yes, ma'am. The case was cut and dry. She was intoxicated and slipped from the bank." Bryan rotated his cigarette and looked at the desk drawer, a fleeting glance that might've slipped by most people—but it didn't slip by Maren. In that moment, the memory punched her: a slamming drawer, a clicking lock.

Holy shit, he'd taken it.

The deputy who'd investigated Renee's drowning was withholding her autopsy report. The question was ... why?

Thirteen

Tension dripped from Cade's body as he handed over the case file. The autopsy report had cemented what he'd always believed: Mom's drowning was accidental. She was at peace, and he could accept everything else as coincidence.

Maren, however, didn't seem convinced. "… and no sign of struggle?"

"Zero," Bryan replied, retrieving another cigarette.

"You sure delve deep into clients' backgrounds," Harlowe said.

Cade laughed. "She's a dog with a bone."

"It's part of the job. May I?" She gestured to the window, opening it when Bryan nodded. Humid air funneled in, cleansing the room's haze. "Who didn't get along with Renee?"

"Like I said before, wasn't one person who didn't like Renee."

"So, nobody wanted to harm her?"

Bryan's eyes turned to slits. "No."

Did Maren ever stop pestering people? The woman had missed her calling; she should've been a horsefly. If he didn't say something, she'd continue questioning the deputy until the wee hours of the morning. "How about letting these two get back to work, huh?" he asked, climbing to his feet.

Harlowe pushed off the wall. "Splendid idea. I'll walk you out."

"I appreciate your time," Maren said to the deputy before following them into the hallway.

"Busy day ahead?" Cade asked.

"Hardly." Harlowe held open the front door. "You need anything else, you know where we are. And hey, enjoy the rest of your time in Penngrove."

"Take care." Cade strutted outside where the sunlight was lathering the asphalt, creating a shimmer above Main Street. Even the flowers, so bright in their concrete beds, wilted in the swelter. Hands on his hips, he inhaled the soggy scent of home.

Maren dropped onto a bench beside him. Not pouting—that would be out of character with her determination, her perseverance—but something was off. Disappointment, surely. After all, she'd spent three days chasing down a bum lead. He shouldn't get involved, shouldn't console or do anything that would establish an emotional connection with the woman.

But he couldn't just leave her there.

Despite his brain hollering for him not to, Cade sat down. "I'm sorry."

She continued staring at the ground. "Why?"

"Because you didn't find anything. Have to admit though, I'm relieved. I've always been told her death was an accident. To discover otherwise ... Not sure how I'd have handled that."

"Would you rather not know? Hypothetically, I mean. If it turned out someone had lied to you about the drowning."

"No. I'd want to get justice."

A candy wrapper skittered down the sidewalk, destroying the conga line of black ants trudging across the cement.

"Why'd you chase this so hard?" Cade asked, breaking the silence.

"I told you why."

"The scrapbook picture? I don't buy that. Something else is driving you."

Maren rested her temple on her fist. "I need a climax, something explosive to attract readers. A suspicious death would've worked wonders."

"Why now? I started reading the McMahon biography and haven't seen any dramatic reveals."

"You're reading my book?"

"For research."

"Research." Her features lifted. "Of course."

Wind mussed her hair, whisking the strands across her cheeks. Desdemona and Memaw would've grabbed a mirror and fussed over their reflections but not Maren. She let it whip and wag, her eyes bright, her smile radiant.

Refreshing, how she accepted what life offered and made do without vanity or complaint. He admired that attitude. Was she content with it as well? Or did she feel inferior to a woman like Desdemona? A little too plain, a little too simple in comparison. Maybe that's why their biography needed to be different. Did Maren hope to impress his aunt by outselling the competition?

"I don't think you have anything to worry about," Cade told her. "My family spent months evaluating biographers, and they chose you. Your style obviously resonated with them, so just do what you usually do."

She picked at her cuticles. "If only."

"Desdemona doesn't need perfection, you know."

"It's not her I'm worried about."

"Then who are you worried about?"

"Nobody."

He searched her eyes. Their corners didn't crinkle, and her irises didn't gleam with that hint of mischief he found so alluring. They looked desperate, hollow. "You're lying."

"Am I?"

"You're turning away, and your muscles are stiff. Those are dead giveaways."

She straightened. "When did you become a body language expert? Besides, you're hiding things from me too. It's only fair I do the same."

Clever tactic: pretending she knew something so he'd divulge information. But he wasn't falling for it. "I've told you all I can. You want more, then ask a question."

"Very well." She scooted across the bench, her expression hardening. "Why didn't you attend Stanford like your cousins?"

"How do you know I didn't?"

"Doesn't matter. You have your question, now where's my answer?"

"I wanted to study elsewhere."

"Why?" Maren withdrew her phone, and pulled up a list of statistics. "Look at this. Stanford had the best business program around your graduation year, yet you went to Hopkins."

Cade wiped the sweat from his brow and shrugged. "So I got it wrong."

"Hard to believe you'd get something like that wrong."

"Shit happens."

"And what about majoring in medicine instead of business? That just more shit that happened?"

"Fuck." He thrust off the bench.

She knew. How the hell did she know? Not long before she discovered everything else, if she hadn't already. His career, his practice, and how he'd destroyed both.

No, those details couldn't get out. He'd make sure of it.

Cade whipped around. "How much do you want?"

"What?"

"Jesus." He belted a humorless laugh. "Can you stop the cutesy innocent act? You found out my secret, great job. Now how much money will it take to keep your mouth shut?"

She approached him slowly, like a farmer calming their skittish colt. "I don't want money."

"So what the hell do you want?"

"Your help."

"Keep dreaming."

A bell jingled above the station door, and Harlowe and Bryan exited onto the sidewalk. Their voices quieted as they headed for the parking lot.

"Stop talking for two seconds, and let me explain myself," she demanded, her tone frantic now. "I don't know why you work in HR, or what you're so desperate to hide from the world but believe me, I could find out if I wanted to."

"You sure know how to sweet-talk a man into helping you."

"And you sure know what 'stop talking' means."

Like twisting a stove knob, that sexy smirk reduced his anger from a boil to a simmer. Maren held the thread that could unravel him, and yet, she hadn't tugged. Why?

"What I said before was true: I need something exciting for my book. And I'm sure I could've found that in your medical background, but I think there's something bigger going on. Something that involves your mother."

"You saw the report, Maren. She drowned. Let it go already."

Maren jumped as the sheriff's car rumbled through the alley and turned onto the street. Shoving her hair back, she said, "Listen to me, okay? Because we don't have much time. Bryan lied to you, lied to us. When Harlowe dropped the papers, I saw a coroner's report that wasn't included in the file Bryan gave me."

"But there was an autopsy report in there. You looked right at it."

She shook her head. "It wasn't the same one. There's two autopsy reports, and Bryan hid the other one in his desk."

"How do you know there's two reports?"

"Because they were in two different fonts. The one I saw was typed in Cambria, but the one we looked at together was in Times New Roman."

"Different fonts," he repeated, skeptical. "And you expect me to believe that you can identify Cambria from a split-second glance?"

"Yes. It's my favorite font."

"Your favorite font."

"Think I'm crazy all you want, but it doesn't change the facts. Bryan's hiding something, and I need your help to find out what. That's why I was upfront about the degree stuff; I want you to trust me."

Cade didn't believe any of it, but there was no harm in playing along. "What'd you need help with?"

"Breaking into the sheriff's station." And that was the last thing she said before taking off toward the alleyway.

Fourteen

"Are you crazy?" Cade shouted, his shoes slapping the pavement behind her. "And just how're you planning on breaking in?"

"Easy." Maren stopped near the station's back windows. Most people kept their windows shut in this heat, opting for conditioned air over fresh, but she'd planned for that. "I opened Bryan's window before we left, but I can't reach it by myself."

"Ah, that's my role then."

Striding to the open window, she smiled over her shoulder. "You catch on quick."

"So I've been told. Hey"—he grabbed her arm, twirling her to face him—"this is a felony, you know. You're asking me to commit a crime."

"Technically, you'll only be the lookout. I'll be the one trespassing."

"Still. You want me to stick my neck out for you? I want assurances." He released her, and she blinked up at him.

"What assurances?"

"The Coulters are close friends, and nobody would appreciate you making accusations against them. If what you're saying is true, I'm with you. All in. We find out what happened to Mom together." He rubbed the back of his neck, glancing toward the trees. "But if you're lying, we terminate your contract, and you head back to New York."

The chill returned, the same one inhabiting her body when he'd accused her of extortion. She understood his reasons for being wary, but it still hurt knowing Cade thought her capable of blackmail. Stupid, to care about his opinion; it'd only get in her way later.

For now, they shared a goal: to verify what happened to Renee. But they weren't friends, weren't lovers. Two vehicles driving in side-by-side lanes, that's what their relationship was. Similar destinations, but eventually their roads would diverge, and she'd be on her own. Best to distance herself, and ignore any strange feelings the man stirred up.

She set her jaw. "I can agree to those terms."

"Then we'd better get moving."

He laced his fingers beneath the window, and she placed her foot in his palm, her hand on his shoulder. His muscles tensed under the cotton, and he thrust upwards, propelling her toward the sill. Her biceps burned as she pulled herself inside, bucking like a beached salmon. He must've been grinning at her graceless scramble, but she had no time to look back and confirm.

Sinking to her haunches, Maren crept to Bryan's desk and tugged the bottom drawer. Shit, locked. With a huff, she looked to where Bryan and Harmony were staring at her from the screensaver. Part of her wished he wasn't involved. At least that way, she wouldn't have to devastate two families: the Thurstans by divulging the truth behind Renee's "accidental drowning", and the Coulters by revealing Bryan's role in hiding the autopsy report.

Stop daydreaming, idiot.

Maren refocused, scanning the desk for anything useful. Pencil cup, stapler, snow globe, ruler—hey, that might work. She wedged the ruler into the slit of the drawer and rattled it back and forth, attempting to jar the mechanism loose. Voices infiltrated the office, and her armpits dampened. *Don't come in here, don't come in here.*

Finally, the drawer's lock clicked, and she stifled a hoot.

Heart battering her rib cage, she rifled through irrelevant papers until she found it. Her gold, her treasure cache, written in beautiful Cambria font. She flipped back the cover page.

And the excitement vanished.

Time of death: blacked out. Cause of death: redacted. All the useful information was incomprehensible. There was nothing here.

"Shit." She combed through the report, flipping so quickly the staple nearly snapped. "Shit, shit, shit!"

She grabbed her phone and snapped pictures; at least Cade would know the report existed. That would be enough to keep him from kicking her out. It had to be.

Maren returned everything to the drawer and headed for the window, but a noise in the hallway made her stop dead in her tracks. Footsteps. Right outside.

Frozen needles pricked the back of her neck as she flicked glances around the room. She needed a place to hide. Now.

The window was too far; she'd never make it. Keys tinkled, and floorboards squeaked. They were coming inside. *Okay, okay. Think.* The bookshelf was too skinny to hide behind, filing cabinet too. Only one option left. Maren stashed herself under the desk, her knees stabbing into her chin.

The knob squealed. The door creaked. And she squeezed her eyes shut as the individual entered the office. *Please, don't stay long.*

"... so no reason to worry." A gravelly voice. Bryan's voice. "She came, asked questions, and left." He walked to the desk, the hardwood screaming beneath his feet. "Yeah.

Cade was with her, but he seemed satisfied with what I provided."

Spurs clanged, and a pair of cowboy boots appeared in front of her, close enough to touch the scuffs. Maren clamped a hand over her mouth, hushing her exhales. Sweat dripped off her earlobe, and exploded on the floor. Had he heard that?

"I took care of everything. Been taking care of everything for twenty damn years ... Don't take that tone with me. You're knee deep in this shit too." Bryan sat down, but he hadn't spotted her. Yet. If he kept rolling, those boots would meet soft flesh, and she'd be finished.

"I don't know where she is ... It ain't my fucking job to keep track of her. Try descending from your throne and ... No. Please. I'm sorry, alright? I'm looking now. Maren won't find her. Promise."

Who was he talking to? And who were they looking for? Maren strained to hear the caller—Male? Female?—but the voice was impossible to identify.

Bryan rolled his chair forward. Ugh, that smell. Dried dirt and acid-washed denim. She packed herself tighter, her organs pressing against her throat. His toe hovered an inch from her thigh. No, no, no.

"Help! Somebody help!"

Bryan's knee jerked, and he hurried toward the window. Her heartbeat decelerated, relief flooding into her body like an eight-foot tidal wave—wait. That scream. That was—

"Cade?" Bryan gasped. "Holy hell. Stay there, I'll grab my gun!"

Gun?

The door shut, and Maren scrambled into the open. She didn't look out the window, couldn't risk Bryan spotting her. What was happening? Was Cade hurt? Guilt cannonballed through her rib cage. If she hadn't asked for help, he wouldn't have been here in the first place.

Unable to wait any longer, she crouched down, and waddled beneath the windowsill. Dog barks echoed through the willow leaves, but there were no voices in the background, no conversations to overhear. She chewed her fingernail. Tapped her thigh. Checked the clock. Tick, tick, tick. She bumped her crown against the wall and blew out her cheeks. What the hell was going on?

"Maren!"

Cade. Her heart sailed into the clouds at the sound of his voice.

"Holy crap, you scared me." She peeked outside, looking up and down his body. No blood, no bruises. No injuries? "What happened? Are you okay?"

"Yeah. Come on, I'll help you down."

She clambered over the sill, and Cade moved to her dangling legs. Chest hair rustled beneath his shirt as she glided down his body, and warmth kindled in her abdomen at the feel of his hands brushing her thighs. Her feet met gravel, but she couldn't speak, couldn't move. Her palms rested on his pecs while his lingered on her hips.

"You good?"

She had trouble summoning her voice, too distracted by the way his tongue swept over his bottom lip. "Yes, I'm good." Her answer was a breath. "Very good."

Her desire stirred. The trance, hypnotizing. Her only thought? Yank him closer and press her mouth to his, collapse into the craving she'd been battling since he'd kissed her among the fireflies.

But she didn't do any of that.

Because he stepped back.

"I'm sorry about Bryan," he said. "No cars pulled in, so he must've walked back."

"It's ..." Maren bit the inside of her cheek. Stop acting like a lovesick schoolgirl. "It's fine. I hid until you—" Her eyes widened. "Wait, you're okay, aren't you?"

"I'm good. Didn't want him seeing you, so I said an alligator lunged at me. He's off searching for it with his shotgun."

She looked toward the tree line. "Do they come that close to town?"

"Sometimes."

"Lovely." She wrapped her arms around her stomach. "Anyway, that was quick thinking. Thank you."

"No problem."

"Should we wait for him to return from his jungle trek?"

"Jungle? Using that term pretty loosely, don't you think?" His smile shivved her heart, had her looking everywhere except him. "But no, we don't have to wait. Bryan loves alligator hunting, so he'll be out there for hours, I'm sure."

"Especially when the alligators are fictional."

"Especially then." He smiled again, then motioned toward the sheriff's station. "You find anything in there?"

"Not what I'd hoped for. Here, take a look."

He accepted her phone and swiped through the images. "It's ... it's real?"

The shock in his voice plunged a scalpel into her sternum. He'd truly believed she'd been lying to him. Ouch.

"Sure is," she said. "Looks like you're stuck with me for the rest of the month."

Cade stopped blinking. "Do you remember the date from the report Bryan showed us?"

"Late August, I think."

"Fifteenth." His head snapped up. "This is from the fifteenth. That means this is the original. Who requested that other autopsy?"

She couldn't voice her suspicions. Not yet. She wanted an ally who was truly invested in discovering what had happened to Renee, and for that to happen, Cade needed to reach his own conclusions, garner his own doubts. But what was the harm in helping him along?

"Your grandparents?" she offered.

"They weren't skeptical people. I don't see them questioning the results."

"What about the sheriff?"

"You heard Bryan, it was an accidental drowning. One hundred percent. Why request another examination if there weren't any doubts?"

"Maybe the coroner messed up and decided to re-examine."

"Maybe."

She recognized that tone. The cogs were rotating in his mind, the questions multiplying. Puzzle pieces were coming together, and finally, he was starting to see the full picture.

She stepped toward him. "What are you thinking?"

"Bryan hid this. Why do that unless ..."

"Unless?"

"Unless he didn't want anyone seeing it." He pushed his curls back and held them for an instant. "Because he's involved somehow."

Bingo. "I'm sorry, Cade. I have no answers right now, but I'll find them."

"*We'll* find them." He looked at her, his ocean-blue eyes swirling her emotions. "I thought you were lying."

She pursed her lips. "You had good reason. I've been keeping my cards pretty close."

"Well, time to lay them down. Let's go."

They walked to the car, and Maren explained everything that had happened, including the phone call she'd overheard.

"... so I couldn't hear who Bryan was talking to, but that's not our only problem." She stopped beside the passenger door. "I also don't know where we go from here."

"I do." He ducked inside and cranked the air conditioning. "That first report had a name on it. Let's find the coroner, see what they know."

"We're not detectives, they won't speak to us."

"They'll speak to me."

"How can you be so certain?"

He shrugged. "People like me."

"Really?" Maren adjusted her seat. "I can't relate."

"Of course you can't." Smiling, he shook his head. "How did I get stuck with you anyway? I'm a good person, strong, hardworking."

"So are dung beetles."

"Sticks and stones, baby," Cade drawled, turning onto Main Street. "You're attracted to me, admit it."

"Wrong. Aren't doctors supposed to be smart?"

"Come on. This"—he gestured to his body—"does nothing for you?"

"Sure, it does." She batted her eyes. "It makes my bile rise."

He chuckled. "Lady, you're so deep in denial you can't even see the surface anymore."

"I'm in denial? You're the one who can't accept that I don't find you attractive."

"Can't kiss me like that without feeling something."

"I never said I didn't feel anything." She pressed her lips together, suppressing the smile. "Is disgust an emotion?"

He laughed again. "You'll learn to appreciate me. Just wait."

No need. Her cheeks were embers. Her stomach, a butterfly conservatory. It was wrong to feel this way. He wasn't some boy next door, wasn't some coffee-shop Casanova she could shag and abandon. Cade Thurstan was a client, and pursuing anything with him beyond professional acquaintanceship would be a terrible idea. And for the rest of the drive, she stared out the windshield, definitely not thinking about that terrible, terrible thing.

Fifteen

THE PARISH MEDICAL EXAMINER was located a few miles east of New Orleans. Steering into the parking lot, Cade glanced at the building. Shimmering windows, ruby-red bricks, trimmed hedges: the place looked too cheerful to house a morgue.

He folded an arm over his eyes as he climbed out of the car. The air was like a preheated oven threatening to blister anyone who lingered too long and yet, he couldn't bring himself to move. He pictured his mother, bloated and swaddled in a black tarp, being rolled through those double doors while strangers in crisp, white coats pricked her with medical tools, not allowing her a moment's peace even in death.

"Cade?" Across from him, Maren tipped her head. "Are you okay?"

"Yeah." He sucked a breath. "Let's get this over with."

Cade accompanied her up the sidewalk, and held the door as she shuffled inside. Goosebumps erupted on his arms as soon as he crossed the threshold. Starch-white walls surrounded a receptionist frowning at her computer, her gray bun rigid against the blasting central air. The chilly interior provided solace for the workers and pre-vented the corpses from decomposing. Win-win.

His stomach spasmed as he walked toward the front desk. Had he known this place would affect him so strongly, Cade would've phoned for the information. Instead, he'd driven an hour to speak with the coroner in person, partly to gauge Dr. Garcia's reactions, and partly so he could show Maren the city.

No Louisiana trip was complete without a visit to New Orleans. He'd give her the tour, stand in the background while her eyes sparkled. It was all strictly professional, of course. He wanted to show her the sights because he wanted to be a good host—not because he wanted her.

But that didn't mean she wasn't tempting.

Man, that laugh; it was mute your favorite song pretty. Cade had taken it one step further and shut off the whole damn radio. Maren hadn't seemed to mind; in fact, she'd appeared to genuinely enjoy their conversations during the drive up here.

Not attracted, his ass.

Any fool could see the pull between them. The way she'd gazed at him back at the station: electric, but he didn't want a repeat of their kiss behind the house. High on emotion, regretful afterward. She'd said she wanted to keep things professional, and he'd respect her wishes. No matter how hard it was.

The old lady rose from the desk, narrowing her eyes. "Can I help you?"

"I'm hoping so, ma'am." Cade tugged on his collar and tried to muster his charm. "May we speak with one of your doctors?"

"You got a body to claim?"

"No, ma'am. We wanted information on a past autopsy."

"This isn't a walk-in clinic. Our doctors won't appreciate you just stopping by."

"I understand, and we won't take too much of their time. Could we—"

"Wait." She patted the sides of her hair, capturing the rogue strands. "You're Kincade Thurstan, aren't you?"

"I am." He grinned. "You can call me Cade if you'd like."

"Sylvia." The old woman giggled, offering her pale hand. "Imagine, Kincade Thurstan in my clinic. The book club won't believe it. Which doctor was it again, sweetheart?"

He propped against the desk, ignoring Maren shaking her head beside him. "Garcia? I only have the last name."

"Name sure sounds familiar." Sylvia sat down and clicked on the keyboard. "You got a date for me?"

"Would've been about twenty years ago. August."

She stopped typing. "Magdalena Garcia. Gotta be."

"Is she available?"

"What is this regarding?"

"We have some questions about my mother's autopsy."

"Your mother?" She touched her collarbone. "Oh my word, Renee."

"You knew her?"

"Not personally. My church used to hold our annual picnic in Penngrove, and Ian and Renee would stop by sometimes to speak with the pastor. I was so sad to hear about her passing."

"That's actually why we're here: we'd like more info on her death. Maren's writing our biography, but it's tough finding records. We were hoping Dr. Garcia could shed some light for us."

"I'm afraid that's not possible." Sylvia lowered her head. "She no longer works here."

"Well, that really puts a stick in our spokes."

"Did she transfer somewhere?" Maren asked. "Leave a forwarding address?"

"I really shouldn't share details, but ..." She checked the hallway to her left and leaned forward. "Maggie was one of our best doctors."

Maren mimicked her hushed tone. "We can assume she wasn't fired then. What happened?"

"A month before she left, Maggie started acting real strange. Wouldn't chat with me anymore, kept to herself. Worked different hours and wanted to be walked to her car. Scared off her biscuit."

"She never told you why?"

Sylvia glanced at Cade. "No. Then, she just disappeared one day. Didn't show up for work, didn't answer the phone. Gone." Sylvia clasped her hands. "God bless her. I hope she's safe."

He twiddled his thumbs. "Did she have a place she liked to go? Someone she liked to talk to?"

"Heavens, it was so long ago, I don't think—wait. Maggie had a sister, just a bitty thing. Let me think now, what was her name?" Sylvia tapped her lip, and he held his breath.

If she didn't remember the name, he would hire an investigator to find the doctor. But how long would that take? Maren had three weeks left in Louisiana—precious little time to vet a P.I. and get them up to speed on what's happened—and with nothing to distract her, she'd switch focus. To him, his past, his degree. And he didn't plan on just rolling over and letting her ruin him. No, if Maren came after him, she'd be gone. Contract terminated. To hell with his family's opinion on the subject.

"They had cute nicknames for each other," Sylvia said. "The girl would call her Magpie. And Maggie said ... Ana Banana! Ana Luisa, that was her name. Ana Luisa Garcia."

"You're a lifesaver. If there's anything you ever need, call me." He handed over his business card and tried to keep his cool. Inwardly, he whooped and whistled, cheered and cartwheeled.

"Take this before you go," Sylvia said, chasing after him. "Good luck with the biography. Safe travels."

Cade unfolded the paper and grinned. Now they were getting somewhere.

Outside, Maren hooted a laugh. "Is it always this easy getting what you want?"

"I believe I got what *we* want." He unlocked the car doors and dropped into the driver's seat.

"I thought for sure she wasn't giving us anything. Did you see the scowl when we walked in?" She scrunched her nose and pinched her lips, and he smiled at her impersonation as the vehicle rumbled to life. "One look at your handsome face and she melted."

"Aha!" He snapped his fingers and pointed at her. "Attraction. There it is."

"That really should've been obvious. I kissed you, remember? Why kiss a man you're not attracted to?"

"Charity work." He cranked the wheel, heading for the interstate. "And you're remembering that wrong. It was I, who kissed you."

"In that case, I guess I owe you one."

His ears heated. "Thought we were keeping it professional?"

"We were." She smirked. "So, what's next? Visiting every Ana Luisa in the city until we find one who responds to Ana Banana?"

"Tempting, but I say we head for the source." Cade passed her the folded paper.

"An address?" She cast her eyes upward. "Unbelievable."

"Do you appreciate me yet?"

"Maybe."

Chuckling, he shook his head. "Man, you're hard to please."

A CRACKED CONCRETE ROAD led to the Garcias' trailer. Two mighty oaks banked the driveway, blocking the sun with their creeping branches. He drove into the shade and parked his sedan behind a corroded station wagon.

"Looks like someone might be home." Cade climbed out. Maren, however, did not. He rounded the hood and opened the passenger door. "Maren?"

She panned the property. "I don't like this place."

"Why?"

"Something feels off."

The area wasn't exactly charming: overgrown lawn, moss-infested trees, a fence coiled by vines and rusted by rain.

She stirred. "It's too quiet."

"You're in the countryside, remember? It's supposed to be quiet. Come on, city girl, we'll be quick." He forged ahead. The porch was covered in junk. A mold-speckled stroller sat in the corner, framed by two mop buckets, and beside them, a wicker bookshelf loaded with crusty garden tools.

When his knock went unanswered, Cade tried again. "Ana Luisa? Sorry to bother you, but do you have a minute?"

Maren stuck close, her breath tickling the back of his neck. "I'll go around, check the windows."

"Sure. Be careful."

"Thought you said there's nothing to be afraid of?" She flaunted a teasing smile, and disappeared around the corner.

Nothing moved. No birds cooed, no breeze billowed. Graveyards were livelier than this place. He cupped his hands like binoculars and peered inside, but the window grime was too thick to see anything. No big deal. They'd head home and come back tomorrow. He glanced around, frowning when he saw Maren hadn't returned yet. Then, a scream rattled the trees. Her scream.

Cade broke into a sprint, tearing across grass and mud as fast as his shoes allowed. In the backyard, he slid to a stop. "Maren!"

She had her nose squished against the back door, her left hand pounding the glass, her right jostling the knob. And her entire body was vibrating like gelatin during a hurricane.

He grabbed her elbow. "Maren? What's wrong?"

"There's someone in there."

"What?"

"There's someone in there, Cade!" She exhaled in rapid spurts and her fingers trembled as she pointed. "On the floor. Oh my god, she's on the floor. We have to get in, we have to help."

He peeked through the window, and his heart dropped when he spotted the woman sprawled on the linoleum. Was she alive? Shit, he couldn't tell.

"Take a deep breath, Maren. In." He inhaled, gesturing for her to do the same. "And out. Do that a couple more times for me, okay?"

Cade tapped the glass, but the woman didn't look over. Didn't move, didn't twitch. His vision tunneled, and in that moment, a switch flipped inside of him. He was no longer the bored Human Resources Director; he was a doctor, and he had a patient to save.

He rammed the door with his shoulder. Once. Twice. The hinges snapped, and he stumbled into the kitchen, falling to his knees. With his fingers pressed against the woman's carotid, he glanced at Maren. "I need you to call 911. Can you do that?"

"Yes. I can do that." She was blinking too fast. Her skin, too pale. But he couldn't worry about Maren right now, not when this woman was laying incapacitated on her kitchen floor.

A weak pulse beat against his fingertips. She was alive, but just barely. He moved his hands down her arms, noting how her skin roughened near her inner elbow. Fuck, needle tracks. Probably an overdose then, which meant he needed to move her into recovery position. Cade bent her right leg and rolled the woman onto her side. He adjusted her chin, ensuring her airway was clear.

"Ma'am? Can you hear me?" He looked around at the dishes towering in the sink and the pill bottles littering the counters. It was a damn pharmacy in here. Obviously something was in her system, poisoning her. Had it been ingested or injected? Impossible to tell.

She groaned, and Cade said, "Help is on the way, ma'am. What's your name?"

"I don't ..." Her eyes were hazy, unfocused. "Ana. My name's Ana."

"Ana Luisa?"

She groaned again, and he had to stop her from flipping over.

"Try to lie still, Ana. Keep your head on its side. Just like that, good. Good. Do you remember what happened?"

Tears seeped from her eyes and dribbled onto the floor.

"Let me help you," he pleaded. "Tell me what you took."

"I don't know. It wasn't—" She retched.

Vomit. A death sentence had he and Maren not been here. Cade filled a glass with water and stayed close as Ana rinsed her mouth. She was still groggy, but a touch of color was returning to her face.

"I'm tired. So tired." Her eyelids sagged.

"Don't fall asleep yet. Focus on me, and answer my questions, okay? Was it heroin? Meth?"

"It wasn't mine."

"Stay awake. Hey." He patted her cheek. "What wasn't yours?"

"The drugs. He gave them to me."

"Who?"

Her fingers jerked. Trying to point at something? Following her finger, Cade looked backward, but there was nobody behind him. "Ana, is there someone else in the house?"

The door crashed open, and he flew to his feet. Paramedics, just paramedics. While they carried a stretcher into the kitchen, he hurried through the living room. He ripped open the front door, expecting to see Maren composing herself outside. Except the lawn sat empty. Was she waiting in the car? No, he'd locked that, and the keys were still in his pocket. So where was she? Lurking in the house somewhere. Must be.

He poked his head into the bedroom, bathroom, and backyard. "Maren?"

But nobody answered. Maren was gone.

Sixteen

WHILE CADE DOCTORED THE woman in the kitchen, Maren paced the living room, gripping her phone tightly enough to bruise. Finally, an emergency operator picked up, and she hurled out her words. "I need an ambulance! There's an unconscious woman here."

"What's the location of your emergency?"

"Dammit, hold on." She raced across the porch, relaying the house number as soon as it came into view. Luckily, the mailbox listed the street name, so there was no need to jog to the end of the block. With the emergency called in, she held her kneecaps and stared at the grass. Her legs were slippery with sweat, her breath wheezing. Please, let that woman be okay. Let them have gotten to her in time.

Crows cawed, their beady eyes tracking her around the yard. A shiver of apprehension crept up her spine, but she dismissed her instinct to flee. It was just leftover unease. After all, she'd been correct before; things had been off—a woman had been lying unconscious fifteen feet away. But there was no reason to be wary now, no reason for her gut to stir.

She pressed on as the clouds eclipsed the sun, plunging the front yard into darkness. The air adopted a new scent, and she recognized that fresh, earthy musk.

A storm was coming.

Halfway to the house, she quickened her pace. Winds whipped up, billowing a plastic bag across the yard and careening it toward the trees. Thunder grumbled in the distance, and the downpour began. Raindrops slipped off the leaves, moistening the dirt and plopping onto the car roofs.

Something else sounded too. Hoarse and high-pitched, like the screech of a barn owl. Maren paused, listened, angled left.

No, not a bird. A window.

A leg dangled from the first story, blurred by sheets of rain. The rest of the dark figure scuttled from the opening, and landed in the mud with a sopping splash. Thunder drew closer, its menacing growl throwing off her concentration. The person snuck around the rear of the building, ducking through the trees and sliding into the marsh that bordered the property. She swiveled, intending to tell Cade where she was going, but there was no time. She had to move. Now.

Easing down the slope, Maren vanished into the tree line. She weaved through the trunks, the razor-like bark grazing her biceps. She kept her pace steady and her footsteps even. The pounding rain muffled her hiss of breath and her stampeding heart. Keep quiet now, don't follow too close. A violent wind clobbered the treetops, and water gushed from the undergrowth, suffocating her sneakers.

Why did this person sneak out of the house? Had they hurt that poor woman? Did it have something to do with their investigation, with Renee?

Cade called her name somewhere in the darkness. Close enough to hear, but too far to go back. And she wasn't the only one who heard; the figure locked eyes with her, then broke into a sprint.

"Stop!" She propelled forward, leaping over bush and bramble, puddle and stone. Damp ropes of willow sliced her cheeks and nipped at her shoulders. Her flabby muscles burned, struggling to maintain this speed. Using her final ounce of strength, she sprinted faster. Inches away now. If she could just reach out and grab their shirt ...

A root ensnared her, and Maren sailed to the ground. Air whooshed from her lungs as her chin smacked against a rock, shooting painful tingles down her neck. Panting, she curled into a fetal position. Her mark's footfalls quieted before disappearing completely, leaving her alone with dripping leaves and throbbing limbs. The clouds parted, but a dark storm still raged inside her.

That person could've been the key to her problem. She could've brought peace to Cade, funded school for Minowa, appeased Primrose. And she'd failed them all.

"Fuck." Because it felt good surrendering to anger, she smashed her fist against the ground. "Fuck, fuck, fuck!"

She lay in the brushwood until her wounds dulled to an ache and her hostility reduced. Kneeling, she swiped the blood from her face and rubbed it on her shorts, adding another stain to the mud-caked denim. She climbed to her feet, and heaved her arms forward. Shit, this was going to be an uncomfortable walk. Her head was pounding, her legs felt like they'd been carved from uranium, and there was so much water in her shoes, she was convinced her toes might become permanently raisined.

Sunshine lightened the woods but failed to lighten her mood. If only she'd followed closer, pushed harder.

A menacing growl pulled Maren back to reality. She spun around, studying the trees and bushes, searching for the source. And her fingers numbed at the sight of scales. A massive reptile lay prone in the cattails, rumbling like a car engine. Mighty snout, golden eyes, and teeth that sent spiders of fear scurrying over her skin. The beast was close. Too close. One lunge and the alligator would have her in its jaws. Her veins thrashed against her wrist as she stood still as cement, unable to tear her eyes from the alligator. Impossible for her to run away—with those thick hind legs, she'd be gator chow in seconds—and though survival programs said to attack the snout, there was no chance in hell she was going to test that theory. No fight. No flight. What else could she do?

She caught movement in her peripherals and, for one bone-chilling instant, thought death was near. Instead, she spotted a mop of blond, a blink of blue. Could it be—

"Stay calm," Cade said. "No sudden moves. Back up, slowly."

Despite her clenched muscles, she managed a backstep. Another. The alligator grumbled, observing her careful retreat.

"Don't these things live near water?" she whispered.

"Half this state is water. Keep moving."

"And if it follows?"

"We die."

"That's not funny."

"Wasn't supposed to be."

He continued coaxing her backward until the creature was out of sight. Safe for the moment, Maren covered her face with trembling hands. Alive. She was alive.

"You look like shit."

Her fingers slackened, and she released a shaky laugh.

"What's so funny?"

"I don't know." She dropped her arms, giggling. "I thought I was dead. I couldn't even move, I—" She leaned her head back until the laughter subsided. "You saved me. Thank you."

"Anytime. What're you doing out here? You scared the hell out of me."

She looked at him then. Really looked. Sweat idled in the creases on his forehead, and his shirt, drenched by rain, clung to every dip and ridge of his chest. He'd come for her. In the rain and mud and thunder, he'd come for her.

"I saw someone sneak out of that woman's house." Maren gasped. "She survived, didn't she?"

"Yeah. This person you saw, what'd they look like?"

"I didn't get a good look; they were too fast. Couldn't even tell if it was a man or woman."

"What's your gut say?"

She rolled her lips together. "A man. He moved like a man."

"I'd put money on it being a man then. So far, your gut instinct has been pretty spot on."

"Too bad it can't tell me what his name is." She hurried to keep up as Cade started through the trees. "The woman back at the house, you said she'll be okay?"

"She was talking by the time paramedics showed up, alert and conscious."

"Thank goodness. Do you know what happened?"

"Bits and pieces. I think someone drugged her."

"Drugged?" Her voice wavered. "The man I chased, that man in the house—"

"Was likely an attempted murderer? Yeah, I figured as much."

"Cade." She lunged for his wrist, bringing him to a halt. "Tell me what you're not saying."

"She told me her name."

"Ana Luisa. It was her, wasn't it?" She rattled his arm. "Answer me."

"Yes."

"Someone tries to kill her the day we visit? That can't be a coincidence."

He edged forward. "This isn't on us."

"Bullshit it's not on us." Recoiling, Maren pressed her hands to her eyes. "Jesus Christ, I almost got a woman killed today. Maybe not directly, but you can't convince me that, had we not been here, this would've still happened."

"You saved her life, Maren. I would've knocked a few times and left. You're the one who went to peek in the windows, you're the one who found her on the floor."

"Doesn't mean much if I played a part in putting her there."

Cade gripped her shoulders, leveling his gaze with hers. "You're really upset, aren't you?"

"Of course I'm upset!" She shoved away from him. Shock, anger, regret: unsure what to do with the cocktail of emotions, she paced. "I've got my reasons for being down here, but I never intended to get anyone killed."

"You didn't."

She glared at him. "I almost did."

"What if it wasn't you? No"—he held up his forefinger—"shut up for a second and let me speak."

Typically, she would've told him where he could stick it, speaking to her that way. But his expression held no trace of annoyance or smugness, only concern.

"This could've had nothing to do with you. Maybe she has an abusive ex or maybe she needed a fix, got mixed up with the wrong people. She's a drug addict, so it's not a radical theory. If we weren't here, she would've died. We might've saved her. You, might've saved her."

She lowered her head. "I don't buy it, but you're sweet for saying it."

"We're not finished," he said as she began to walk away.

"Oh?"

"You saw a man breaking out of a house that belongs to a woman you don't even know, then pursued him with no regard for your own safety. Why would you do that?"

"Wouldn't anyone?"

"Hell no. Call the sheriff and report it, sure. Book it into the bayou over a stranger? That's not a normal response. You're too smart for that."

She studied the worms wriggling in the puddles. "I wanted his story. Maybe it had something to do with your mom."

"Want to know what else I don't understand?" Cade pitched his hip against a willow trunk. "Why you aren't pursuing easier leads. Your boss wants scandal. Okay. But you're not at the office pestering us about shady business deals. You're not at the house monitoring who's coming home with who. You're out here. With me."

"What's your point?"

He shrugged. "Just doesn't make sense, you doing this solely for your boss or my mom. I think there's a bigger reason."

Maren wrung her hands. "With my sister getting into law school—"

"Minowa."

"Yes." An ache blossomed in her chest. Why did it touch her that he remembered her sister's name? "Her acceptance means tuition bills. She'll get a few scholarships, but there will still be some leftover and since I'm the only one working I need these books to sell. So yes, I'm slightly impulsive at times but with Min's future on the line, there's no other way."

"You're a talented writer." He stepped toward her. "A good sister." Another step. "And a good person." Only a hair of distance between them now, he smirked. "But a terrible liar."

Her eyes held his. "What do you want from me?"

"So many things." He tucked a lock behind her ear, and her toes curled. "Honesty, for starters. I want to know you. Tell me what's going on up here." He tapped her temple.

"I don't want to slander your family."

"Why?" He caught her chin between thumb and forefinger. "Look at me."

"Because I don't want to hurt you, Cade. This is the best course of action; if it turns out there's something more to Renee's death, we both get what we want."

"And what's that?"

"I get my bestseller, and you get to find out what truly happened to your mother."

"Exposing how the people I trust lied to me all my life, that won't hurt me?"

"Maybe. But I asked you back at the station if you'd rather live in ignorance, and you said no. You said that you'd want to know what really happened, that you'd want justice for Renee. So you could say, I asked permission before involving you."

"You did, didn't you?" He blew air from his nose and shook his head slightly. "Dammit, Maren."

"What?"

He traced a finger up her arm. "I meant it when I agreed to stay professional with you."

"I did too. Oh—" Her breath caught as those strong fingers moved to the curve of her neck, a simple touch that jumbled her every nerve.

"But to tell you the truth, I'm having a real hard time keeping my end of the bargain."

"Maybe we shouldn't."

He stilled. "You want to stop—"

"No." She touched his forearm, his hair tickling her palm. "Maybe we shouldn't hold on to that bargain any-more."

Her words seemed to spur him. His finger curled in her belt loop, tugging her against him, and her breasts collided with his chest. All toned pecs and hard lines, and—she smiled—a soft belly further down. Maren noticed nothing else as he pressed his mouth to hers.

Seventeen

Maren had been kissed before. She'd endured her fair
share of after-school pecks behind the football bleachers
and messy smooches in the backseat of station wagons.
Had experienced the yearning, the arousal, the desperate
fumbling of buttons.

But she'd never experienced this.

Cade's mouth was hot and demanding. His tongue
brushed the seam of her lips, teasing her, urging her open.
He cradled the back of her head with one hand, while
the other dug into her hips, caging her against the rough
bark of the willow. She broke away, sucking in air as he
moved to the hollow of her throat. His kisses seared; a
delectable inferno that burned every inch of her, had her
pulse pounding and her breath quickening. Different from
the kiss they'd shared behind the house, but she couldn't
put her finger on why.

He captured her, claimed her in a way that felt deliciously foreign. A weightiness settled in her belly, intensi-
fying as his mouth found hers again. His hand abandoned
her hair and glided down the side of her body, skimming
her breast with his thumb. Maren shivered at the touch.

"So responsive," he murmured, grazing his teeth over
her lower lip. "We'll have a lot of fun together, you and I."

She could only laugh. The man wasn't lying. He knew
how to touch a woman; no doubt he knew how to plea-

sure one too. Excitement rushed through her at the thought of it: tender kisses turning her insides molten while skilled fingers pushed her to carnal pleasure. Her muscles clenched, aching for him.

Her physical response was familiar, but Cade provoked an emotional reaction too. A longing. A desire for something more than make-out sessions and noncommittal sex—and that was downright terrifying. She had responsibilities back home; she couldn't want anything from this man.

Maren pushed on his chest, and he stepped back immediately.

"Are you okay?" He asked cautiously. "It wasn't too much, was it?"

"No." She licked her lips, cherishing the taste of him. "It was perfect. A whopper of a kiss. Thank you." Shit, did she really just say that? Maren covered her eyes, and a blush grilled her cheeks.

"Are you ... thanking me for kissing you?"

"No."

"I think you are."

"You must've misheard me." She hurried past him, a fruitless attempt to avoid further embarrassment since he set off right behind her.

"I don't think I did. In response I say, it was an absolute pleasure kissing you and I plan to do it again very soon."

"How irritatingly polite."

"Hey, you're the one thanking me. I'm just returning the favor."

"I guess chivalry isn't dead."

"Never was. You're just dating the wrong men."

She responded by lengthening her strides. Space and time: those were what she needed right now. A few hours to think and stew, and figure out what the hell that was back there.

She didn't do the mushy thing with men. Didn't have time for it. She had biographies to write and a sister to support, so late-night booty calls suited her just fine. She'd slip from strange beds with her shoes in her hand and her head held high. It wasn't a walk of shame; it was just a walk. That lifestyle had never bothered her because she knew her purpose, had known it from the day her sister entered the world: she'd do whatever it took to make sure Minowa got everything she needed. And for three decades, Maren had stood by that goal.

But doubt had reared today. It was flowing through her system now, seeping into every fiber, every cell. Her body wanted more than gentle caresses from strangers, wanted more than what New York life offered; it wanted Cade. Luckily, the poison hadn't reached her brain yet. There was still time to reverse these effects. She just needed to call her sister.

The paramedics had vacated Ana Luisa's home by the time they reached the yard. The land gurgled underfoot as Maren hurried for the driveway. In the car, she cranked the radio to drown out any attempts at conversation. Her defenses had been stripped, and she feared what she'd say if they discussed their kiss. Too new, these feelings, and she didn't know how to cope. But once her resolve strengthened, she'd figure it out. She'd figure everything out.

SUNLIGHT STREAMED THROUGH THE crack in her bedroom curtains, setting the room ablaze with orange hues. Maren hung her muddied clothes on the bathroom door and showered. Clean, she picked up her phone and stabbed the first name on her contact list.

Minowa answered immediately. "Hi, Mare! I was about to call you."

"Great minds." Smiling, she opened the curtains and bathed in the light of early evening. Outside the glass, a pair of dragonflies tangoed in the wind. "How are things?"

"Things are good! I'm just getting dinner going."

"What're you cooking?"

"Steaks."

She winced. "What credit card did you put those on?"

"Why?"

"I'll have to pay it off. We're running pretty close to our limit, and I don't want it getting denied on you."

"Um ... Visa, I think. How's your trip?"

She scrolled her credit card account and updated her sister on the happenings. "... but luckily, Cade and I finally found a way to get along."

"That'll make things more bearable down there."

"Definitely. He's not as bad as I thought. And I'm not as bad as he thought, apparently."

"Wait ... what's that in your voice?"

"Hm?"

"Holy crap, you kissed him."

"How did you—"

"Please. We've lived together far too long for me to not know your just-kissed voice."

"God, you're a creep."

Minowa laughed. "Don't keep me in suspense. How was it?"

"Nice."

"Nice?"

"Yep."

"Nice is how you describe flower bouquets and finding designer brands in a thrift store. It's not a word to use when describing a kiss from Cade Thurstan. I'd be swooning."

"Really? You guys would be really cute together. Come down and I'll introduce you." Before Minowa acknowledge her joke, she added, "I don't see any charges from your card. Are you sure you used the Visa?"

"It should be there. Don't." She cut off, speaking to someone in the background.

"Who's that?"

"Nobody."

"You're chatting with ghosts now?" She examined her fingernail. "Come on, tell me."

"It's nobody you'd know. Can we just leave it alone?"

Maren scowled at her sister's sharp tone. Something was wrong; Minowa didn't keep secrets from her. "Min, you're scaring me. What's going on?"

Minowa sighed so heavily she swore it heated her cheek.

"I wasn't going to say anything, but since you're so insistent ... Mom's here. With Oliver."

The words hit harder than a jetliner in freefall, and the only response she could manage was, "Oh."

"We were going out for dinner, but I thought it'd be nice to cook something. Oliver brought the steaks."

She squeezed her eyes shut and channeled a positive tone. "I'm glad things are going well."

"You'd like him, Mare. Oliver's really friendly, and he just adores Mom. She's been asking about you too."

"That's nice." What else was there to say?

"She wants to see you," Minowa said carefully. "Or talk to you at least."

"She has my number. But I suppose if she hasn't used it in the last four years, she's not about to start now."

"I don't think you're being fair."

"Fair's a pretty subjective word." Maren breathed deeply as her temperature rose. "You were right. Let's talk about this when I get home. It's not a conversation to have over the phone."

"She's told me stories about her vacation, showed me pictures too. You wouldn't believe how far in the back-country they went. No wonder it was hard to find cell signal."

"I think most airports have signal nowadays. Unless she walked to every country?" The dragonflies' dance trans-formed into a duel. "Don't force this, Min."

"I'm not forcing anything. I'm trying to help you."

"Could've fooled me. Look, just because Rebecca is ready to reconcile doesn't mean I am. She's shown her true colors, and I don't want any part of that toxic rain-bow."

"She did nothing wrong."

"What?"

Louder now, Minowa said, "She did nothing wrong."

"Did nothing—" Unable to digest the outrage flooding through her system, Maren paced. How could her sister say that? "You have no idea what I've had to give up so she could take this little tropical vacation. No idea."

"Because you've never told me! You never tell me any-thing. You're so constipated with communication. Asking what's bothering you is like asking a grizzly bear to hand over her cub."

She opened her mouth, closed it. "I did that to protect you."

"I don't need you to protect me, I need the truth."

"The truth." Maren chuckled dryly. She'd already ex-hausted her brain determining what to do about her at-traction to Cade. Now, her sister was picking a fight. Too much. It was too much. She was confused, tired, and sexually frustrated; emotions which, she decided, were valid excuses for her next outburst.

"You want the truth, Min? Fine. I took dead-end publishing jobs to pay for college and get my dream career. Graduation day Mom says, 'Surprise!' and leaves the country. I had desires, goals. Plans that were put on hold because I had to house us and feed us and buy your school supplies." A geyser of anger exploded. Impossible to plug the hole now. "I've put up with a boss who blackmails me and insults me every damn day, but I do it with a smile on my face because I have to provide for you. Protect you. But hey, you don't want to be protected? Fan-fucking-tastic. I'll depress you with this shit every day until you're as bitter as I am."

Silence. Maren removed the phone from her cheek, and confirmed the call still ran. The timer clocked sixty seconds before her sister spoke again.

"You should've said something." Her voice was quiet. Defeated. "Goddammit, I wish you'd said something."

"I didn't want to upset you."

"But if I'd known how unhappy you were, I'd have never ..." Fabric rustled in what sounded like her sister moving to another area of the apartment.

She'd never vented to Minowa before—bottling her emotions was far easier—but damn, it felt good to share. Surprising too, her words. She'd always adored caring for her sister but now, looking back on the life they shared, she felt only resentment. When had that changed?

An ache bloomed in Maren's chest when she heard her sister's quiet sobs. "Don't cry, Min. I'm sorry. Those things I said, those aren't me. I'm stressed about the biography and losing my mind in this heat."

Minowa sniffled. "That's not true, you know it's not."

"It doesn't matter. I'd be miserable every day if it meant you got a minute of happiness. I love you, and I'm sorry for making you cry."

"I love you too." She took a shaky breath. "I'm not crying because of what you said. We need more of that. Promise you'll tell me the truth more often."

"I promise."

"And I'll do the same thing, starting right now."

Maren curled her legs underneath her. "What's going on?"

"Mom called. Regularly."

She blinked once. Twice. Had she heard incorrectly? Of course, she had. Minowa would never hide something like that. Would she?

"I didn't know things were so bad," Minowa explained. "After everything Mom did for us growing up, she deserved some fun. This adventure brought her smile back."

Maren said nothing.

"Are you still there?"

"Yes," she squeaked out, her lungs aching with every expansion. "How could you keep this from me?"

"You were working so hard. I knew if Mom talked to you, she would've come home."

"Four years. You said nothing for four years."

"I'm sorry!" Tears muffled Minowa's voice. "I didn't want to make you mad."

This wasn't happening. This could not be happening. She needed to get off this phone call, needed time to process this earth-shattering news. "I have to go, Min. Enjoy your dinner, and tell Mom I say hello."

"Maren, wait."

She ended the call and stared at the phone until her eyeballs dried out. She didn't blink. Wasn't sure she could.

Her heart felt like a jack-o'-lantern. Sliced open, hollowed out. Empty.

Maren had forgone everything for her sister. She'd shelved her dreams, stifled her emotions, swallowed her complaints. And the payment for her sacrifice? Betrayal.

Minowa had always been her anchor, but now the chain was severed, and Maren was swirling in a dark ocean, shocked, disoriented. And utterly alone. She needed something to ground her, something to make her feel valued, make her feel wanted. Something.

Or someone.

Eighteen

CADE OGLED MAREN AS she ascended the stairs, her thighs jiggling while strong, mud-speckled calves propelled her up each step. She was a pretty woman—any fool could see that—but the substance of her character, now that was her golden glow.

He'd misjudged her, had assumed her greedy and callous. But she'd disproved that theory today. Far from selfish, Maren was dedicated to protecting those she cared about. It was rare for Cade to witness a display of genuine devotion. His aunt put on a convincing show, preaching about charity and community, but her acts of generosity always involved the company. And was it truly compassion if Desdemona profited from her endeavors?

His stomach grumbled. Should've grabbed takeout on the way home. With dinner being prepared, a snack would have to do. He headed into the kitchen, and found Peter manning the stove. His butler turned around at the sound of the squeaking door.

"I'll fix that soon. Fresh out of grease for those hinges."

"Why didn't you tell me?" Cade asked, grabbing an apple from the fridge and hopping onto the counter. "I've been in and out of town for the last few days. Would've happily picked some up."

"Plum slipped my mind. Besides, you've had your hands full dealing with Maren." He swirled a cast iron pan, and placed some raw chicken to sizzle. "How's it going with her anyhow?"

"Rough at first, but I think we've bridged the gap."

"Good to hear. Mona was worried about how you'd behave."

"I'd never piss her off intentionally. I just want what's best for the family." He crunched the apple and pointed it in Peter's direction. "A fact you agreed with."

The breasts browned. He pricked them with a fork, flipped them. "As does Mona, but you know how she is. If it's good for business ..."

"It's good for her." Cade chuckled under his breath. "Was she always that way?"

"She had other passions once." His smile was weak and as cheerless as the color gray. "When her life didn't revolve around profit margins."

"It's hard to picture."

"They loved the arts, Mona and your mama. Acting, painting, dancing."

"That I believe. Seemed all our parties ended in fox-trots." He twisted the apple stem. "Been a while since we last entertained."

"Hard to organize something with how busy everyone is."

"I miss those days. Memaw used to pack this place to the gizzard."

"She did, didn't she?" Peter brightened. "She was a social butterfly. Like your mom."

"I loved that about them."

"They had good energy. Desdemona, on the other hand, she took after Ian. More reserved and serious. Oldest-sibling syndrome, I call it."

"Lawrence must have a chronic case."

"You may have a point there." He laughed. "I remember when we were teenagers, Renee and I used to." He stopped talking and flicked his wrist. "Never mind. I'm sure you've got things to do."

"No. Tell me."

Peter poked his tongue into his cheek. "You really wanna spend your evening walking down memory lane with this old-timer?"

"What old-timer?" Cade discarded his core and leaned back.

Peter plated the chicken and rested his elbows on the countertop. Conversation flowed easily, a pleasant surprise. Maybe everyone would finally stop tiptoeing, and Cade's life could return to normal.

"... and Bryan—boy could that guy throw a football. He should've gone pro."

"Why'd he stop playing?" Cade asked.

"Life, I suppose. Married Harmony, joined the academy. You know how it goes."

"Were you guys close?"

"Bryan was a good friend. We've drifted some, but I guess that's normal once you get older."

He inched forward. "Did he get along with Mom?"

"Real well, but then again, who didn't get along well with her? Renee could step on a black mamba and still befriend the damn thing." Peter angled his head. "Why're you asking about your mom all the sudden?"

"Maren brought the memories back."

"She still asking about Renee? Mona won't like that."

"Why?"

Peter rubbed his neck. "I think she's afraid the bedlam will start again. Newscasters, journalists. They hounded us for months after Renee passed."

"I never noticed them."

"Boy in mourning doesn't need that hassle. We chased them off the property. Hired people to guard the gates. Protected you the best we could."

"I ... I don't remember any of that." Acid burned his throat. What other childhood memories had grief hidden from him? Did he even remember the night of the birthday party right?

Cade headed outside. He longed for fresh air and space to think. Seated on the patio swing, he retrieved a cigar and whiskey tumbler from the cabinet. Poured. Lit. Then eased back, inhaling puffs of smoke and honeyed air, but his alone time didn't last long.

The screen door slapped, and Maren exited onto the porch. She sunk down beside him, barefoot and sparkly eyed, with a rosiness flourishing in her cheeks. He resisted the urge to touch her; she'd been standoffish in the car, and he didn't want to press.

"Can I have some of that?" She gestured to the bottle, and took a swig when he handed it over. Her face squished, and she coughed.

"You okay?" he asked, patting her back. "I should've specified that's a sipping whiskey."

"Yeah, no kidding," she rasped. The wheezing stopped, and she dabbed her tear ducts. "What made you hate yourself enough to drink that?"

He tapped his cigar on the bottle where the liquid sloshed at the halfway mark. "Got a long way to go before I'm drunk enough to answer that question. What's up with you?"

"Nothing." She flumped against the chain suspending their seat.

"Doesn't look like nothing."

"Rough day." She offered a smile that looked far too fragile. "Endless questions and no answers."

"We'll fix that."

"When? Our big lead is in the hospital."

"Let's go visit her."

"Really?"

"Why not?" He stretched his arm along the back cushion. "I'll make some calls, find out where she is."

"That would be amazing." She glanced at him. "Did you ever work in one?"

"A hospital?" He sipped his whiskey. "Nice try."

"You're no fun," she said, nudging him with her elbow.

The sun was setting, pilfering the sky of its blue, and birds were erupting from the treetops. How many nights had he spent out here since closing his practice? Dozens. Had to be. Always with a drink in his hand and a frown on his face. Tonight though, he smiled. "Is this the way all your projects go?"

"What do you mean?"

"Uncovering conspiracies, chasing down leads. That a regular thing?"

She shook her head. "You're my first."

Was that an innuendo? How unprofessional. He could've just let her statement hang, but that embarrassed blush of hers was just too damn cute to resist. He'd never forego an opportunity to see it again.

"Your first, huh?" he asked, combing a lazy hand through her hair. "I'll have to be gentle."

Her fingers brushed his thigh, and she wetted her lips before whispering, "Not too gentle."

Holy shit.

Cade clenched his stomach and turned away from her.

"You're blushing," she teased, laughing and tugging on his shirtsleeve. "Stop hiding it, you coward."

"I'm not hiding anything. A rare bird just flew past."

"Which bird?"

He scratched his throat. Name a damn bird. "An Arctic tern."

"An Arctic tern. In Southern Louisiana."

Dumbass. "I told you, rare."

"Uh-huh. Not to mention made up."

Her smile sent his heart spiraling, and in that moment, he nearly relented. Forgot where they were, who they were, and what obstacles lay between them. He wanted to cradle her neck, and take that sassy mouth—and everything else she had to offer. Except he couldn't. Not yet. This wasn't the time, and it sure as hell wasn't the place.

He eased away from her, picking up his drink. "You really think Bryan's been hiding something all these years?"

"Oh. Um." She tucked her hair behind both ears and made space between them. "I guess we'll find out once we speak with Dr. Garcia."

"Peter says he got along well with Mom. If he did something to her—"

"Hey." She grasped his hand. "We don't know anything yet. No use rattling off the what-ifs."

He nodded. "You're in the wrong career. Should've become a detective."

"With those uniforms? I'd sweat like a mule. Biographer suits me all right for now."

"There something else you'd rather be doing?"

"There was, once." When he indicated for her to continue, she explained, "I wanted to be a historian. Got my degree and I was raring to go, but things fizzled out."

"That about the time your mom left on her grand adventure?"

Maren widened her eyes, a regular reaction for her when he recalled an intimate detail about her life. It was as though she believed he didn't listen—or didn't care—when she shared personal information. A huge misjudgment; learning more about this woman was quickly becoming his favorite hobby.

"Yeah, it was. With one income, I couldn't leave Primrose Publishing to pursue an entry-level historian position. What about you? Has this place always been the dream?"

"Once. But a lot changed after Mom died. That's why I went into medicine, actually. Kind of like a lasting tribute to her."

"Then you stopped practicing."

"Then I stopped practicing." He poured another glass. "I'd like to live in a cabin in the woods. Hunt and fish for my food."

"Do you know how to cook?"

"I can build a fire. Can't be too hard from there. Besides, all else fails, I slice up some fish and I've got homemade sashimi. Delicious."

"Doctor, aspiring woodsman. Is there anything you can't do?" A quiet moment passed, and she waved toward the lawn. "I didn't realize how beautiful this area is."

"And you've only seen this. I meant to show you New Orleans today, but it slipped my mind."

"We had bigger things to think about."

"This weekend." He angled his glass toward her. "Put on something nice because I'm taking you out."

"You don't have to."

"I want to."

She fluttered her lashes and gave a shy smile. Then, ever so slowly, she tipped her chin and met his lips. A soft, slow kiss that set his juices to bubbling and promised something more.

The driveway lights triggered, and in their dim glow, moths flitted as quick as floating scribbles. Lulled by the crickets and other singsong creatures, he nursed his liquor in relative comfort. He didn't think about the upheaval that would embroil his life upon finally connecting with Dr. Garcia. Wasn't bombarded by thoughts of the past: his failures and mistakes. His brain only registered the choir of the night, the burn of alcohol on his tongue, and the warmth of her body beside his.

What a wonderful way to end the day.

Nineteen

"I APPRECIATE YOU MEETING with me so early," Greg said, striding into the library and claiming the chair opposite Maren.

She rubbed her eyes and wrestled with a yawn. She and Cade had chatted for hours yesterday. It'd been half past midnight when she'd finally crawled into bed. Had she ever enjoyed a man's company that much? All the clever quips and insightful remarks. Her brain screamed warnings, saying these feelings were a mistake, but it'd also said Minowa would never lie to her. No, Maren wasn't listening to her brain anymore. Her heart had the wheel now, and it was charging full speed ahead.

She opened her laptop. "Of course. Busy day ahead?"

"That's an understatement. Ma and Lawrence are working on this charity event. And guess who's in charge of creating promotional materials."

"The marketing head having to market?" She smiled. "Travesty."

He leaned back, his eyes gleaming. "Cade said you were quick."

"He did? I'm surprised he's mentioned me."

"You're all he talks about."

She pursed her lips to suppress the grin, and ran through her regular questions. With those finished, she asked, "What do you remember about Renee?"

Greg stared at his thumbs. "Not much, terrible as it sounds."

"That's understandable. You were pretty young when she died."

"That's true. Plus, Ma makes it easy to forget. She doesn't even keep pictures of her around."

"I noticed." She jerked her chin toward the shelf. "Those scrapbooks are the only trace of Renee's existence."

"Kept in a room nobody uses."

"Why does Desdemona want to keep her memory contained?"

"She doesn't want to be reminded of Renee. Makes her too sad."

"Still?"

He nodded. "She never got to mourn the loss of her sister. The morning after Renee died, Ma was thrust into preparing for CEO."

"Quick transition."

"Pepaw demanded it. Our family lost an aunt, a sister, a mother. But the company lost its future CEO—that took priority for him."

Her head jerked up. "Over his own daughter's death?"

The air conditioning ruffled the drapes, and sunshine invaded the room. The light skipped across the glossy spines, illuminating dust particles in the air.

Greg squinted. "You have to understand. TIG is our legacy. It's handed down, generation after generation. You let the company fail, you're not only disappointing your ancestors, you're disappointing your children, your grandchildren. Pressure like that changes a person."

She tapped the edge of her laptop. "Ian was that far gone? Couldn't allow his family to mourn?"

"He trusted his faith. Found peace knowing Aunt Renee was with God. Thought we should too."

"Desdemona hasn't found that peace?"

"Hasn't had time to try." His smile was dull. "It's unhealthy, how she copes. I know it. Lawrence knows it."

"Try talking to her. Families can solve anything"—her tapping quickened—"if only they'd communicate."

"Ma doesn't talk. She orders."

"What happens when people disobey?" Like Maren was doing right now. Surely, the punishment couldn't be that bad; Desdemona seemed rational.

"They die."

Maren yelped, bouncing to her feet as a book crashed to the floor behind them.

"Jeez, are you okay?" Greg's tone held worried amusement. "Didn't mean to scare ya."

"You didn't." Idiot, idiot, idiot. She returned Jane Austen to her spot on the bookshelf.

"To clarify, that was a joke." He grinned, and Maren wanted to sink through the chair. "If people disobey, she fires them. Simple."

"You're very candid. Getting information from your brother was like herding piglets."

"Lawrence is a lollipop. Born with a stick up his ass." She laughed, and he said, "I don't mind talking about Ma. She's a good person, and she's there when we need her."

"And if TIG needs her at the same time?"

He dropped his gaze to the floor. "TIG comes first. Always."

Company needs outweighed Greg, Lawrence, and Cade. Had they outweighed Renee too? As the oldest, Desdemona would've had expectations from day one. Future CEO of Thurstan Industrial Group, her birthright. She would've spent years fantasizing about the power and prestige. Then Ian announced Renee would inherit the business. Hopes dashed, dreams decimated, Desdemona would've been furious. Furious enough to harm her little sister? No. Ridiculous. This wasn't Hollywood; this was real life.

Without facts, her imagination was running wild. She needed to speak with Ana Luisa and read the real autopsy report. After finishing up the interview, she stored her laptop and went to find Cade.

SEATED ON THE FOYER tiles, Maren slid her foot into the rubber boot. "You're sure Harmony won't mind if we cut some flowers?"

"Positive." Cade offered his hand and helped her up. "She's got flowers coming out the wazoo."

"Maybe we should ask. It's her garden, her space."

"She's working anyway." He held open the front door. "We'd better get moving if we're making it to the hospital before lunch."

A blossom-scented breeze enveloped them as they trailed through the trees. Greenhouses in sight, Maren paused. "Which one is Harmony's?"

"The far one."

Inside, the temperature rocketed fifty degrees. Dirt piles speckled the floor, and on the walls, muddied spades and shovels hung in disarray. Harmony Coulter was a caring woman, a terrific baker. She was not, however, a clean gardener. Foliage spilled out of splintered wooden boxes, colorful petals dangling like elaborate wedding bouquets.

"She's talented." Maren palmed a tomato suspended within a metal cone. "I wish I could garden."

"Never had a green thumb?"

She snorted a laugh. "I kill everything I touch."

"That's very reassuring." He snatched a pair of shears from the tool pile and kneeled beside a planter. "You like these?"

"Pretty. Does it say what they are?"

"Nope." He snipped a couple. "Hibiscus, maybe. Wouldn't call myself an expert."

"Me neither. We could pair them with those." She pointed to a cluster of waxy leaves, and Cade harvested some.

Maren passed several planters crammed atop tables or huddled on the ground. How did Harmony remember it all? Plant names, watering requirements, and soil preferences: it sounded like algebra to her.

After a quick pit stop to change shoes, they were on the road. They'd contacted five hospitals before finally finding the one treating Ana Luisa. Even then, it'd taken time for Cade to convince the physicians to let them visit her. Eventually, his charm had won out.

At the hospital, he turned into the underground parking, and reached out the window to snag a ticket from the tollbooth.

She winced at the parking prices. "I'll pay you back for this."

"Don't worry about it."

The gate arm rose, and they parked the car. Flattened gum stuck to the cement, adding a pop of color to the canvas of oil stains and discarded receipts. While the elevator dinged its descent, Maren picked at her fingernails.

He grabbed her hand and lowered it. "You're nervous."

"I'm scared. What if she won't speak to us? This is the only chance we have to find out what happened to your mom and if it doesn't pan out ..."

She tore her gaze away. They both knew what would come next. She needed her story, and he had something to hide. Her heart was strapped to a guillotine, and Ana

Luisa held the rope. Would she help them or release the blade?

The elevator opened on the eighth floor. Cade approached the desk and asked for the doctor he'd spoken to. After a brief discussion, he beckoned her over, and they walked down the hallway in silence.

"This is it," he said. "You ready?"

She nodded, and stepped inside. Two beds occupied the room. The first one sat empty. In the second, Ana Luisa lay, staring out the window.

Crinkling her nose against the scents of bodily fluid and antiseptic, Maren headed for the bed. "Ana Luisa?"

"Hm? Can I help—" She looked at Cade and touched her breastbone. "It's you."

He sank into the armchair near her pillow, placing the flowers on the bedside table. "How're you feeling, Ana Luisa?"

"Ana, please. You were in my house."

"Yes, ma'am. I'm Cade Thurstan. This is Maren Sharpe."

She returned Maren's wave, her gaze volleying between them. "Not that I'm uninclined to visitors, but can I know why y'all are here? And why you came to my home?"

"We're looking for your sister," Maren said. "Do you know where she is?"

"What do you want with Maggie?"

"We wanted to discuss my mother's autopsy."

"Renee, right?"

Cade nodded. "You have an excellent memory."

"Hard to forget when she died. Her face was everywhere back then."

Yet the local paper held no trace of the woman. Maren pushed those thoughts away as Cade spoke again.

"Will you help us?"

Ana Luisa pulled the blanket to her chin. "I'm sorry to disappoint y'all, but I haven't seen Maggie in years."

The words were a mallet to the gut. Maren's posture crumpled, and she squeezed the bedrail. Dead end. What could they do now? Confronting Bryan would be useless. He'd been keeping secrets for decades; it'd be difficult getting answers from someone so accustomed to lying.

Cade's shoulders remained set. "When was the last time you saw her?"

"We met for coffee a couple Christmases ago."

"You two weren't close?"

"We were. Once."

"What happened?"

"I'm not sure. She left home one day, wrote me a note saying she was moving out but didn't tell me where. Still won't."

He leaned forward. "How do you know when to meet her?"

"She calls."

"You have her phone number?" Maren released the bedrail, relaxing her hands. "Could we have it?"

"I don't know." She nibbled her bottom lip. "Maggie is real private about that stuff."

"We just want to know what happened to Cade's mother."

"Thing is, I don't call her. She calls me. That's the way she wants it." Ana Luisa pulled up the sleeves of her cardigan. Bruises purpled her arms, and rashes reddened the creases of her elbow. She scratched the area and yanked her sleeves down.

Cade glanced at the doorway. "Do you know who broke into your home?"

"No." Ana Luisa peeled one of her split ends.

"We're not law enforcement, not looking to get you into trouble," he said. "Maybe we can help."

"You can't. You have no idea what I'm going through."

"That's not entirely true." He edged forward. "I studied medicine for a long time. Volunteered at local shelters between my exams. I've seen what addiction does to people." His voice was gentle and sympathetic. "Let us help you."

Maren's heart floated in her chest. She couldn't take her eyes off Cade. He cared for people. Genuinely cared. Hard to believe he'd leave the medical profession willingly. Something must've forced him out. But what? She ached to know the truth. Not for Primrose but for herself.

"Why would you care what happens to me?" Ana Luisa asked.

"I've seen too much death in my life." Cade stared at his laced fingers. "The world is a cruel place. I try to offer kindness when I can."

"And if I don't help you find Maggie? Would you still offer that kindness, Mr. Thurstan?"

He lifted his lashes. "In a heartbeat."

Tears welled in Ana Luisa's eyes, and she jerked her head toward the television murmuring near the ceiling. Maren angled her body, giving the woman some privacy. No family came charging into the room. The visitors' chairs sat empty, save for Cade's. Did Ana Luisa have any other loved ones? Or was it her and her sister against the world? Pain flared behind Maren's ribs. She knew how it felt, being torn from a sibling. The emptiness. The loneliness. How long had Ana Luisa been alone?

Maren grabbed some tissues from the bathroom and handed them to Ana Luisa. "We didn't mean to upset you."

"Not your fault." She blew her nose. "Crying is just what I do now. Once the high wears off, it leaves you feeling pretty damn low."

Cade inclined his head. "What've you been using?"

"The better question is what haven't I been using." She moved her hand and swore when it started vibrating. "Had my addiction under control once. Then Maggie left, and it was so hard not having her around. Fell into old habits and well, look how that turned out."

"Did you know the man in your house?"

She looked at Maren. Nodded. "He was my boyfriend."

Cade tensed his jaw. "He left you for dead."

"Never said he was a good boyfriend. But he kept me supplied, so I didn't complain. Drugs come first." She balled her tissue and whipped it into the wastebasket. "Drugs always come first."

The knot in her stomach loosened. It wasn't their fault Ana Luisa got hurt. Thank goodness.

"Does Maggie know you're using?" he asked.

"I told her I quit. Didn't want her to worry, y'know?" She toyed with a thread on the blanket. "It's been one battle after another since she left."

"I get that. I don't know what's keeping her away, but it might have something to do with my mother's death."

"How do you know that?"

He explained what Sylvia had shared. "I'd like to know what's going on. Maybe we can work on making your sister feel safe again. Bring her home."

Her eyes narrowed. "How do I know you're not the one who's after her?"

"You don't. But I did save your life." He stood up and removed a card from his pocket. "This is my phone number, and I'll write Maren's on the back. We can't promise we'll be able to help. But we'll try."

She twirled the card. "I'll pass it along."

In the hallway, Maren hugged herself. "I hope she calls."

"She will."

"How can you be sure?"

"Call it a hunch. Listen, I'll meet you by the elevator. Have to take care of something before we leave."

"Does this have anything to do with your hunch?"

Walking backward, he grinned. "It might. See you in a sec."

She watched him turn the corner. Please, let his hunch be right. The last thing she wanted to do was hurt that man.

Twenty

HIS HUNCH WAS WRONG. Friday arrived, and they still hadn't heard from Dr. Garcia. To distract from the ache in her chest, Maren had stayed in her room for most of the week, trying to piece together a rough draft for Primrose. He and Minowa had lit up her phone several times. For Primrose, she'd answered. For Minowa, she'd texted; her messages confirmed she was alive, but they hadn't incited conversation. Once back home, Maren would speak with her sister. Voices would raise, tears would roll, and love would prevail. They'd repair their relationship, and life would return to normal. Which meant that now, she really needed a break.

"Ring." Sitting on the duvet, Maren stared at her phone. "Ring, you stupid thing!"

Sunday. If the doctor didn't call by then, she'd pursue other avenues. Come hell or hailstorm, she'd depart Louisiana with a secret to sell. But whose secret? Her grip tightened on the phone. Don't let it be Cade's. Please, please don't let it be his.

Footsteps sounded, and her eyes popped open. High heels. Maren scrambled off the bed and tidied her flyaways.

"Hello, dear." Desdemona beamed on the threshold of the guest room.

"Good afternoon. You're home early." During writing breaks, Maren had recorded the mansion's comings and goings. Useful knowledge should she need to snoop again.

"I wanted to speak with you." She frowned. "You look stressed. Is something the matter?"

"Everything's fine. Just tired."

"Is it the mattress? I can have Peter drive into the city and purchase a new one."

"That's generous, but completely unnecessary. I've always struggled to sleep in unfamiliar beds. What was it you wanted to talk about?"

Glee brightened Desdemona's features. "Cade let your Saturday plans slip. I thought why not skip out this afternoon and go shopping. Just us girls. Judging by the size of your suitcase, I assume you didn't bring any formalwear?"

"*Formalwear?*" Maren swallowed. Her definition of formal was the biweekly wearing of her sole set of matching lingerie. Surely not what Desdemona was referring to.

"Don't faint on me now." Her face barely moved around the laugh escaping her lips. "Meet me downstairs, and we'll go into town to get you all set up. How does that sound?" Without waiting for an answer, she swept from the room.

THE BOUTIQUE'S FRONT WINDOWS housed several mannequins dressed in a rainbow of gowns. Maren followed Desdemona inside where polished racks were chock-full of silk, lace, and chiffon, all perfectly aligned. Even the air smelled good, like vanilla birthday cake. This was a place with wooden hangers and upholstered stools in the fitting rooms. A place where salespeople pounced the moment a toe crossed the threshold. This place, she couldn't afford.

Desdemona didn't notice her apprehension. Striding to the middle of the store, she placed a hand on her hip. "What color are you partial to? I love a good navy blue but for you, perhaps, a lavender?"

"That sounds good." Maren nipped her instinct to bee-line to the clearance section. Instead, she stayed close to Desdemona who was inspecting the garments. "I'm surprised this place hasn't gone under, given how small Penngrove is."

"They have an affordable lease. Besides, I spend more than enough here to keep the place afloat. Speaking of which, Anya!" She waved at the frail lady behind the counter. "Come over and meet Maren."

Anya obliged, scurrying across the pine floor. She was a bitty thing—eyeline barely reaching Maren's chest—with thin, gray curls and a face grooved by wrinkles. Her smile was warm, like a cozied mug of hot chocolate.

"You're the owner?" Maren asked.

"Sure am," Anya said, shaking her hand. "Had this place nearly forty years now. My, has it really been that long?"

"You're getting old," Desdemona teased with an affectionate rub of the woman's shoulder.

"Hush you. I like to think you're only as old as you feel and that wouldn't put me a day past fifty. Now, did you come in here to buy something or just tell me things I already know?"

Ten minutes later, dozens of gowns heaped the women's arms. To be polite, Maren took all the suggested dresses into the fitting room, but she already knew which one she intended to purchase: a blush number which was on sale. It still surpassed her monthly dress budget of zero dollars, but it beat the other inflated prices she'd seen.

Anya's biceps twitched as she dragged the velvet curtain closed. Maren tossed her clothes onto the tufted stool in the corner, slipped the first dress on, and stepped out.

"This one is beautiful," Desdemona said, accepting the flute of champagne offered by Anya. "Do a spin. Show us the whole thing."

Anya made a choked sound. "Stunning." To Desdemona, she said, "Seems like yesterday it was you girls in here, getting all gussied up for prom."

Their reminiscing continued as Maren stripped and slid into her next dress. She adjusted the fabric over her hips, listening.

"You remember the apple cider you gave us?" Desdemona asked. "And Mama thought it was alcohol. She was about ready to tan your hide."

"Perla always had a burr in her saddle about something." The two shared a laugh. "That's one swell thing about getting old. We're one step closer to seeing 'em all again. Perla, Renee. My Pierre." She turned when Maren drew the curtain. "Oh my. Pretty as a spring daisy. What do you think?"

"I like it." She brushed her hand down the pink lace.

"I'd love to see the lavender," Desdemona said.

Maren wrangled the garment off the hanger. An exquisite—and expensive—piece. She couldn't purchase this but, to please Desdemona, she squeezed into the dress and opened the curtain.

Desdemona gasped. "This is the one. Isn't it breathtaking, Anya?"

"It's sensational." Anya sighed. "Shall I ring it up?"

"The dress is stunning, but out of my price range. I'll take the pink one."

"Nonsense." Desdemona waved her back to the changing room, and she scrambled into her street clothes. "Anya, please add it to my bill."

"Wait, hold on." Maren stumbled out, her laces untied and her hair staticky. "You don't have to buy that." The lavender gown lay crumpled on the stool behind her. Anya bustled past and gathered the garment. With a nod at Desdemona, the woman headed to the front of the store. Resisting the urge to tackle her, Maren sank into the chair beside Desdemona.

"I know I don't need to. I want to. Think of it as a gift." She tipped the champagne bottle, offering Maren a glass.

"I can't accept gifts from clients. It's unethical."

She swirled the alcohol. "Your ethics confuse me."

She heard it then: the veiled bitterness. Not red-faced anger or desperate frustration, nothing to give the illusion Desdemona wasn't in control. But something brewed. Her eyes held a cool intensity as if she was staring at a wasp's nest knowing she had insecticide in the garage.

Maren scratched the goosebumps on her arm. "Why is that?"

"Client gifts cross your moral boundary." She cocked her head. "But kissing my nephew does not."

Her spine turned to titanium. Dummy. She should've expected Desdemona would find out. Wealth made the woman all-powerful and all-knowing—abilities augmented by the gossipy tendencies of small towns. Of course, making out with a client wasn't explicitly forbidden—slimy as Primrose was, he'd probably approve—but it could damage her professional reputation. She had to fix this.

"I'm sorry," Maren said.

"I understand the attraction. Cade is handsome, eligible." She fired a look. "Rich."

"I'm not interested in his money." Maren kept her voice calm, her posture poised, and her smile bright. Inwardly, however, she raged. Such a cruel insinuation, as if Cade had no attractive qualities other than his pocketbook. She hadn't kissed him because she longed for his money or the power to be gained from his last name. She'd kissed him for his cleverness, his protectiveness, his determination. And because she'd wanted to kiss him. Simple.

Desdemona white-knuckled the champagne flute. Odd. She'd voiced her concerns. Why was she still irritable?

Renee. Had to be. If Desdemona knew about her kissing Cade, she'd know about their investigation too. Might as well get it out in the open.

"It's Renee, isn't it? That's why you're upset."

Desdemona shut her eyes. "I'm upset because you ignored my instructions. Renee is not to be included in this biography."

"You have a roster of dead relatives that'll be included in my book, why not Renee? If you're afraid I won't handle the subject matter delicately—"

"The only thing I'm afraid of is you hurting my family."

"How would this hurt them?"

The front door rattled, and Anya welcomed the new patrons: women, judging from the murmurs. Fabrics rustled, and hangers squeaked. Maren rested her chin on her hand, waiting for an answer.

"Her death broke us," Desdemona began. "Mama barely spoke, and Cade stayed in his room. My boys cried every time I left; they were terrified I'd die like their auntie did. And Daddy ... well, he was never too good with emotions. Chose to hide at the office."

"You went with him, right?" When her forehead wrinkled in question, Maren added, "Greg mentioned it."

"Daddy was a good businessman, and he doted on TIG. Didn't let personal issues get in the way. Renee had worked alongside him for years, readying herself to take over. Then she died, and everything fell apart. He needed—we needed—to fix things. I didn't have the luxury to prioritize my feelings, not when there was work to be done."

She squirmed. What if Minowa died, and her parents didn't allow her time to grieve? What would she do with the emotions, the regret? Learn to compartmentalize. She'd stuff everything into a mental suitcase and lock it away. It'd be the only way to cope with such agonizing loss. Was it similar for Desdemona? Maybe this wasn't about protecting Renee or Cade or Greg; it was about protecting herself. That, Maren could work with. She wasn't a therapist, but she knew how to get people talking; hundreds of biography interviews had honed that ability. A few more chats and Desdemona might warm up to the idea of embracing Renee. But there was still one last thing to clear up.

"Why'd your father choose Renee for CEO?"

She shifted, focusing on a fixture of bridal accessories. "I'm not sure."

"He must've had a reason."

"She was the better choice."

"That's hard to believe. You've done such an amazing job with the company. Almost like you were born to run things."

"He didn't think me stable enough."

"Stable enough?"

"My husband's death affected my mental health. Daddy saw what I was going through and knew I was no longer an optimal candidate. He chose Renee, and I got to spend more time with my boys."

"Renee must've worked long hours. How did Cade cope?"

"Fine. Whenever she wasn't at the office, she was with Cade. My sister was an exceptional mother." Desdemona rubbed her knuckles. "Loved her children very much."

"Children."

"Pardon me?"

"You said children. Plural."

She reached for the alcohol bottle. "I meant Lawrence and Greg. Living in the same house like we did, parenting was a joint effort. Both of us had three children in a way."

Fair enough. "How did you feel when Ian announced you wouldn't become CEO? It must've been hard to swallow."

"If you say so."

"Renee must've been ecstatic though." This next bit was tricky. Had to keep her voice pleasant and non-accusatory. "Were you happy for her?"

Her mouth flattened. "These are odd questions."

"They're part of my job."

"Enough." Rising, Desdemona fluffed her hair and hand-ironed the creases from her skirt. "I like you, Maren. I truly do. But I'll terminate your contract like that"—she snapped her fingers—"if you continue obsessing over my sister. This is your last warning. Is that clear?"

"Crystal clear."

"Delightful." She floated toward the cash register, and Maren traipsed behind her. "Anya, we're about done. Have you prepared the gown?"

Excusing herself from the other customers, Anya hurried to the checkout. "I steamed it, so it's fresh for dancing. Did you want me to carry it out?"

"No need. I'm sure Maren can handle it. Do you still have those bridal candies by chance? With the day I'm having, I could use some sugar."

"Rough one?" Anya fumbled behind the counter and removed a packet of gummy roses.

"That's putting it mildly."

Maren flipped through wedding magazines without paying them any attention. Desdemona acted like a woman with something to hide. It had to relate to Renee—why be so against including her otherwise? They needed the autopsy results. If foul play was evident … had Desdemona been involved?

"Peter and the boys, how're they doing?" Anya handed over her change.

"Peter's well. Lawrence shadows me at work most days, chomping at the bit to take over. Still some learning to do, but he's doing great. Greg is, well, Greg. You know the way he is." Desdemona zipped her purse. "As for Cade, he's hanging in there."

"Poor thing." Anya shook her head. "Never felt right, what happened to him."

Maren's ears perked up.

"He blames himself nevertheless," Desdemona said.

"Wasn't his fault. Wasn't anybody's fault. That little girl would've died either way."

Little girl?

"He just needs time." She popped a candy in her mouth. "I'd best be getting on. Maren, go ahead and grab the dress. I'll meet you at the car." With that, Desdemona sailed onto Main Street.

"Mona's lovely, isn't she? We're so blessed to have her in Penngrove. Very charitable, very kind." Grinning, Anya cradled the dress. "This looked beautiful on you."

"Thanks. Anya?" Maren waited for the woman to stop fiddling with the garment bag. "Who was the little girl you were talking about?"

Her face scrunched. "Best be asking Cade about that. Now, take this dress and go have a good time tomorrow night."

"I will have a good time"—she plopped her purse near the register—"in the pink dress."

"Wh-what? I've already added this one to the Thurstan account."

She sifted through her wallet. "Do you prefer credit or debit cards?"

A few minutes later, Maren hauled out her purchase. She didn't need Desdemona's permission on what to wear. She especially didn't need it on what to include in their biography. Cade deserved to know the truth.

But for now, she'd forget about the stress, the pitfalls, the future. Forget about everything except enjoying a night in New Orleans with Cade. The man who challenged her mind, stole her breath.

And, she feared, captured her heart.

Twenty-One

MAREN GRIPPED THE EDGE of the bathroom sink with a mouthful of bobby pins. She'd spent the last hour failing to style her hair; it resembled a burl rather than an elegant updo. Adding cakey foundation and smudgy eye shadow, she was a sight to behold. And she was out of time. Maren entered the bedroom and squeezed into the dress, adjusting the cowl neckline and spaghetti straps. She glanced at her reflection. Frowned. Her back fat bulged around the bra band, and her belly popped out like a sausage encased in lace.

Groaning, she sank onto the bed and pressed her fingers into her eyes. Why was she so nervous? She'd been on dates before. Music, dancing, moonlight: she'd done it all—just never with him. So far, it'd been stolen kisses and soft touches, but tonight was a black-tie dinner in New Orleans. Tonight, was serious.

A serious dead-end. What else was she expecting? This wasn't some fairy tale where he'd profess his love and she'd stay in Louisiana. Things were never that perfect, not for her. Maybe she shouldn't go. Spending quality time with the man would just make returning home that much harder.

No. Tonight was about the moment. Living in it, basking in it. There was no room for doubt and second-guessing.

She jumped to her feet and descended the stairs, her heels clicking and her heart thumping. Cade stood in the foyer with a tux jacket draped over his shoulder, staring out the window. His hair, gelled and swept to the side, lacked its usual curls. She admired the point of his ears, the way his white dress shirt tucked around narrow hips. Then he turned, their eyes met.

And her uncertainty dissolved.

This wasn't the lustful ogle a man sent a woman across a crowded nightclub. This stare warmed her blood and pinkened her cheeks, its intensity making her feel so wanted, so beautifully feminine. Stopping in front of him, she swallowed hard.

"Wow." He bobbed the ringlet that had escaped her hair pins. "You. This dress. I can't find the words."

A breathy laugh escaped her lips. "How do you do that?"

"Do what?" He offered his arm, and she looped her wrist through the crook.

"Make me feel so beautiful."

"Is that what I did?"

"Uh-huh."

"You deserve to feel beautiful, Maren. Every second of every day." He opened the door and steered them toward the idling car. "I've got the air conditioning on. Didn't want your thighs sticking to the leather."

Goddamn. Could he be any more perfect?

"You've got good manners," she said.

"I live to please."

"Do you?" She blocked his path. Whether it was the kind gesture, the night air, or the heat pooling in her belly, she wasn't certain; all she knew was she wanted this man. Now. "Would you care to prove that?"

His gaze slid up her body. "I was thinking about it."

"We could forget New Orleans." She fisted the fabric near his hip and tipped her chin up. "Crawl into the backseat, see where the night takes us."

"You're so indecisive." He cupped her jaw and traced a finger down her throat. "One minute, you're calling me a dung beetle, and the next, you're asking to be fucked in my backseat."

Tingles scampered over her skin. "I've learned to like dung beetles."

He leaned in, his lips whisper-close. "You know what you'll learn next?"

"What?"

"Patience." Grinning, he stepped back and patted the sedan's roof. "Get in the car, woman."

Her eyes narrowed. "I hate you."

"Ah, see? There's the Maren I know."

As promised, the leather was cool against her legs, and a guitar twanged on the radio as Cade swung around the fountain.

"Are you going to tell me where we're going tonight?"

"No, I like making you wait." He winked. "How was shopping yesterday?"

"It was ..." She twirled her hand, searching for the right word. "Interesting. Mona tried to buy me a dress with far too many zeroes."

"You bought another one?"

"Had to. It felt like she was trying to buy my silence."

"Bold move." He stopped at the end of the driveway, and his eyes consumed every inch of her. Caressed her legs, glided up her belly and across her breasts. "I'd say you made the right choice. Any word from Dr. Garcia?"

"Nothing." She fumbled with the hem of her dress. "If she doesn't call—"

"We'll find out the truth another way. If Mom's death wasn't an accident, I want to know. No matter how hard it might be."

Two songs ended before she spoke again. "I'm sorry."

"For?"

"Coming here and dredging up the past. Turning your life upside down."

"You? Apologizing?" He inclined his head. "Where'd that come from?"

"I'm trying to voice my feelings more." Maren drummed her fingers on her kneecap. "Minowa recently told me I'm constipated with communication."

"That must've upset you."

Nodding, she relayed the conversation with her sister. "I put my life on hold when Mom left. But I kept my head down and worked my ass off because I didn't think there was another choice. I never mentioned anything to Min: the hostility at work, how tired I was, how badly I needed change. Little did I know, maybe things would've gotten better if I had."

"She didn't say anything either. Seems there was a lack of communication on both sides."

She leaned against the seat belt. "I guess there was. Anyway, I wanted you to know that if I could do things over, I never would've accepted this contract. I would've bitten the bullet and bared my soul to Min."

Cade itched his chin. "Not sure I like that alternative."

"No?"

"There are a lot of things about this situation I'm unhappy about, but meeting you isn't one of them. Besides, I didn't have much of a life to ruin before you arrived."

"I'm here if you ever want to talk about your past." Maren squeezed his hand, and he dabbed kisses on her knuckles.

They rode the rest of the journey in comfortable silence, and soon, lights were glowing on the horizon. New Orleans. She opened the window, and peered out. The area mirrored New York with its skyscrapers and vehicle-clogged streets. A few blocks in, however, the city transformed.

"This is the French Quarter," he said.

Transfixed by its beauty, she hardly heard him. No towers tickled the clouds. Bi-level homes hedged the road in a mosaic of pink and yellow plaster. Intricate iron arches fenced the second-floor balconies, and leafy hanging baskets swayed to the jazzy tunes pouring from nearby restaurants. It was a medley of music and color and life.

With windblown hair, she ducked inside. "The pictures don't do it justice."

"You should see it around Mardi Gras. Hot as hell and can't move an inch, but you're loving every minute of it."

"Sounds wonderful." Outside, steaming dishes packed the patio tables, and her stomach rumbled. "Are we stopping soon? Bet the food is divine."

"I have something in mind."

"What?"

He smiled. "You'll see."

A few minutes later, she did. The riverboat floated on the water, white and magnificent. It had three decks with a raspberry-red paddlewheel connected to the stern and two soaring steam valves on its bow.

"You're not afraid of water, are you?"

Maren shook her head. They parked, and Cade rounded the trunk to open her door. Laughter filled the syrupy air, and the river gurgled against the bank. Passengers, dressed formally, filed through the boat doors like ants to the hill. She patted her hair, twisting any loose strands around the bobby pins. Hand in hand, they shuffled to the attendant's booth where Cade gave their tickets to a man who greeted him by name.

"Do you come here often?" she asked.

"Mona holds a quarterly get-together for investors on these cruises. Very Southern, she says."

"I agree. Can't say I've seen anything quite this colorful cruising down the Hudson."

He smiled. "This way."

Tables draped in white linen and centerpieced by vases of carnations speckled the ballroom. Near the window, the band swayed, playing the blues on stringed instruments.

"If I had a dollar for every time I thought something was beautiful, I'd be rich as you."

He laughed, squeezing her hand as they weaved to the room's far side.

"Aren't we grabbing a table?"

"Not here. Upstairs."

The guests' murmurs quieted as she emerged onto the upper deck, gasping at the awning of string lights dangling overhead. In the corner, a private table and server awaited them.

The server pulled her chair out. "Welcome, Ms. Sharpe, Mr. Thurstan. May I interest you in a cocktail?"

"I could go for some white wine, please." She ran her hands over her butt, flattening the skirt before sitting down.

"Certainly. And yourself, sir?"

"Make it a bottle. Thank you."

The server nodded and retreated downstairs.

Maren sipped her water. "Private deck. Bottle of wine. Dinner under string lights. You sure know how to impress a date."

"Is this a date?"

"Let's say it is. What's your next move? How does Cade Thurstan seal the deal?"

"I don't think you want to play that game with me."

The rumble of his voice had her gut twisting in anticipation. "Why not?"

"Because I always win."

Before she could tug on that conversation thread, the waiter returned with a chilled bottle and poured them each a glass. After delivering a basket of bread and announcing dinner would arrive soon, he exited back down to the lower decks. The paddle lapped on the river, each splash complementing the downbeat of the music playing beneath their feet. Blankets covered the grassy shore, a tapestry of summer picnics.

Beautiful views, fine food, expensive wine: easy to get used to, this life he led. So exotic and opposite her own it didn't feel real. She couldn't allow herself to want this, to want him beyond a physical connection. The heat between them was temporary, a summer fling at best. Soon she'd return to her life, and these four weeks spent with Cade would be nothing but a pleasant memory.

"Here we are." The waiter set down two plates. "Grillades served over garlic mashed potatoes with a side of charred carrots and asparagus." He turned to her. "As Mr. Thurstan requested, we've served your tomato gravy on the side. Was there anything else I could get you?"

"This is excellent," Cade said.

"Bon appétit."

They picked up their forks, and he dug in while she toyed with the food.

"Not hungry?"

"No, I am." Maren speared a carrot. "You put my gravy on the side."

"You didn't take tomato on your po'boy. I figured you wouldn't want your food doused in it."

"That's sweet of you." She picked up the ramekin and dolloped some of the sauce over her meal. "I dislike the texture of tomatoes more than the taste. I'll still eat sauces with them."

"You must be fun to cook for."

"It's my one dislike. Do you enjoy all foods?"

He shrugged. "I'm not picky."

"Liver?"

"Love it."

"Snails?"

"Escargot. Yum."

"Frog legs?"

Cade drummed the tabletop. "Never had them, but I don't think I'd object."

"Wow." She bit into her meat. "You really are perfect."

"I'll take your word on that." He undid his top button to reveal a hint of blond chest hair curling near his clavicle. He took leisurely bites, his burden of sadness seemingly dispelled for the moment. Because it pleased her to see him this way, Maren kept the conversation light and playful, leading to the question she longed to ask.

"How come you're not married? You're successful, good-looking, funny."

"Careful with talk like that. Stroke my ego enough and it'll sink this ship."

She wagged the fork at him. "I'm serious."

He finished his dinner and settled back. "I've dated here and there, just never met the right one."

"Ever come close?"

"Nah. You?"

"I'm too busy for romance."

"You've got time now." Cade crossed to her side and stretched out his hand. "Dance with me."

A blush scorched her neck. "I don't think so."

"There goes that ego."

"No, it's not that. It's, well …" She fidgeted with the tablecloth. "I don't know how."

"I'm an excellent teacher."

On a deep breath, she touched his palm, and he whisked her away from the table. Plenty of space to humiliate herself over here. Wonderful.

He placed a hand on her hip, guiding them into a dance. "Look at me."

"I don't want to step on you."

Cade slid his hand up the side of her body and tilted her chin up. "I brought my steel-toed dress shoes. Relax, keep your eyes on me. The only witnesses up here are the stars."

He expertly led her around the floor, stepping into her, pushing her out, spinning her back in. She squished his loafers twice, wincing each time. He only shook his head and laughed. The sound made her heart tremble.

"You okay?"

She nodded. "Where'd you learn this?"

"Mom taught me." He twirled her again.

"She put you in lessons?" Maren stumbled but caught herself. He drew her close, his fingers splaying on the small of her spine.

"No. My memaw used to throw huge parties. When the sun went down, we'd crank up the tunes and flock onto the driveway. Mom forced me to dance with her. Crucial knowledge, she'd said."

"You had a great connection with your mom."

"You could have that. You've got a second chance now. Release that toxic shit, start over fresh. Start over happy."

"Good advice."

The music slowed, and Cade pulled her close. She laced her arms around his neck and pressed her ear to his chest. His heart pounded. For her? The thought warmed her every limb. They moved, a soft sway under starlight, his breath warming her hair and his slacks teasing her thighs.

"What're we doing here?" he asked, his voice quiet and husky.

"Some kind of slow dance."

"I'm talking about you and me. How far are you wanting this to go?"

How was she supposed to answer that? Was it like putting in a deli order? One pound of kiss her, two slices of ravage her. Instead of making a complete fool of herself, Maren flipped the question. "What do you want to do?"

"Currently?" He dragged his teeth across his lower lip. "I'm thinking about what's hiding beneath this dress." He traced the seam, leaning toward her. "About what you'd do if I pressed you against that railing, slipped it off, ran my tongue over every delicious curve of your body." He touched her shoulder blade and brushed up to hold her cheek.

A shiver coursed through her.

"How you'd respond when I slip two fingers inside you, make you pant and moan." His mouth was close, his eyes scorching into hers. "So how about it, Maren? You really want to see how I seal the deal?"

Twenty-Two

Yes.

The word undid him.

Cade dipped his head and trapped her mouth. It'd taken all his strength to resist her demands earlier tonight. Now, he couldn't combat his need to touch her, to hold her, to taste her.

He pressed in, ensuring she felt every inch of his arousal. She gasped, and he capitalized on her parted lips, swiping his tongue inside. Sweet, addictive. Cade stepped forward, forcing her against the railing. Prisoning her. His hands skimmed her waist, gliding over her ribcage. He closed over her breast, and—holy shit. That sound. Breathy little squeak. It awakened something within him, something fevered and intense and wicked.

He moved to her neckline, traced the lacy edge. "I need this off."

Her eyes snapped open. "Here? Now?"

"Does that scare you?"

Maren looked around. No guests occupied the deck, and no airplanes vandalized the sky. The air was still and quiet, apart from the waves slurping the boat's hull and the gentle bob of the string lights. Her eyes flickered, but her smile? That gleamed, wide and radiant. The stars should be ashamed.

"What if I get cold?"

Cold? Precious. Could she not see it in his eyes? How badly he yearned for her. He'd worship every freckle on her exposed skin, keeping her warm with his breath if he had to.

"Are you cold now?" He moved to her shoulders and slid off the straps.

"No."

"You sure?" Cade brushed her lips with his, shimmying her dress down. He grazed the top of her breasts, his thumbs teasing her through the bra. "Because you have goosebumps."

"Not cold." Her knuckles whitened on the railing.

"That's good," he whispered against her chest, and traced her bra with his tongue. His hand slipped beneath the cup and squeezed. Warm, soft. Knew she would be. "I never want you cold, understand? I want you hot and desperate and begging for me."

He rolled her nipple between thumb and forefinger, and she nuzzled his neck, quiet moans for his ears only. But that wouldn't do. That wouldn't do at all.

"Don't hide, pretty girl." Cade rocked his shoulder, and she straightened. He pinched her chin, gazing into her wide eyes. "I want everyone onboard to know I'm fucking you."

Maren paled, but nodded. His heart skittered. Strange, this power she possessed; it roused his every desire. He longed to cradle her, take her to bed. Make love to her, gentle and slow. But he couldn't control this carnal instinct, this need to fuck her against a wall until she was writhing and raw. No walls up here, so he'd make do with the boat railing. He was nothing if not resourceful.

Cade kissed her and journeyed downward. Murmured over her jaw and throat, sampling the tender skin of her breast. His mouth found her nipple, and Maren arched her back. Her hands turned needy as his tongue circled. She pawed at his waistband, but he moved out of reach. No way was he rushing this. He dropped an arm and brushed his fingertips up her thigh, lifting the fabric. In that melody of moans and pants, Cade knocked out reality.

But it came back swinging.

A door creaked open, and he lurched upright, shielding Maren as she frantically covered herself. His jaw hardened. He'd rented this deck for the night; whoever thought to interrupt them had one hell of a death wish. He spun around. Froze.

Not a staff member. A woman stood on the port side, staring at him with a face devoid of color. Shit, what was she doing here? He wasn't ready for this.

Maren touched his bicep. "Are you okay?"

He tried to form words, but his tongue refused to cooperate. How was he supposed to explain this woman? The emotions she incited, the insecurity and regret and—

"Dr. Thurstan?"

Rubbing the back of his neck, Cade forced a smile. "Hi, Alice. How've you been?"

She twisted her fingers. "Fine."

Didn't look fine. Gray had dulled her fiery, red hair, and bags, dark as charcoal, weighed down her once bright eyes. The bones of her hips and ribs protruded through her dress as if she hadn't eaten for months. She was the image of a broken woman. A childless mother.

"I didn't know anyone was up here," she said, turning away. "I'm sorry to intrude. I'll go—"

"That's alright." He looked at Maren. "Could you give us a minute?"

She squeezed his hand. "I'll be downstairs if you need anything."

"Do you want to sit?" Cade walked to the table. "Is Henry here? I can bring another chair."

Alice looked at her shoes. "We've separated, actually. Divorce will be finalized next year."

Steam pumped from the crowned valves, and liquid dribbled off the paddle wheel. Calm waters made for a safe, smooth voyage—but Cade was drowning. His throat was tight, and his lungs ached. He'd ruined this woman. Destroyed her marriage, killed her child. How could he ever come back from that?

"It's good to see you."

He forced down saliva. "You too."

"You don't have to lie." She rubbed her upper arms. "I've been meaning to call, but time kept passing, and it never felt like the right thing to do. Then there was the funeral then the lawsuit then the divorce. It was too much, and I couldn't bear to ..." She sighed. "I'm insane, aren't I?"

"No." He jerked forward. "I can't imagine how painful this year has been."

"Only a year?" Her posture slumped. "It feels like a lifetime since Chelsea died."

Cade reached for the bottle of wine. Liquid courage—liquid defense, really. His chest had been pried open, leaving his heart on full display. Why wasn't she yanking his organs out? Why wasn't she angry? He deserved every insult and unkind word for what he'd done. What he'd failed to do.

"It would've been her tenth birthday last month." Her voice cracked. "She was so excited about double digits."

"It's a big deal."

"Isn't it? She was obsessed with the zoo. You should see how many stuffed giraffes—" She choked back tears, and Cade bit his lip.

He couldn't do this, couldn't watch her break down, knowing he caused that pain. The wind was batting the buoys around, and he wanted nothing more than to commandeer one and row to shore, escape these feelings, this situation.

Instead, he pummeled the words out. "I'm sorry."

Her sobs quieted.

"I should've looked harder. Should've run more tests or monitored her overnight. With her cough and those sniffles." He paused and pressed his fist against his mouth. "I thought it was the flu. Maybe if I'd examined closer, I would've seen the signs. She might still—"

"Don't do that."

"What?"

"Blame yourself." Alice grabbed his hand. "We can't carry this burden with us for the rest of our lives. Chelsea wouldn't have wanted that. You need to forgive yourself."

He shook his head. "I don't think I can."

"You have to. Henry couldn't release his anger. He blamed me, blamed himself. Blamed many people—including you. The loss changed him, made him bitter and mean." She wrapped her arms around her stomach. "I couldn't live that way. I need to heal, and so do you."

"I admire your strength."

"I don't feel strong. Every day is a struggle and every night is lonesome. But we have to try and get through this. Promise me you will."

"I promise."

"Good." She gazed at the stars. "Chelsea loved visiting the doctor's and getting a lollipop for her efforts."

"The dentist paid me to give those out." He swirled his wineglass. "It's one big racket."

Her laughter sounded sad and dusty. He doubted it was used much anymore. "You're a good person. You helped the less fortunate and never made us feel lesser for it. I'm sorry for treating you like I did."

"You were mourning your child." Cade forced a brittle smile, emotion stinging the back of his throat. "No apology needed."

"Thank you." She glanced at the door. "I'm glad you have somebody. Venting does wonders for the healing process."

Wrong on both counts. He didn't have Maren, nor had he discussed his troubles with her. But it felt like the next step. He wanted more than a scorching physical connection. He wanted to confide in her, share with her. Had he ever felt like this before?

Cade escorted Alice downstairs. She rejoined a group of women, and his eyes locked on Maren. She was at the bar, straw-stirring ice cubes and bobbing her foot to the jazzy tune. Several locks had escaped the hair pins and were drifting past her nape. Her dress rode high to reveal a pair of plump thighs. When she swiveled, his entire body responded. His mouth returned the smile, and his abdomen tightened with lust. Even his heart, which had never been involved in his previous affairs, battered a bruise against his ribs. Yeah, he could trust this woman, finally reveal his past.

First, however, he needed to take the edge off.

"Is everything all right?" Maren asked. "The way you responded to that woman, I thought ..."

He looped his right arm around her waist and towed her in for a kiss. So good, the taste of her. She molded into his personal space like she was made to be there. From personality to body shape, this woman complemented him perfectly.

He signaled for a drink from the bartender and slid onto the stool beside hers. "Now, what was it you thought about that woman?"

She nibbled on her lower lip. "I thought she was an ex-girlfriend. You were pretty shocked to see her."

"You think I'd stop what we were doing because of an ex?" Cade smiled wryly and sipped his cognac. "I'd have thrown her off the boat."

He couldn't take his eyes off her as she shrunk away and covered her mouth. She didn't laugh enough. Usually, it was smiles or smirks. He'd change that. Given the chance, he'd make her laugh every day if only to revel in the enchanting sound.

"Okay, so I was wrong. Who is she then?" At his silence, she added, "You don't have to tell me if you don't want."

"I do. Just need a minute to collect my thoughts."

"Let me know when you're ready." On the counter, her hand covered his. "Until then, cheers." They clinked glasses.

And Cade began to drink.

Twenty-Three

"HOLD ON TO ME," she said.

"I'm fine." Cade stumbled up the hotel stairs, grasping the banister tight enough to suffocate the wood. Watching him, Maren shook her head. They'd spent the rest of the cruise at the bar, chatting, laughing. Drinking. Knowing her limits, she'd stopped after a few. He, however, had not. She'd still had fun—he was a happy drunk. After disembarking, he'd asked one of the crew members to arrange a taxi to the hotel.

It was an impressive place with burgundy walls and furniture a combination of wood and velvet. She'd nearly fainted when the concierge quoted the price for two rooms. Cade had simply handed over his credit card and headed for the stairs.

It'd been a glorious night—until now.

She sported a smile, but the knot in her stomach soured her joy. Who was that woman, and why did she affect him this way? Cade usually wore self-assurance like a fitted suit, so this vulnerability worried her. She wanted to erase his hurt, to soothe and comfort. But first, she needed to know what happened.

Maren scurried behind him, holding out her arms in case he toppled. "Stop the macho act and lean on me. I'll keep pestering you otherwise."

"Now that's a terrifying threat." He paused at the newel post, allowing her to slip into his armpit and place a hand on his chest. The plush carpet swallowed her heels.

"Some night, huh?"

Reaching their rooms, she fumbled for the key cards. "It wasn't so bad. I tried new food, learned to dance—or how to mash toes anyway." She bumped his bicep. "You lead some life, Cade Thurstan."

He chuckled. "You're tellin' me."

"Your nights in New Orleans always this exciting?" She wrestled the door open, and they wobbled inside.

"No." His grip on her tightened. "Usually I get lucky."

She tipped her nose up. "I think you're a bit inebriated for that tonight."

"Let's test it out."

"Sure." She dashed to the window on the room's far side. "If you can walk in a straight line from there to here, we won't sleep in separate beds tonight."

"Straight lines are hard even when I'm sober."

Game for compromise, she grinned. "Forget the straight line then. Walk over here without looking like a newborn giraffe and I'm all yours."

He ambled three paces and grabbed the wall for support. Poor guy. His heart must really be hurting. Maren pulled back the duvet and helped him to bed.

"I'm sorry." He crawled over the sheets, and collapsed onto the pillow. "I didn't mean to drink this much."

"There's no reason to apologize."

"There is." He propped an elbow behind his head. "This isn't how I envisioned tonight ending. You, helping my drunk ass to bed."

"I've had worse first dates." She loosened his laces and removed his shoes. Smiled at the boats sailing his blue dress socks. "I'll let you sleep. If you need anything, call me. I'm right across the hall."

"Maren?"

"Hm?"

"Thank you. For everything. You're an incredible woman."

"I ... You're welcome." She plucked at the skin on her throat. "You're very complimentary when drunk."

"I didn't say it because I'm drunk. Just want you to know it. Want you to believe it." He cocked his head. "You don't get compliments often, do you?"

"Is it that obvious?"

"M'hm. You look like you just swallowed a bug."

"Look about as good as you, I suspect."

He chuckled. "God, you're cute. Come here."

"Cade."

"I won't try anything. Promise."

Cautiously, she approached the bed and perched on the edge. A wordless minute passed. His eyes were closed, his breaths long and deep. Deeming him asleep, she started to stand.

"That woman on the boat was Alice. She's the mother of a former patient of mine." He opened his eyes and she sat back down. "I used to dream of the day I'd join TIG. Work alongside my family, continue making them richer."

At his hesitation, she said, "You don't have to tell me."

"If I don't do it now, I never will. You need to hear it."

"Okay." She settled. "Go on."

"Losing Mom changed me. I didn't want to sit behind a desk, employ a bunch of locals, and think I was something special. I wanted to be in the community, making her proud. That's when I decided on medical school. I had the brains to get through the curriculum and the money to pay for the education, so I moved to Maryland. Completed my degree, my residency."

She didn't dare interrupt. Learning about this man filled her with ecstasy, and there was no way she'd ruin it.

"I opened my practice soon as I got back. A family came in one day. They had a daughter, Chelsea, who'd been having intense stomach pain. I'd treated her before, mild stuff like pink eye and chicken pox. She was a sweet kid. Had the bluest eyes I'd ever seen. I performed a couple x-rays—found nothing—and gave her parents some medicine to take home." He studied the wainscotting. "She died two days later."

She touched his thigh.

"It's rare to die from the flu, but I swear that's what it was. Still bothers me to think I could've helped her. Saved her. If only I'd been more observant."

"I'm sure you did all you could. Her death wasn't your fault." When he didn't reply, she captured his face between her palms. "Tell me you know that. Tell me you know that little girl didn't die because of you."

"I treated her, then she died. How could I not feel guilty about that?"

Maren laid her head on his shoulder. "That shows you're human." Silence swallowed the room, and she angled to look at him. "That's not the end, is it?"

"No. A few weeks after the funeral, Alice and her husband served me papers. Suing me for negligence."

"That must've been hard."

He shrugged. "I couldn't hold it against them. They were grieving their only kid. But when Penngrove found out what was happening, hell broke loose. Alice and Henry's home was vandalized. The shops refused to serve them, and the sheriff's office turned a blind eye to it all. Eventually, they left town."

"How long ago?"

"Ten months." His chest rose beneath her hand. "Took me another four to shut down the practice. Alice lost her daughter and her home because Penngrove has a toxic sense of obligation toward my family."

"You were afraid it might happen again. That's why you closed your practice."

He nodded.

"What about the lawsuit?"

"They dropped it."

"You hadn't seen Alice since?"

"No. I was expecting anger or sadness. Indifference, even. But she was apologetic. She told me to forgive myself."

"Will you?"

He nestled into the pillow and pulled her close. "I'm trying."

"Sharing is a good first step. I know you didn't want anyone to find out. Especially me."

"Yeah well, I was helpless against your moves. Damn temptress." Cade kissed her hair and murmured something against her scalp.

"What?"

"Will you write about it? My past?"

She cuddled into his side. "No."

"Readers would eat that up."

"They would." She traced the floral design on the duvet. "But I won't betray you."

He sighed in relief. "Mission accomplished then."

"What mission?"

"To seduce you into never disclosing my secrets. No woman can resist my manly wiles."

"Your manly wiles."

"Yes, ma'am."

"Hate to burst your bubble, but you haven't seduced me. That would involve nudity and subjects of a sexual nature. You'll notice I am fully clothed and we have yet to"—she waved a hand—"engage in adult subject matter."

"Adult subject matter?" He touched her nose. "Love it when you talk dirty."

"Shut up." Grinning, she bopped his arm.

They lay together for a while, and her eyelids sagged. She couldn't find the strength to leave, so she kicked off her shoes and climbed under the covers. Judging by the way he embraced her, Cade didn't mind sharing the bed.

She'd nearly drifted off when he whispered, "Promise me something."

"Sure."

"Promise me, if you need it, you'll publish my story." The arm looped around her waist tightened its hold. "You've always put yourself last, and I won't have you do that for me."

She clung to him. "I promise."

Now, more than ever, she was determined to discover what had happened to Renee. If only so she could leave that promise unfulfilled.

SUNRISE CAME TOO EARLY. Maren twisted her head into the pillow, groaning against the light glimmering through the blinds. The duvet was soft and warm on her skin—but it failed to compare to Cade's body. His arm was hugging her waist, his exhales tickling her nape. She released a happy sigh. Had she ever slept beside someone without abandoning them come morning? What a pleasant change.

She frisked her phone off the nightstand. No missed calls from the coroner. Without Dr. Garcia, they'd be running around all week trying to find another angle to pursue. A lazy Sunday might not be so bad. She cuddled into the blanket cocoon. Stilled.

His dress pants were tented against the small of her back. A normal occurrence for a man, but she accepted the compliment nonetheless. She stirred, gauging his length. Not too big, not too small.

He grumbled, yanking her closer, and she stared at the hands dangling near her ribs. Gentle, healing hands. But she'd glimpsed their other capabilities last night. Excitement jolted through her, remembering those fingers thumbing over her breasts, that mouth roaming her body, such sensuous torment.

She shouldn't be doing this. Shouldn't allow these fantasies to fester. Cade Thurstan was a client. Sleeping with him? Off-limits.

Shit, why did that turn her on more?

"You're killing me, woman," he said, his voice hoarse and tinged by sleep.

That did it. Decision made. She wanted him to whisper filthy things in her ear, to drive that erection inside her. She wanted to feel the pleasure, the intimacy, the ecstasy.

"Killing you?" She didn't turn around; not seeing him heightened the tension somehow. Grasping his hand, he trailed upward. "I wouldn't want that." Their fingers skimmed up her ribs and closed over her breast. She sighed, arching her back against him, and Cade brought his mouth to her nape.

"Then what do you want?"

"Adult subject matter."

"Ah." He sunk his teeth into her earlobe. "You want to be fucked, Maren?"

Desire clogged her throat as his fingers worked over her body, the pace torturous. His palms were smooth and uncalloused. Pampered. These weren't working hands. Shouldn't she want that? Someone who worked hard and fought for everything—someone like her.

But nobody made her feel like this. Maren inhaled sharply as he squeezed her ass. The arousal was overpowering, but it wasn't just physical. The ache in her thighs, she was used to. The ache in her heart? Not so much. They'd deal with that—she'd deal with that—later. For now ...

She reached backward, grazing him through the pant fabric. Solid. The touch ripped a feral sound from his throat, and he thrust lightly.

"Say it, sweetheart," he whispered. "Say you want me to fuck you."

"I want you to—" she sucked a breath as he worked his thumbs over her nipples, the lace of her dress like a barrier between their bodies. "I want you to fuck me."

He smiled against her throat. "Where are your manners?"

"Cade."

"Come on." He licked the sensitive flesh just below her jaw. "I'm Southern, remember? Politeness is important to me."

"Fuck me, Cade—please."

A deep chuckle slipped from his lips, and he billowed her dress. "Let's get this off then."

It landed on the floor a millisecond later. She was decked in mismatched lingerie and topped by a tumbleweed of day-old hairspray and erratic bobby pins, but Cade didn't seem to notice. Good sport. His eyes twinkled in the faint light, like a tourist admiring the cherry blossoms. She arched her back, and he unhooked her bra, dragging his fingertips down her spine.

"So soft." He brushed his lips over her midriff and planted kisses along her stomach. "How do you get so soft?"

"Vaseline." She grinned. "From the dollar store."

He laughed, and the roughness of his stubble against her breast provoked goosebumps. His mouth on her nipple? That provoked so much more. He moved his tongue in slow, wet circles. She inhaled, her hands jetting to his hair, tangling in the sleep-softened gel. God, his mouth felt good. She moaned his name, and his head lifted.

"I knew you'd be like this. Responding to every lick, every touch." He accented his words by nudging her thighs open, grazing her. She bucked, and heat burned her cheeks. What the hell? She wasn't a sexual novice. Shouldn't react this strongly to a simple caress. Her need for the man was driving her crazy, that was it.

Cade dragged his thigh between her legs, and her eyes popped open. He wasn't naked.

"This isn't fair." She grabbed his waistband, intending to strip off his shirt, but he snatched her wrists and pinned them above her head.

"It's not supposed to be." He slipped a hand beneath her hips, encouraging her to rub against his pant leg and dampen him with her arousal. "That's something you'll have to get used to."

The fabric was deliciously rough. Erotic, to be naked—bared to him—while he still sported clothes from the night before. She whimpered at the feel of him, the scent of him.

"I love your sounds." He nosed her throat and slid his tongue up her jaw before at last, taking her mouth. This kiss did not simmer—the lid had covered the pot too long for that. Their lips met in an explosion of yearning and emotion, of passion and heat. She melted into the mattress, dissolving into the pleasure of an encounter that had barely begun.

"How long have you been thinking about this?" When she didn't reply, he snaked his way downward. Spread her legs, settled between them—then bit her thigh. She yelped. "Answer me, Maren. Open your eyes and answer me."

"Shit." Breathless, she drew out the word. "All morning. Last night. Days before last night."

Her bed-headed man bellied between her legs. What a sight.

Wait, when had she started thinking of him as her man?

Her brain shut off when he pushed her underwear aside and drew his tongue across her mound. He breathed against her wetness, his fingertips tracing her stretch marks. This man of medicine, torturing her. Go figure. Lava pooled in her abdomen, and her body teetered on a cusp. Cade was the catalyst, building the pressure, inching her toward eruption. He licked her slit, seeking out where she yearned to be touched, and when he found it, she jerked her hips.

Cade indulged. A flick of searing tongue. A gentle—oh, so gentle—graze of teeth. He slipped his hand beneath her buttocks, orienting her body. And pushed two fingers inside her. She clasped the sheets in a death grip, her toes curling into the crumpled duvet. His mouth was hot and urgent. He stroked her with his fingertips, and fuck, was she panting? The weightiness grew within her. Close. So close. He caught her clit between his lips, and her body quaked. She bucked and twisted, mangling the bed coverings.

Shit. The man was good.

She refocused as he crawled to her. Like magic, there he was, warm and tan and naked. She grasped him, and he sucked air through his teeth, pressing a kiss to her mouth.

"You're so sweet. So fucking sweet."

She longed to look at him, to drink in the dusting of chest hair and caress the lines of his spine. But not right now. Too hot, they were running too hot. He hovered inches from her entrance. She hesitated and glanced around.

"Do you have ... well ..."

"Oh. Yeah." He leaped from the bed, rustled the condom from his pocket, and returned to her sheathed.

"Quite presumptuous, aren't—" Her words disintegrated as Cade thrust inside her.

A perfect fit: filling but not overbearing. In slow rhythm, he rocked back and forth, stifling her moans with his mouth. Detaching from the kiss, he increased his speed. He pumped his pelvis and brushed her sweet spot, and her inhibitions crumbled. Fiery tingles floated under her skin, and her mind went fuzzy. She saw him, only him. His muscles flexing, his eyes fixed on their connection. The sensations built inside her like delicious pulses of electricity. Then, a power surge. Warm pleasure zinged across her body, had her writhing and crying out his name. She clenched him, and he swore, finding his own release. The mattress squeaked as he toppled to the sheets beside her and tugged her against him.

Sweaty, satisfied, content, Maren sighed. "You're not all talk. I'll give you that."

"Glad you enjoyed yourself," he said, nuzzling her hair.

She rolled away, and winced at the bobby pins littering the floor.

"I'm not done with you, y'know," he called as she headed for the bathroom. "Not by a long shot."

God, she hoped not. Smiling at his promising threat, she shut the door. Compared to the Thurstan's guest bathroom, the hotel's facilities were lackluster. Black dual vanity, monochromatic images of local hotspots—or, what she assumed were local hotspots—and a walk-in shower. Her destination.

Maren adjusted the temperature, waiting for the hot water to kick in. Her arms and face were gritty from dried sweat. Soap bar in hand, she worked a lather over her skin. Sore, where he'd filled her. So completely. So perfectly. As was everything about him.

Therein lay the issue.

They complemented each other, sure, but they also had an expiration date. She'd return to New York soon, and never see him again. Emotions bombarded her at the thought of it, but Maren locked them away. She brought this on herself. Could've stopped everything after the first kiss or returned to her room last night, but she hadn't. Now, she'd suffer the consequences.

Lost in contemplation, she jumped at Cade peeking through the door. "Mind some company?"

"There's room enough for two." She rinsed out the shampoo and ogled him as he stepped in. Toned pecs and thick legs. She licked her lips.

"You sleep okay last night?" he asked.

"Yeah. Usually, I don't in a bed that's not mine."

He slicked her hair to the side and pressed his lips to her nape. "I have that effect on women."

"You put them to sleep?"

"Exactly." Grinning, he tugged her sopping strands and moved under the water.

She slid her hands up his back. "What're the plans for today?"

"Let's grab breakfast. I don't know about you, but I worked up quite an appetite."

"Me too. I'd kill for a mountain of bacon right now." And more sex. But she'd give him another minute.

"Leaving so soon?" he asked.

Stepping onto the bathmat, she smiled over her shoulder and swaddled herself in a towel. "I warmed it up for you."

"I was hoping for something hotter than a warm-up."

"Rain check?"

"Promises, promises."

The smile stayed on her face as she exited the bathroom. Later, she'd cash in that rain check. She planned to make the most of the time they had left.

Maren frowned at the dress strewn on the floor. She hadn't brought extra clothes—or anything—in her purse for an overnight stay. No alternatives, she wrangled the garment over her head. She needed to brush her hair and teeth. First, she checked her phone. Nine in the morning. Two hours till checkout. The shower stopped, and she opened her emails, humming a song from last night. Birds chorused. Cars honked. A towel dried skin.

And the phone rang.

Her temperature plummeted. Blocked number. Could be a phishing call, but her gut said otherwise. This was Dr. Garcia. Her coroner, her savior. Every answer she needed was on the other end of the line.

She swiped to accept the call, leaving a sweat mark on the screen. "This is Maren Sharpe."

"You're real," a woman said.

"Dr. Garcia?"

"Yes."

Relief filled her body, fast as a tropical tsunami. "Thanks for calling us back."

"Ana said it was urgent."

"It is"—she held up a finger to Cade who walked toward her—"Do you have time to talk about Renee Thurstan?"

"We shouldn't discuss this over the phone."

"Can we meet somewhere?"

A loud crunch. Biting her nails? "How do I know you're being honest?"

"Hard to prove honesty over the phone, but we did save your sister's life."

"Paid her hospital bill, too. Why would you do that?"

Had they done that? Maren spun around and nearly knocked heads with Cade. He flashed his palms in apology.

Silencing the call, she asked, "You paid Ana's hospital bill?"

He shrugged. "Trying to tip the scales in our favor."

"It worked." Smiling, she unmuted the call. "Cade Thurstan paid it. He wants to know what happened to his mother."

"I don't like involving myself with the Thurstans again, but y'all did help Ana." The line quieted, and after several minutes, Dr. Garcia asked, "You work somewhere up north?"

"Yes. New York."

"You got ID?"

"I do."

"Twenty minutes and I'll call with an address. Meet me there. Fast as possible."

"Twenty minutes. Got it." She resisted the urge to cartwheel. "But why the secrecy?"

"Some people wouldn't appreciate me talking to you."

Her pulse partied in her ears, and Cade stood beside her with clenched fists. She'd convinced him to doubt everything—and everyone—while they investigated. He deserved something. A nibble, a taste. Maren reached for his hand and asked the ultimate question.

"Dr. Garcia, was Renee's death an accident?"

"No."

Twenty-Four

Five miles north of Gulfport, Cade chucked the gearshift into park. "I don't like this."

"You've been saying that since we left New Orleans."

"That was about the car." To save time, they'd left his sedan at the docks and hightailed it to the rental agency. A stupid decision. This jalopy had an interior that smelled like a chain-smoker's living room, and it took thirty minutes to go from zero to sixty.

"We don't have a choice. She knows what happened to your mom."

He clasped one of the hands brawling in her lap. "I'd feel better if I could come with you."

"Let me build rapport first. I don't want to spook her."

"Isn't this a little much though?" He gestured to the empty parking lot. "I can't even see the restaurant from here."

"It's right through those trees. I'll be fine, don't worry."

"Be careful. Please."

"Of course." She dialed his number, plucked his cell from the cupholder, and accepted her call. "I'll keep you muted. This way, you'll hear what's going on." She stuffed her phone into her bra.

"Don't make that a habit." He pointed to her breasts. "Could be cancerous."

"Look at you, the little conspiracy theorist." She grinned. "Better keep those comments to yourself, or people might start thinking you're growing fond of me."

"Would that be so bad?"

Maren looked down at him. A breeze ruffled her dress and sent her hair into a flurry. Honey locust trees stretched and swayed, their leaves a backdrop of lush green. They were in unfamiliar territory, and she was traipsing through the brush to meet a stranger. Awful idea. If anything happened to her ...

The realization hit him like a tire swing to the gut. This wasn't fondness. The way his chest seared at the thought of her hurt, the way his heart lightened when she smiled—this was far deeper than fondness.

"You okay?"

"Yeah." He blew a breath. "You should get going. Watch yourself."

"Aye, aye, Captain." She saluted, slammed the door, and strode out of sight.

He leaned against the headrest, listening to the leaves crunching in the breeze. No rubber peeled down the road, and no tourists loitered at the rest stop. Hopefully, the restaurant would have patrons at least.

Her voice echoed in the cupholder. "Stop worrying."

"I'm not worrying."

"Yes, you are."

He grabbed his phone and pressed it to his ear. "For all you know, I've left you here. Freed at last from the thorn-in-my-side biographer."

"But you didn't. Face it, my friend, you've shown your cards. Peel away that grouchy exterior and you're a bowl of jelly."

For her, maybe. But he couldn't say it. Wasn't sure if she was ready to hear it. Instead, he impatiently tapped on his thigh. "Are you getting close?"

"Crossing the lot now. I don't see—" Silence.

"Maren? Are you okay?"

More silence. She must've muted him.

His knuckles whitened on the phone. Five minutes. She'd get five minutes before he barreled through those trees. The thigh tapping grew frantic, and a bead of sweat dribbled down his spine. "C'mon Maren. Give me a sound. Anything."

She came through for him—a habit of hers. "Dr. Garcia? Nice to meet you."

"Get in. You bring your ID?" Something slammed. A car door?

No, no, no. What the hell was she doing?

"How'd y'all find me? Thought I covered my tracks," Dr. Garcia said, her voice weak and nasally.

"We talked to Sylvia. Do you remember her?"

"Sweet woman. How's she doing?"

"She's worried. Where have you been all this time?"

"Here and there. Don't stay in one place for too long."

"Why?"

"I can't take the threats. Feels like anywhere I go, he always finds me."

Cade dragged his hands down his face. How the hell was he supposed to sit here and listen to this? Hoping air might help, he exited the car, and the hood seared his ass. Still, there was room to rotate his neck and kick out his legs, work off the stress.

"Who's threatening you?" Maren asked.

"Never asked his name."

"You saw him? What'd he look like?"

"Tall, handsome. Someone you'd never expect."

Fabric swished, and Maren's breaths became louder. Probably using her phone. "Is this him?"

"What the hell? How did you know?"

"He's the reason we found you."

"Who is he?"

"Bryan Coulter."

Cade paced. What was this? What was Bryan trying to hide?

"He's told everyone Renee died by accident," Maren said. "What really happened?"

"See for yourself."

Papers shuffled. "Is this your report?"

"Yes, ma'am."

"No signs of sexual assault. No water in her lungs ... Is that typical of a drowning?"

"Drowning is difficult to prove. Most times, we're figuring out what didn't happen. Once everything else is eliminated, we can conclude a drowning if the circumstances warrant it."

"I see." She paused. "Did this warrant it?"

"My results were inconclusive."

Maren's heavy breath rattled the speaker. Cade swore, covering his face with his arm. Three minutes, and he'd crash their little meeting.

"You said it wasn't accidental. Why?"

"Two reasons. That." The pages crinkled again. "And this."

Maren gasped, and his cellphone vibrated.

"Shit!" Cade rammed his dead cellphone into his pocket. To hell with waiting. He locked the car and broke into a run. Leaped over nettle, weaved through spicebush. The dirt tried to seize his shoes with every step, and he nearly lost his balance twice before reaching the restaurant's parking lot. He peered through the window of a minivan. Finding it empty, he moved to another. Empty. Had they left? Was Maren alone in some backseat while he was wasting time inspecting vacant cars? He picked up the pace, flying through the vehicles, dodging side-view mirrors. Only one left to check. Please, let this be it. He approached the driver's side—and the door crashed into his nose.

"Fuck!" Cade fell over.

"What the hell you think you're doing, sneaking up on us like that?" A woman loomed over him, wielding a tire iron. Her hair was black and fluffy, her eyes wild.

"Stop!" Footsteps battered the pavement, and Maren ripped the weapon away. "This is Cade."

"The son?" Dr. Garcia paled. "I saw him creeping through the cars and I thought ... I'm so sorry."

Maren bent, helping him to his feet. "Are you—"

Whatever she intended to say got lost in the flesh of his neck. He held her, buried his nose in her hair and inhaled the flowery scent of the hotel's shampoo. "Is everything okay?" he asked. "The call dropped and I couldn't wait anymore."

"I'm fine. You, on the other hand, don't look great." She touched his chin, and blood reddened her fingertip. "Let's go inside. Get you cleaned up."

"What about her?" Cade scowled at the doctor.

"She's coming with us." Maren rubbed her lips together. "There's something you need to know."

THE DINER WAS A hotbed of bacon grease and cracked vinyl seats. Families occupied most of the tables. Road tripping, probably: two major highways intersected just west of here. Condiments cluttered the bar top, their labels obscured by syrup dribbles and crusted ketchup. Cade grimaced. Where was LaSalle when you needed him?

He settled in the booth beside Maren and laced his fingers. Across the table, Dr. Garcia kept a tentative eye on the door.

Maren slid over a porcelain cup. "I got you this."

"Thanks." He drank. At least the coffee was decent. "You going to fill me in?"

"Yes. Maggie?"

Dr. Garcia handed him a manila folder. "Second page, near the bottom."

The server approached, and scribbled down the women's orders before turning to him. "For yourself?"

"I'll stick with coffee."

Maren looked over. "You're not eating?"

"Not here." Cade opened the file. At the bottom of the first page, a bunch of toxicology information. He read on. "Blood alcohol level ... zero percent? How is that possible? Everyone said—"

"They lied," Dr. Garcia said. "She was sober as a church fly."

"What're all these here?" He motioned to the list of chemical names.

"Stuff that shouldn't be in the human body. Especially not in those quantities."

He pried his tongue off the top of his suddenly dry mouth. "She was poisoned? Jesus Christ."

"Not necessarily."

"Meaning?"

"Cade." Maren rubbed his thigh. Her voice was tight, her eyes tender with sympathy.

"What's going on?"

"Someone could've poisoned her. Or this could've been ..." Dr. Garcia toyed with the ring of condensation left by her water glass. "Self-inflicted."

"You think she killed herself?"

Heads turned, and dozens of faces grilled him with their stares. Cade shrunk into the seat, heat creeping up his neck. Lowering his voice, he said, "Mom would never commit suicide."

"She was going through a stressful time. Working long hours. Overtaking the company and—"

"She was happy, Maren. There's no way she'd do that." He rubbed his temples. "What about Bryan? If she killed herself, why was he hiding the autopsy report?"

"Someone might've forced him to do it," Maren suggested. "Keep the suicide out of public eye."

He scoffed. "Or?"

Maren waved to the file. "Last page."

He sifted through the papers, and the color drained from his extremities. He stared at the word until his eyes dehydrated. No. It wasn't possible.

"Pregnant." His head popped up. "How? Whose?"

"Think you're old enough I don't have to explain how." Dr. Garcia dumped four sugar packets into her tea and stirred. "As for whose, that's what your lady here wants to find out."

"She's agreed to help us." Beneath the table, Maren grasped his knee. "On one condition."

"Condition?"

"I want my sister clean." She laid her spoon on the table and sighed. "Maren said Ana's been using again, so I need her checked into a facility. For that, I need money."

"Anything you need." Cade blinked away the haze. "But how can you help us?"

"I'll tell you who the father is."

The door crashed open, and Dr. Garcia surged upward, her legs rattling the table. The shakers tipped, spewing salt and pepper everywhere. A server glared at them before hustling to greet the new arrivals: teenagers. The doctor heaved a breath and unclenched her jaw.

Cade waited for her to settle. "That's quite the paranoia."

"You try hiding for twenty years. See how you handle it."

"Fair enough," he said. "So, how are you going to identify the father?"

"May not seem like it now, but I was a competent coroner. I've got blood samples from the baby and the mother."

"Where?"

"Don't you worry about that. They're uncompromised."

The food arrived, and Maren dug into her blueberry waffles, Dr. Garcia into her omelet. He sipped his coffee, ignoring the rumbling in his stomach. Pay for rehab and find answers. Could it be that easy? The pregnancy changed things. It revealed a motive for murder—and a prime suspect. This wasn't a suicide. Pepaw wouldn't be happy with a baby out of wedlock, but Mom would never kill herself because of that. Would she?

No. This was homicide, plain and simple. If they could confirm the father's identity and find out which poison was used, the sheriff's office might reopen the case. Dr. Garcia had saved their asses, but curiosity still yanked on his sleeve.

"You've held onto this for twenty years," he began. "Why talk now?"

"Wasn't going to." Dr. Garcia chewed her food. "But Ana told me how you saved her life. Said you seemed like good people. Plus, if y'all can end this and bring me home, it'll be worth it."

He leaned back. "Excuse me for being skeptical, but you can't just analyze blood and find DNA similarities. You need something to compare it to."

She smirked. "That's where you come in."

Twenty-Five

"WHAT DO YOU THINK?" Maren asked from the passenger seat.

"I think you're crazy." Cade strangled the steering wheel. Mashing the accelerator, he overtook the turtle of a Toyota in the left lane. He needed to drive. Craved the rev of the engine, the whoosh of air darting past the windows. But he slowed—slightly—when she gripped her knees like they were life jackets.

"We haven't established that already?" she asked.

"You were sexy crazy before."

"Flatterer."

"Now"—traffic stilled, and he pointed at her—"you're insane. Full stop."

Her laughter mended the tension in his neck. "Don't you love it?"

Didn't he? Cade looked at her. The pink cheeks, the pursed lips, the frizzy hair highlighted by late-morning sunshine. Damn, there it went again—his heart tripping.

A car horn blasted, and he signaled an apology in the rearview before moving the car forward.

Maren fidgeted, her eyes fastening on the windshield. "Bryan has to be the father, and we'll need his hair for Maggie to do a DNA test."

"I know, but I'm not fond of breaking and entering again. We should find another way to prove it."

"Let's decide later."

"Why?"

"Because there's something else we need to discuss." She exhaled heavily. "I think Desdemona knew about the baby."

Damn. Another dropped stitch.

Memaw had taught him how to knit when he was a boy. He'd spent hours on the porch with his grandmother, listening to the birds, and fashioning scarves to donate. Holes had always defiled his creations, and Memaw would wait for his fussing to cease before leaning in to help. She'd said their family was like a knitted blanket. It was warm and comforting, a protection from the elements.

That blanket was falling apart now. The colors were fading, the yarn fraying, and the damage worsened with every secret that surfaced. Every lie, another dropped stitch. The results of this investigation could destroy his family, and he may be forced to make a new blanket.

Did Maren know how to knit?

"Did you hear me?" she asked.

"Yeah." He gave his head a good shake. "Why do you think Mona knew?"

"At the dress shop, she mentioned Renee's children. She corrected herself, and I thought it was a mistake. Now, with the pregnancy—"

"I wouldn't exactly call that definitive."

"I know."

"If you were pregnant, would you tell Minowa?"

She blinked hard. "Yes."

The highway bottlenecked. Drivers panted and stuck their arms out the window. Heat radiated from the asphalt, fuzzing the license plates and corny bumper stickers. Cade cranked a dashboard dial, but the AC failed to cool him; it sizzled off his skin like eggs on a too-hot pan.

"Why would Mona hide it all these years?" he asked.

"We'll figure it out. For now, let's get those DNA samples."

The front tire belched and sputtered out air.

"Really?" He thwacked the console, flicked his hazards on—and almost laughed. This day. This fucking day. He stopped on the shoulder and said, "I'll call a tow."

"A tow?" Her face scrunched. "I'm sure we have a spare."

"Maybe."

"Yet, you want to spend money on a tow truck."

"I don't know how to change a tire."

She batted those enchanting eyes. "Are you serious?"

"Yes, ma'am."

"Okay." She nabbed the cell from his hands and set it back in the cupholder. "Then you, sir, will learn something new today."

"It's not nece—"

"No arguments. Come on."

With a heavy sigh, he slunk outside and met her at the trunk. Maren peeled back its lining, revealing the skinny tire.

"Take this." She handed him the tire, snagged the jack for herself, and walked to the hood. "Don't look so glum, chum. This is a vital life skill."

"A vital life skill I could pay somebody else to do for me."

"It'll build character. Humor me."

Cade twisted out the lug nuts. "How'd you learn this? Thought a city girl like you would take the subway everywhere."

"I do." She grunted, removing the flat. "But I've dated people with cars."

"Me too, but that doesn't make me a mechanic."

"Fair point. Lift that"—she pointed to the spare—"and I'll screw it on." Her forearms flexed, and he licked his lips.

A beholding sight: her kneeling on the road, toting that pink lace and lugging tires around.

"There." Grinning, she eased back. "I like knowing this stuff. It's helped me out of a few scrapes in the past. The only person you can rely on is yourself, right?"

"Right." Watching her swipe grease off her hands, steeped in a prideful glow, Cade knew one thing: he could rely on her. She was the seawall to his coastal shore; every revelation was a wave threatening to erode him, but she softened the blows. Whether a ripple or tsunami, she guarded him, lightening the mood with laughter or cheeky retorts. And she was going to leave him. Expressionless, Cade slid into the driver's seat.

How was he supposed to let her go?

AN EMPTY HOUSE GREETED them a few hours later.

Sunday afternoon. Desdemona would be puttering around town, chatting up locals and strengthening her image. Fueled by dreams of becoming CEO, Lawrence would be poring over documents at the office. Greg, on the other hand, would be waking up in another city—and another woman's bed. Cade would've remained at home, phone in one hand, bourbon in the other.

Work, women, alcohol: Thurstan men had their vices.

Today was different, however. His step had pep, and he wore a smile that would put the Mona Lisa to shame. Hot air coated his lungs, and seeped into the threads of his day-old dress shirt. Inside the house, he found salvation.

"I'll run up and change. You want to head out right now?" Maren asked, yawning and putting her shoes away.

"I have to eat something first. Do you want to lie down? I can wake you up in a bit."

"Sounds good." She stopped at the landing. "You could join me, you know. Help put me to sleep."

"You looking for a lullaby or a bedtime story?"

"I'll take whatever you give me."

Grinning, he caught her forearm and twirled her into a kiss that dizzied him with desire.

She let out a dreamy sigh. "That. I'm looking for that."

"We do any more of that, and you won't sleep a wink."

"Worth it."

Before he could stalk her up the stairs like an aroused neanderthal, the front door swung open, and Greg paused on the threshold. His eyes locked onto where Cade held Maren's arm.

"Didn't mean to interrupt," he said, crossing the foyer. His shoulders were back, his hair disheveled as if fingers—probably not his own—had raked through it. Some might label it the walk of shame, but they'd be wrong. His cousin relished the hunt, and displayed his bedpost notches with honor. He was too young to realize the emptiness that lifestyle provided. One day, he'd learn.

Greg hitched his hip on the newel post. "You two look cozy."

"Cade treated me to a lovely evening." Blushing, Maren climbed a step. "I have a few things to get sorted upstairs, if you'll excuse me."

Greg, with his shit-eating grin, mocked a curtsy. "He treated me to a lovely evening."

Cade glared at his cousin. "We really doing this?"

"Hell yeah, we're doing this." He practically skipped as he followed Cade to the kitchen. "I haven't seen you this giddy in a while. You fuckin' her?"

"Classy." Cade opened the fridge and loaded his arms with bread, lettuce, tomato, and sliced chicken. A couple of sandwiches seemed simple enough. He arranged the ingredients on the counter and wrinkled his nose. Outside, Peter lounged in a lawn chair, scribbling on a notepad.

"I'm just bugging you." Greg leaned against the refrigerator and crossed his arms. "You are attached at the hip though. Something special there?"

"Maybe." He removed four bread slices, dropped them in the toaster. "Don't see how it's any business of yours."

"Testy."

"Just tired."

"You're lying. What's got you down? Anything you want to talk about?"

"Here he comes." He snatched the butcher's knife and massacred a tomato.

"Here who comes?"

"Greg the therapist. You love that guy. Me? I'm not the biggest fan."

"Whoa, what the hell is stuck up your ass?"

Cade rubbed his neck. He couldn't discuss Mom's pregnancy until he was certain of what had happened. But if it turned out Desdemona knew, who else was privy to the information? Could it be a big family secret he was on the wrong end of? Unlikely perhaps, but he planned to tread lightly anyway. Still, that didn't mean he had to take out his frustrations on Greg.

"Sorry," he said. "Long day."

"It's her, isn't it?"

"What about her?" The toast popped, and he glared at the burned slices. He could diagnose illness and repair broken bone, yet bread troubled him.

"She's under your skin, and you're bummed she's leaving in a few weeks." Laughing, he bopped Cade's arm. "I'm proud of you. You spent so long calling her a snake in the grass. Now here you are, covered in bites."

"Quite the metaphor."

"It's true then?"

"She's interesting, kind, funny." A smile snuck out as he crafted the sandwiches.

"Hell of an ass too." He raised his hands at Cade's glare. "I'm just saying. It helps when the personality's wrapped in a nice bow."

"Hasn't helped you."

"I've got sky-high standards. You're telling me Maren checks every one of your boxes?"

"Yeah." Cade's answer surprised them both. To digest the realization, he repeated, "She does. I love her humor, her determination. Never really felt something like that. With anyone."

"Wow. I didn't think ... You've got it bad, huh?" When he didn't respond, Greg pursed his lips. "You tell her yet?"

"I didn't want to complicate things."

Didn't want to have this conversation either. He bit into his sandwich and watched the leaves dance, hoping his cousin would take the hint, but Greg remained perched on the counter, whistling. Really? How many unprovoked therapy sessions would he have to endure?

Groaning, Cade pivoted. "What?"

"Don't want to complicate things. Is that really the cop-out you're sticking with?"

"You don't understand. She loves her family—it's one thing we've got in common—and I'm not about to put her in a situation where she has to choose between staying with me or returning to them."

"She has to know, man."

"Rich, coming from you. Tell me, what's the name of the chick whose bed you stumbled from this morning?"

Greg trailed him to the door. "If I found a woman and spoke about her like that, no way in hell I'd keep my feelings secret."

"Appreciate the advice." Cade patted his cousin's shoulder and left the room.

Greg didn't know what it was to care for someone, to put someone's needs before his own—but Cade did. For that reason, he'd keep his feelings quiet. How hard could it be?

Twenty-Six

MAREN DUCKED UNDER THE trellis arch as she walked across the Coulter family's front yard. Planters lined the gravel path, and grapevines swallowed the porch railing. Flowers dotted the greenery, vivid as saltwater coral, and there were no soaring pillars or extravagant fountains in sight. She could picture herself here: snuggled in the Adirondack chair, drinking coffee, and waiting for the warmth of sunrise. Easy to get lost in daydreams like that.

But she was forbidden from getting lost in them. She was flying home at the end of the month, even if she had to chain herself to the tail wing.

"You think they're home?" she asked as Cade crossed the porch. "There aren't any cars on the street."

"We'd better hope so. How else are we getting inside?"

"Pick the lock. Scale the house. Where's your imagination?"

"Restrain yourself, Nancy Drew." He knocked. "There might be an easier way."

"Be right there!" a voice called from inside.

"Golly, someone is home." He sent her a smug smile. "Imagine that."

"Yeah, yeah." She looked around. "I could've scaled this. Just needed a rope and gloves. Maybe a pickaxe."

He hugged her waist, pulling her close. "Do you even know how to use a pickaxe?"

"Can't be that hard. Swing and stab."

Cade chuckled and kissed the top of her head. He lowered his arms as the door creaked open.

"What a pleasant surprise." Barefoot in the foyer, Harmony waved them in. "If you're looking for Bryan, you just missed him." They removed their shoes, and followed Harmony into the kitchen. "Y'all want some sweet tea? Whipped up a fresh jug this morning."

"Sounds great." Maren leaned forward, peeking into the hallway. A floral runner blanketed the hardwood, leading past several doors, a surprising number for such a small house. But which one housed Bryan's hairbrush?

"There you go." Harmony gave them each a glass. Hands on her hips, she asked, "So what brings you by?"

Maren bounced an ankle. She hadn't prepared an excuse, hadn't prepared to talk at all, really. They should come back when nobody was home, less risky that way. She was already on thin ice with Desdemona; if Harmony caught her searching the cupboards and reported back to the matriarch …

"My fault, I'm afraid." Cade spun his ice cubes. "Got a hankering for some Harmony originals, and with the bakery closed, I've come to grovel."

Her eyes twinkled. "You'll never have to grovel, honey. All you gotta do is ask." Harmony plated a few treats, and gestured to the sliding glass door. "Why don't we eat these on the patio? Rufus is out playing, and I'm sure he'd enjoy the company."

Cade lifted the pitcher. "Lead the way."

Now or never. She tapped Harmony's shoulder. "May I use the bathroom?"

"Of course, cher. Last door on the left."

Maren nodded at Cade before whisking down the hallway. The bathroom was dingy with barely enough space to fit the tub. Soap dispenser, toothpaste, no hairbrush. She rifled through the drawers. Nothing. Maybe in the shower? She whipped back the curtain and scowled. There must be an ensuite bathroom. She crept into the hall and opened the next door. This was a bedroom but, judging by the size, probably not the master. Maren entered another room, noting the cluttered desk and overflowing filing cabinet—Bryan's office, no doubt. Her palms itched. What secrets lay in there waiting to be uncovered?

Focus. Behind the last door, she found the master bedroom, complete with bathroom. Maren hurried across the carpet, checking her phone. Doing okay time-wise. If Harmony suspected something, she could blame an unruly bowel movement. Real classy. Chuckling to herself, she pulled open the top drawer of the vanity. Ah, there it was, ruby red and stuffed with hair. She dug her fingers between the bristles, and folded the hair into a plastic bag before evacuating into the hallway. The office beckoned her with its siren song, and she was powerless to resist. One quick look, then she'd return to Cade.

The man was a hoarder. His desk was a tornado of candy wrappers, takeout napkins, and yellowing case files. Nothing interesting there, so she tugged on the filing cabinet. Locked. Whatever. She already had what she needed. This cake could forego icing. On her way out, she stopped. The closet bi-folds had been removed, showing off an enclave of bins and cardboard. The upper shelves supported only dust, and still had plenty of room to store more items, yet one box sat behind the office door. Strange.

An icy tongue licked her nape, and she wrenched around. Air conditioning, just air conditioning. A flag billowed outside, its grommets tolling like eerie church bells. Cade laughed somewhere, and Maren latched onto the sound. She grazed the cardboard flaps with shaking fingers and threw them open. Holy shit.

She jerked away, and flicked her eyes to the vacant threshold. If Bryan found her with this ... She shivered. Cade needed to see this. She tiptoed into the hallway, sucking deep breaths to calm herself. If she could get the box to the car, stow it in the trunk—

The front door slammed, and a voice boomed through the bungalow.

Bryan was home.

CADE SET THE PITCHER on the patio table and watched Maren vanish into the hallway. Hopefully, she'd work quickly because he was running out of conversation topics. Funny, he'd grown up visiting the Coulter bakery, yet knew very little about its owner. Harmony liked dogs, baked goods and nature walks; that was the extent of his knowledge. Rufus raced through the backyard, his ears and tongue flailing.

"I'll never understand it." He gestured toward the beagle. "How can they run in this heat? Especially with all that fur."

Smiling, she brought the glass to her lips. "He's just excited you're here."

"How old is he?"

"Six months."

"Huh. Was Dash that big at six months?"

Harmony shook her head. "He was half that size. I miss him. Truth be told, Rufus is a handful."

"He'll grow out of it, I'm sure." He rubbed the condensation off his glass. What else could he say? The Thurstans had never owned pets—Memaw thought them too messy—so he couldn't offer puppy advice. Come on, Maren. Come on.

"Do you think she's all right in there? Maybe I'll go—"

"I talked to Alice yesterday."

"What?" Her eyes widened, and she tabled her drink.

Cade relaxed his fists. Penngrove had its faults—jobs were few, resources were scarce, stores were closed by sundown—but he could always count on residents wanting to gossip. He recounted his conversation with Alice, and by the time he'd finished, Harmony was leaning halfway across the table.

"Poor woman losing her child like that." She placed a hand on her belly, and Cade winced.

He'd been so wrapped up in his own business, he'd forgotten about her medical history. "I'm sorry, Harmony. I shouldn't have brought that up."

"That's okay. It was so long ago." She looked toward the trees. "How different life would've been, had they lived."

He'd treated many Penngrovians during his stint as a doctor, their physical problems, their emotional ailments. For Harmony, it'd always been emotional. Her first baby would've been his age, the other two younger. Hours he'd spent with her, talking through the ordeal and the pain she carried. Each time, he'd encouraged her to see a psychiatrist, and each time, the excuse changed. No money, no time, no desire. Once their time ended, she'd rise, pat his cheek, and say, "Don't tell Bryan. Never tell Bryan." Cade hadn't needed the reminder; doctor-patient confidentiality was vital, especially in small towns. Still, it'd bugged him.

The Coulters appeared unbent by the trio of tragedies. They'd carved out careers and strengthened their marriage, establishing themselves as Penngrove's power couple. All that supposed strength, and yet, Harmony refused to discuss her pain with her husband. Why?

Listening to Harmony illustrate the bakery's upcoming menu changes, Cade surveyed his surroundings. The lawn spanned an acre, lush and green despite record-high temperatures. Above it all, a flapping American flag held no wrinkles—was it ironed daily? A magazine-perfect property, only thing missing was the white picket fence.

"Your yard is breathtaking," he said.

Harmony blushed. "It's nothing compared to yours."

"Sure, but you don't have gardeners on payroll." He grabbed his drink. "Does Bryan handle the yard work?"

She nodded. "He likes a well-maintained home. Me, I'd live in an outhouse."

He snorted a laugh. "What?"

"With Bryan." She grinned. "Long as we were together, I'd be happy. That man is all I've ever wanted."

His chest heaved, and in that moment, Cade wished the suspicions untrue. Wished her husband faithful, her life unshattered. After everything Harmony had endured, she deserved stability. But this situation was a bandaged wound that had festered far too long. Time to air it out, and let all families—Thurstans, Coulters, Garcias—heal.

"Harm, you home?"

"Speak of the devil." Harmony plodded inside, and hugged her husband.

Bryan removed the star from his shirt, and with movements gentle as a father tucking in his sleeping infant, placed it on the side table. "Afternoon Cade. Wasn't expecting to see you."

"He and Maren stopped by for some treats." Harmony covered her mouth. "Sakes alive, I forgot to check on her." She hurried to the hallway, and Cade hustled after her.

"I'm sure she's okay. We should wait on the porch and give—"

Harmony knocked on the bathroom door. "You okay in there, cher?"

No answer.

"Maren, is everything all right?" Silence again. "Something's wrong." Harmony shooed away Bryan and Cade. "Honey, I'm coming in now." She opened the door, and the bathroom lay empty.

Bryan rotated his head. "Where is she?"

"Strange." She scowled at Cade. "What's going on?"

"I-I don't know." Sweat slicked his forehead. Where the hell—

The front door clattered, and they stampeded back to the entrance. Maren stood in the foyer, her pink toenails bright against the tile. Her hair looked like a balloon had rubbed against it, and her eyes were wide and alert.

"I'm sorry, but we have to go," she said.

That intense stare told him everything he needed to know: this was serious.

Harmony flew forward. "What happened?"

"Nothing, everything's fine." She lunged for her shoes, and tied her laces.

"Are you sure?" Bryan asked. "You look flustered."

"I appreciate the concern," she said, inching toward the door. "Please, don't worry. Something urgent came up and—"

Voices layered as they began talking over one another. Asking questions, probing for answers, deflecting inquiries. It was like a damn presidential debate. He looked from Harmony to Bryan to Maren.

Thrusting a hand through her hair, Maren blurted, "I got my period!"

Mouths slapped shut. Harmony tipped her head and pressed a hand over her heart while Bryan scratched his chin, avoiding eye contact. Cade cleared his throat as Maren stepped onto the porch.

"Thank you so much for your hospitality, Harmony," she said. "Sorry to eat and run."

"No apology necessary. You go take care of yourself, cher."

Cade buckled his seat belt. Driving into the street, he glanced at her. "Should we stop somewhere?"

She kept her gaze riveted to the side mirror, as if watching for pursuers.

"Maren?"

"Sorry, what'd you say?"

"Did you want me to stop?"

"No." Her attention drifted to the rearview. "What for?"

"You know." He twirled a hand, heat creeping up his neck. "To pick up supplies for your ... womanly time."

"My—oh." She laughed, and the tightness in her expression drifted away. "I'm not having my womanly time," she said, exaggerating his words with air quotes. "I just needed an excuse to leave."

"Did you get the hair?"

"Yeah." She sobered. "I got something else too. Can you pull over?"

"Sure."

They walked to the back of the car, rocks grumbling beneath their shoes. Maren grasped the trunk handle, and the look she gave him made his fingers go cold.

On a deep breath, she opened the trunk. "I found this in Bryan's room."

Cade opened the box, and picked up one of the newspapers. "These are from the August my mother died ... Bryan stole them?"

"Yes, and not only the Penngrove Gazette." She dove into the box and removed specific issues. "This one is from New Orleans. This is Baton Rouge. Shreveport."

"Why keep all these?"

She toyed with the newspaper's corner. "Trophies."

"Trophies? Fucking hell." He massaged his temples. "Let's say we're right. Bryan kills Mom, keeps these to relive his crime. Where does Mona fit into this?"

"Maybe she covers it up."

"Why? Why would she do that?"

"I don't know." Maren paced. "Your family is pretty religious, yes?"

"Most of us."

"How would they feel about a baby out of wedlock?"

"They wouldn't like it."

"Maybe that's it then. Renee was the hot topic for miles around, and your family didn't want to risk any reporters catching wind of the pregnancy, so they stopped the media coverage."

"How can we be certain my aunt was involved?"

"Reporters are relentless. Stopping them takes serious power." She glanced up. "And serious money."

"That doesn't make any sense. Mona didn't have any power when my mom died. She wasn't CEO yet."

"You're not CEO, but you still hold influence over people in this state. You've proved that over and over again."

"In this state, sure." He lifted one of the newspapers. "This was published in Miami. They're not going to stop national coverage because my aunt said pretty please. She didn't have that kind of sway."

"Your grandfather did."

He scoffed. "So every member of my family was involved. Is that what you're trying to tell me?"

"I don't know." She closed the distance between them. "What I do know is that things aren't adding up. Bryan couldn't have done this on his own, and he wasn't the only one with a reason to hurt your mother."

"What're you talking about?" Cade asked, fighting to keep the venom out of his voice.

"Desdemona was the oldest child. She should've gotten the company, but her father gave it to Renee. That's a billion-dollar motive. What if she—"

"No."

"Just listen to—"

"Get in the car." Cade marched past the backseat. He didn't want to do this anymore. The questions were multiplying, the suspicions deepening. What would happen once they uncovered the truth? Would his family survive the fallout? He pictured his mother then: her blonde hair bobbing, her smile brightening her face. He'd solve this. Despite the pain and the torturing possibility of losing whatever family he had left, he had to trudge forward and find answers. For her.

"Let's send those hair samples," he said, sliding behind the steering wheel.

"Then what?"

"We talk to the sheriff."

Twenty-Seven

"Do you know when he'll be back?" Cade asked, scowling at the officer manning the desk. Maren stood to the side, watching the door. They both knew Bryan could charge inside at any minute. Surely, he'd noticed the newspapers were missing by now.

"I don't. Let me call Sheriff Harlowe. I'll need a moment, Mr. Thurstan." The officer reached over the desk and fumbled the pencil cup, spilling pens on the floor. "Shoot, I'm sorry. I'll come around."

"No need," Cade said. "We've got this. If you could get an ETA on Harlowe, I'd appreciate it."

"Yes, sir. Right away."

Maren crouched and helped him collect the pens. "You say jump, huh?" She smiled, setting the pencil cup on the desk.

"Afraid I can't take credit for that. This kid's always been a bundle of nerves. Cowers at the sight of butterflies."

"He chose the right career path. Nothing frightening in law enforcement."

"Not in Penngrove." Cade sighed. "Not usually, anyway."

"What'll we do if Harlowe isn't around?"

"Wait."

She gripped her elbows. "I'm not crazy about that idea. What if Bryan comes looking for the newspapers?"

"Are you ..." He stepped closer. "Are you afraid?"

"Does that surprise you?"

"You didn't bat an eye at searching Bryan's office or chasing a drug dealer into the bayou. I was beginning to think you weren't capable of fear."

"We knew nothing back then. Now, we've got this baby which—let's be honest—will turn out to be Bryan's. Who knows what he'll do now that the secret's out."

Cade gripped her shoulders and pressed his lips to her forehead. "Nobody's going to hurt you."

Except him. Maren swallowed the words on her tongue. He'd never hurt her directly; of that, she was certain. But leaving him ... that would puncture her chest, leave her bloody and broken.

She could pretend that Cade didn't affect her, that she didn't stay awake at night picturing their future together, the laughs they'd share, the family they'd build. She could insist her life's compass was still intact, that it said to return home, to the boss, the noise, the unhappiness. Because Cade Thurstan was not her true north.

A momentary crutch, that denial. She was shoveling sand into a sieve and couldn't see the bottom yet, but part of her knew. A small, hidden part that never voiced its opinions. Soon, her time with Cade would end, and she'd board the plane with a mangled heart and a brain full of memories of the man who'd stoked her every desire. Years from now, when Minowa was graduated and life less hectic, she'd unpack this. This something that could've been beautiful if only she'd been brave enough to pursue it.

"Cade, I—"

The officer hung up the phone. "Looks like Harlowe ain't getting back until tomorrow. You wanna speak to Bryan instead?"

Cade shook his head. "Could we set up an appointment with Harlowe?" The officer nodded, and they arranged the meeting. "If he gets in earlier, call me."

"Will do. Take care."

Outside, the evening was gray. Store awnings creaked, flower baskets whispered, and moisture clung to the air, making Main Street smell like unwashed towels.

"How're you feeling?" Maren asked as they walked to the parking lot.

He rubbed his eyelids. "Tired. Frustrated. You?"

"Same. Think we've done all we can for today. Want to grab dinner?"

"Yeah. You craving—" He turned his head and froze.

"Cade?" She followed his gaze to the black truck. "What's wrong?"

"That's Bryan."

The deputy emerged, and slammed the door hard enough to rattle the truck. He marched across the lot, impaling Maren with his glare. A serpent of fear slithered down her spine, and her nails bit into her palms. Stay calm, stay calm.

"Cade," he said, stopping a few feet away. "Mind if I talk to you? Privately."

"Whatever you've got to say, you can say in front of Maren."

Bryan stared at her, his jaw ticking. "You've taken something that doesn't belong to you."

"Not sure what you mean." She wasn't about to confess to stealing something in front of a deputy—especially this one.

He looked at Cade. "Did you know about this? She entered my office without permission and went through my things."

"Seems to me those weren't yours to begin with. Why don't we visit Waldo? I'm sure he can straighten this out." When Bryan stayed silent, he added, "Tell us about the newspapers. Why'd you take them?"

"I don't answer to you."

"True," Cade said. "It wasn't official business though, am I right? Wonder how Harlowe would feel, knowing his deputy is abusing power and looting local businesses."

"Tread carefully, boy."

"You needed those papers, needed to relive the crime," she said.

"You're out of your depth." Bryan frowned as Cade chuckled. "What's so funny?"

"You. Your dedication to this."

"I don't kn—"

"Aren't you tired?" Cade stepped forward, crowding him. "All these years, all these lies. Can't imagine it's been easy keeping track of everything."

Blunt approach. Maren forced herself not to fidget. They were so close to learning why Bryan had concealed Renee's pregnancy. Seconds away from having the answers she sought. She should be thrilled. Instead, her stomach was in knots. Once the truth was revealed, she'd head home—and leave her heart in Louisiana.

"I didn't come here to be interrogated. I came to tell you"—Bryan thrust a finger at Maren—"to stay the hell away from my home. Hear?" He stomped away, grinding the gravel into powder.

"We found the coroner," Cade called.

The wind stopped blowing, and the sun ducked behind an oak tree. Goosebumps played hide and seek on Maren's arms. Her breaths were shallow, but they sounded like foghorns in the quiet.

Bryan rotated. Shreds of sunset mottled his face and flickered over his eyes, but his dilated pupils extinguished every trace of light. Why weren't his hands fisted? Why wasn't he rushing toward them, spewing threats and insults?

"She showed us the report—the real one." Cade crossed his arms. "We know how you've been threatening her to keep quiet. We know everything."

The deputy kept his gaze pinned to the ground, his body stiff and motionless. She inched forward. Maybe they wouldn't have to wait for the DNA to come back. Maybe they could find out the truth right here, right now.

"You were sleeping with Renee, weren't you?" she asked.

Bryan nodded slowly.

Cade sighed. "When did it start?"

"Long before you." He dragged his hands down his face. "I fell in love with your mama when I was twelve. We were inseparable for years but drifted apart. She met your daddy, and I married Harmony. We'd talk in passing." He shut his eyes. "Then your daddy left."

"You saw your moment, huh? Pursued Mom when she was weak and alone." Cade flexed his fists. Maren sidestepped, placing a hand on his lower back. His shoulders lowered, and underneath her fingers, his tense muscles relaxed.

"How dare you?" Bryan's tone was sharp, piercing. "I'd never do anything to hurt Renee. Never. We were both hurting, and we supported each other."

"What was hurting you?" Maren asked.

"Three miscarriages. It was around that time Harmony and I stopped trying." Bryan paced, massaging his temples. "I loved Harmony with every bone in my body. Still do. But during those years, she changed. She never left the bedroom. Didn't shower, refused to communicate, and

I"—he inhaled a shaky breath—"I needed someone. That's when I reconnected with Renee. I'd heard she was dealing with some issues too, so I reached out."

Unbelievable. Maren pictured Harmony swaddled in bed, her cheeks streaked by tears and her body wrapped in week-old pajamas, wondering where her husband was. Meanwhile, he was across town flirting with an old flame. The image sliced her last thread of restraint, and she launched toward the deputy. "Was Harmony too sad, too broken? She wouldn't step up the wifely duties, so you stepped out on her?"

"No, that's not—"

"Were you disappointed? You wanted a family, and she failed you three times. No choice but to look elsewhere."

"Stop!" Bryan backed away. "I love my wife. Through all the ups and downs, I remained faithful. Renee and I were just friends—for a while, anyway."

"Until you slept with her," she bit out.

"I made a mistake. One stupid, stupid mistake."

"Tell us what happened," Cade demanded.

"It was after TIG's annual gala. The whole town attended. Harmony was tired, but I didn't want to leave yet, so Rhonda May drove her home. Renee and I got to talking about old times, old memories. She was staying at a hotel down the block, and I didn't want her walking by herself, so I went with her. Lobby drinks turned into mini-bar drinks. She was stressed and looking to blow off steam, and I wasn't exactly thinking clearly. I kissed her, and one thing led to another." He hung his head. "We regretted it immediately."

Cade's expression was unreadable. "And the pregnancy?"

"She told me about it later. I was still trying to wrap my head around it when she died."

"Did Harmony know?"

He shook his head. "I couldn't tell her. We'd been through so much together ... I didn't want to hurt her. So, I did what needed to be done."

What needed to be done.

Maren wanted to scream. Why had Bryan betrayed his wife? Why had Renee slept with a married man? Valid questions, but there was only one question that mattered.

Lamps burned in the station's windows, and the air, breezy and cool, was ripe for an evening stroll—an opportunity many capitalized upon. Cade stood close behind her, radiating with warmth and strength. She wasn't alone. She could do this.

"Bryan." Maren swallowed. "Did you kill Renee?"

"Did I kill Renee?" His mouth dropped open. "Are you serious?"

"We believe Mom's death wasn't an accident. You just said you'd do whatever was necessary to ensure Harmony didn't find out about the affair, so—"

"Not murder!" He shoved his hand through his hair. "I can't believe you'd accuse me of that."

Cade counted on his fingers. "You hid the newspapers, you lied about the autopsy report, and you were having an affair with the victim. Tell me, Deputy, does that sound like motive to you?"

"Go to hell." Bryan unlocked the truck and climbed inside.

He grasped the door, preventing it from being slammed shut. "The truth's coming out, Bryan. No way you can stop it."

"I wanted to come clean! Tell Harmony everything, get this weight off my chest before it crushed me."

"Then why didn't you?"

"She said she'd ruin my life if I came clean. Said I had to keep an eye on Maren as well. That's why I was in the newspaper archives that day. I had to see what you were doing. I burned most of the newspapers a long time ago, but I kept one box. Just in case things went wrong and I needed some reporters on my side. Just in case she went back on her word."

"Who? Just in case who went back on her word?"

"Go home and find out." He started the engine. "And stay away from my wife."

Together, they watched Bryan rumble onto Main Street and out of sight. She eyed Cade through her peripherals. His posture was stiff, his cheeks drooping and covered in stubble. Her palms itched, but she didn't touch him. What gave her the right to comfort him when she was the reason for his suffering? She'd kindled this pain. Every frustrating fact, every exhausting truth, all her fault—and it wasn't over yet.

They still had to face Desdemona.

Twenty-Eight

THE MOON WAS MISSING. Cade leaned forward and frowned at the empty sky. Shadows terrorized the trees, and their branches wavered in the wind like skeleton fingers against a vast, foreboding blue. Driveway lanterns blazed, the only protection in this darkness. A pitiful defense. Cade was already consumed. His heart, blackened. He wanted to grab a sledgehammer and break something. Instead, he parked near the fountain and pried his hand off the gearshift.

There it was. A spectacle of wood, marble, and glass radiating like a mirage in the desert. Luxurious, welcoming. It'd been his sanctuary, a haven where he could forget the troubles of the day, laugh with people he loved. Now, it was just a mansion with unfamiliar inhabitants. So many secrets, so many twisted truths.

A stranger's house.

"It'll be fine." Maren patted his thigh. "We'll go in, ask our questions, and be done."

"She won't admit anything. If there's one thing I know about Desdemona, it's her ability to keep cool under pressure. She'll humor us." Cade glared out the windshield. "Toy with us like pawns."

"Then we'll get Harlowe to bring her in."

"On what grounds?"

"I don't know. Lying to her family?" She bit her lip and looked away. "That should be illegal."

He kissed her hand. "I know."

They climbed the porch steps in silence. He inhaled deeply, unlocked the door—and tripped on the suitcases. "What the hell?"

"Are you all right?" Peter dashed across the foyer and snatched Cade's elbow, helping him to his feet. "My apologies, Cade. I'm loading these into the car."

"What's going on?" He looked at the suitcases. Stained bottoms. Zipper pulls replaced by colored paper clips. Too shabby for his family. Which meant—

"Ms. Sharpe will be leaving us." Desdemona emerged from the parlor, and he raised his eyebrows at the whiskey glass in her hand. "Her plane departs at midnight."

Peter corrected the overturned luggage and faced Maren. "I got all your belongings, but I'll escort you upstairs for one last look."

He slanted his arm, blocking her path. "She's not going anywhere."

"Please." With a dismissive wave, Desdemona sashayed into the dining room.

"Stay here," he demanded, marching after his aunt. Walking backward, he pointed at Peter. "You don't touch those suitcases, hear?"

Desdemona was perched behind her laptop, so calm and proper it made his temperature boil. "I'll be terminating our contract with Primrose Publishing. I'm afraid Ms. Sharpe is no longer welcome here."

"I'm afraid"—Cade whipped back a chair and sat down—"that's no longer up to you."

Desdemona stopped typing and lifted her gaze. He'd witnessed this stare before, but had never been on its receiving end. It was reserved for arrogant boardroom members, for enemies requiring elimination. It put men in their place and made warriors tremble. But Cade didn't retreat.

He saw his mother in those irises, her body floating, him diving in and gasping for air as he desperately tried pulling her to shore. He saw a boy on his knees with hands clasped, begging God to give his mom back, a boy losing faith in the Lord but never his family. He saw his aunt stroking his hair, telling him that it'd be okay, that his mama was at peace. Sweet, empty lies. He saw every sleepless night, every unanswered prayer, every tear-stained magnolia.

He saw red.

"Don't let your affections for the girl cloud your judgment." Desdemona linked her fingers. "I'm only protecting you."

"Protecting me," he spat the words out like they were acid on his tongue. "Is that what you tell yourself?"

"Her behavior is unacceptable. She disobeys orders and pokes into things she shouldn't. She's ruining this family."

"You're ruining this family."

"I beg your pardon?"

He had to admit, she'd perfected this performance. No slumping posture or wavering voice. She was the personification of sincerity and virtue, but Cade wouldn't fall for it; he knew better now. Her innocence was a costume stitched together by years of deceit. Luckily, he had the seam ripper.

"You spoke with Bryan, I suspect," he said. "Which means you know exactly what I'm talking about."

"I assure you, I do not."

"Jesus Christ."

"Cade, don't use—"

He shoved to his feet. "When were you going to tell me about the baby?"

A clock ticked on the wall, counting off five seconds of silence, ten. Footsteps made the ceiling creak. Someone else was home. Greg, must be; Lawrence rarely left work this early. Who would they side with? Cade's gut stirred, because he already knew the answer. His cousins would defend their mother, and he'd be left with the woman who'd started it all. She'd be enough. His heart pulverized his rib cage, thinking of Maren. Yeah, she'd be enough.

"How much do you know?"

"Does it matter?" Cade scraped his curls back. "Were you ever going to tell me?"

Desdemona neatened her sleeves. "Renee didn't want anyone knowing."

"You're a medium now? Speaking for the dead?"

"Can we not be civil about this?"

"Civil?" The laughter was dry in his throat. "We had twenty years to be civil, but you chose to lie." He slammed his hand on the table as she raised a finger. "Lying by omission is still lying."

She straightened her shoulders. "Did you expect me to share everything? You were a child, Cade."

"No, that's just another excuse. I'm not a child now. What, did you forget to tell me?"

"It's what Renee would've wanted."

A weight settled in his abdomen. She'd never explain herself. They'd circle forever, and he'd be no closer to finding out why she'd hidden this. Idiot. Why had he expected a different outcome? How naïve, hoping she'd grow a heart, confess her sins, and choose to wrestle this as a family. He'd been the dedicated nephew. Supported every endeavor, applauded every speech. And it was all for nothing.

The heat evaporated from his body, replaced by a debilitating emptiness. This couldn't be happening. This woman was his rock, his second mother. She'd reveled on his good days and coddled him on his bad days, always desperate to heal his pain.

Why wasn't she healing his pain?

He couldn't handle this. Without a word, Cade left the dining room.

"Get your stuff," he said quietly, touching Maren's arm.

She paled. "You're trembling. What happened?"

"Doesn't matter. Get your things. I'll meet you at the car." He handed over the keys and hurried upstairs. Minutes later, he returned with his packed bag. Through the open door, he spotted Peter helping Maren heave suitcases into the sedan. Nails clicked on a keyboard in the dining room, and Cade swore. His aunt hadn't moved. That solidified it. All her acts of love and compassion were just that: acts. Very well. He could be cruel too.

"We'll be talking to Harlowe tomorrow," he called.

"Whatever for?" his aunt asked.

"Murder inquiry."

The typing stopped, and a chair screeched. Desdemona walked into the foyer and crossed her arms, studying him. "That's serious."

"Isn't it?"

"I understand you're upset, but—"

"Goodbye, Auntie."

"Cade, wait."

He paused on the porch and glanced over his shoulder.

"Who?" Desdemona rubbed her arms. "Who was killed?"

"Mom."

"How could you say that?" She glared in Maren's direction. "Has she poisoned you with this nonsense? She only wants an intriguing story, don't you see?" Desdemona followed him onto the driveway. "She's using you, trying to pull us—"

"Enough!" He hurled his suitcase into the backseat and slammed the door. "Lie to me again, Auntie. Tell me her drowning was accidental."

"It was. Baby, it was."

"I don't believe you," he snapped, avoiding her comforting hand. "Mom was an excellent swimmer. If she couldn't escape, she could've treaded water or floated until help arrived. And how'd she end up in the water in the first place, huh?"

"It was a party. She was drinking."

"While pregnant? Yeah, okay." He grasped the driver's handle. "I'm done buying your bullshit."

In the rearview, he watched Peter drape an arm around Desdemona as she covered her mouth—showing emotion, finally. But it was too late for that. Cade wouldn't be suckered anymore. He pushed the gas pedal and sped into the darkness.

"You need any help with those?"

Cade looked at Maren over the trunk lid. This was the first time she'd spoken since they'd left the house. "I got them. Can you grab the door?"

She walked up the front steps, and he hauled their suitcases through the entrance of the Penngrove Inn. He frowned. These accommodations were ... humble. No bellhops, no baggage carts, and dusty depictions of tropical shorelines cluttered the walls. Cade rang for service and drummed his fingers on the desk. "Sorry about this,

I'd suggest going somewhere else, but it's the only hotel in town."

Maren smiled tightly and returned to studying the floor.

"Hey." He tapped the bottom of her chin. "Something bothering you?"

A door swung open. "My sincere apologies!" Arnold Blackburn waddled behind the desk and pulled out a binder. "Wife's whipping up scones for tomorrow and just about burned the kitchen down. Now, how may I—" He looked up, and his eyes widened. "Cade. Can't say I was expecting you."

"Hi, Arnold. Do you have any rooms available?"

He glanced at Maren, and back at Cade. "One or two?"

"One works," she said.

Arnold nodded, noted Cade's payment information, and led them down the hallway. Unlocking the last door, he handed over the keys and bid them good night. Maren sank onto the end of the bed, and tucked her hands between her legs.

He abandoned the suitcases and sat beside her. "What's going on?"

"It's nothing, I'm fine."

"Maren."

Her spine deflated. "I'm ruining you."

"Ruining me?"

"I've brought you nothing but pain. All this shit, this unhappiness ... it's because of me."

"Who says I'm unhappy?"

"Aren't you? You've left your home, your family." She shook her head. "I did that."

"No, you didn't." He touched her knee. "Look at me."

She met his eyes, and warmth filtered through his chest. Ruined him—that was laughable. If anything, she'd rebuilt him. Picked up the ingredients of his life and baked something beautiful. Didn't she notice it, the hold she had on him?

Cade wiped away the tear rolling down her cheek. "Don't blame yourself for that, hear me? Bryan and Desdemona were the ones who lied. They kept me in the dark. You..." He touched his nose to hers. "You brought back the light."

Her chest fell on a contented sigh. "Better be careful. Women will fall at your feet with lines like that."

"Really?" He leaned away. "How come you're not?"

Streetlamps glowed behind the curtains, and leaves tip-tapped against the glass, buffeted by the breeze. The bed creaked as Maren rose and walked to the opposite wall. Avoiding him? His stomach sank. She wasn't ready for this conversation; he shouldn't have—

"Is that what you want?" Maren turned, running her tongue over her bottom lip. "You want me falling for you? On my knees for you?" She lowered to the carpet in front of him and looked up.

"This isn't what I meant."

"I know." She brushed his thigh with her hand and trailed higher. "Should I stop?"

Cade caressed her temple, letting her hair sift through his fingers. "No. You're good."

His abdominals tightened as she unbuttoned his pants. He bent forward and whispered, "You can't escape this conversation. We need to talk about what'll happen with us."

"I don't feel like talking." Her kiss hypnotized him. So hot, so sweet. It was unquenchable, his thirst for this woman. How was he going to convince her to stay?

That question wouldn't be answered tonight because when Maren dragged his pants off and took him in her mouth, his mind went blank. He could think of nothing but the warmth of her palm, the slickness of her tongue, and the sultry glint in her eye.

God help him.

Twenty-Nine

Maren woke to the smell of coffee. Groaning, she stretched and patted the left side of the bed. Empty. She jerked up, and Cade smiled from the desk in the corner.

"Morning, sunshine." He tipped his nose at the nightstand. "Got you a coffee."

"I knew there was a reason I liked you." She snatched the paper cup and sipped, hoping the caffeine would provide a boost. Her eyelids were anvils, her yawns relentless. They'd stayed up way too late last night. Pillow talk, that's all it was, casual and noncommittal. She couldn't offer anything else. If Cade suggested it … well, hopefully he wouldn't. She'd already tossed his life into a bonfire, and she didn't intend on stoking the flames any further.

"What time is it?" she asked.

"Eight-thirty."

She checked her phone. No missed calls. Strange. She'd been expecting a slew of angry voicemails from Primrose. Either Desdemona hadn't made good on her threat, or he was waiting to chastise her in person. No use worrying about it now. She peeled back the blanket and rubbed her eyes. "Any word from Harlowe?"

"Not yet." Hee tossed his cup in the trash and strode to the suitcases. "I was thinking we'd grab something to eat and head over to the station. Somebody has to know where—" His phone vibrated. He pulled it from his pocket and pressed it to his ear. "This is Cade."

Maren slithered off the bed. In the bathroom, she cranked the shower faucet, drowning out Cade's murmurs. Once the water pressure had blasted away the tension in her shoulders, she stepped onto the bathmat. Clean, refreshed—and content. This past week had been filled with turbulence; she shouldn't feel this comfort in her belly, this lightness in her chest. Cade's voice drifted through the door, and she smiled. His fault, this giddiness. Maren wiped the condensation off the mirror and stared at her reflection. Her smile wasn't forced or fake; it was wide enough to make her cheeks ache. Bizarre. Who was this happy woman?

A knock sounded, and Cade peered in. "That was the officer confirming our appointment. I think I'll go grab breakfast."

"You want me to go with you?"

"That's okay. Getting some air helps me clear my head, and I could use some normalcy right now. These past few days have been a little ... much."

"Tell me about it."

He enveloped her in his arms. "We'll head to the station when I'm back. Deal?"

"Deal." She locked the door behind him and retrieved her laptop, but she couldn't focus on her emails. Normalcy. What a funny word. Her normalcy had been a dingy New York apartment, pinching pennies with mother and sister, and coping with tyrannical bosses. Now, that life felt wrong. Like ketchup on rice or chocolate in grilled cheese. This—she looked around—this was right. Tangled sheets and heaped clothes, air scented by coffee and cologne. Cade's cologne. Maren leaned against the pillow and inhaled. His scent was her nicotine. She loved the color of his eyes, the sound of his voice, and the way he made her laugh. How he'd—wait, was this too many loves for a fling?

The warmth in her belly, the pattering in her chest. This was no fling.

Maren paced, trying to calm her breath. These emotions, such sweet poison. What the hell was she supposed to do? Stay in Louisiana and trust her heart? What a ludicrous thought.

Then again, what was holding her back? She hated the city, and her career would end after this contract got canceled. With their mother home, Minowa wouldn't be alone, and that was most important. Maren would miss her sister, but she could visit frequently. If she left Penngrove without communicating her feelings to Cade, she'd regret it forever. Her sister would understand, right? Probably, but she had to be sure.

She scrambled over the bed and grabbed her phone. Tumbleweeds bounced around in her stomach as the line connected.

"Maren? Is that you?"

That voice. The air ripped from her lungs. Not ready for this. Goddammit, she wasn't ready for this. Sinking onto the duvet, she sucked a breath through her teeth. "Hi, Mom."

"Thank goodness." Rebecca laughed dryly. "We were so worried. Minowa's paced tracks into the carpet. Why weren't you answering your phone?"

"I texted."

"Even kidnappers can text. I was expecting a ransom call any minute."

"Ransom?" She smiled tightly. "I'd be killed for sure."

"We'd scrounge. Have a little faith in your family."

Maren clung to the phone. She'd been marooned for four years, alive but never living. Laborious days, lonesome nights. Now, a boat floated off the coast. She could hear the music, see the sails. All she had to do was run to shore, release her heavy grudges, and swim for it.

"I missed you, Mom."

"I missed you too. Min told me what happened, and I feel terrible. I should've called you directly."

"Why didn't you?"

She sighed. "Min told me how busy you were and how you rarely answered your phone. I didn't want to risk one of my calls being missed. We did lots of backpacking and outdoor adventures, off-the-grid stuff. It was hard to predict when I'd get cell service again."

"It's all right."

"It's not. It's really not." Her voice trembled, and she sucked in unsteady breaths. "Can you forgive me?"

Was ... was she crying? Maren dropped the phone.

Rebecca Sharpe was unbreakable. She'd juggled multiple jobs, stomached pitiful pay, and returned home dead tired, somehow still finding the energy to smile. That was routine. A single mother struggling to provide, shedding blood and sweat—but never tears. No, she must've hidden those. Must've waited for her children to fall asleep, for darkness to quiet the world. Then, the tears must have come. Standing in the kitchen, countertop covered in overdue bills, maybe that's when her body would vibrate and her chin would tremble. And she'd cover her mouth to stifle the sobs, making sure her family didn't know. Nobody could know.

Like mother, like daughter.

Maren rocked, the lump in her throat expanding with each sounding sniffle. She yearned to reach through the phone and embrace her mom. Instead, she pressed it to her cheek and choked out, "I love you."

The dike crumbled, and she curled into a ball. Loving sentiments passed between them, again and again. She cried for the sacrifices given, the dreams lost. For every morning she'd woken up corrupted by hatred and contempt. For being so unapproachable her sister felt it necessary to spout lies. She wept out the anger, let regret dampen the sheets. Finally, her bitterness was gone.

Their conversation was like helium to her heart. By the end, she felt light and free. Mom's hotel story cracked her up and she fell against the pillows, breathless. "I can't believe you said that."

"I know. So unlike me. I can't wait for you to meet Oliver," Mom said. "And I can't wait to meet Cade."

She smiled. "Not sure if it's meet the parents time yet."

"Baloney. I hear the way you talk about him. Min did too, she's already picking out her bridesmaid dress."

What dress would her sister choose? Something pink and frilly. Meanwhile, Maren would opt for conventional and cheap, maybe mermaid cut. Oh, and sequins!

She shook her head. Too early for marriage—she knew that—but fantasizing about becoming Cade's wife ...

Mom squealed. "You should come to Europe with us next time. And invite Cade. How fun!"

"You're leaving again?" Maren jerked upward. "When?"

"Couple weeks. But don't worry, we won't be gone long. A month at most."

"Are these trips going to be a regular thing?"

"Oliver has a couple of vacations planned. Oh, Maren." She sighed. "I've never been so happy."

"That's ..." Her throat thickened, and she squeezed her eyes shut. Get it together, woman. "That's wonderful. I'm happy for you."

"Thank you, sweetheart. Min's out of the bath now. Did you want to talk to her?"

Did she? If Maren left New York, her sister would come home to an empty apartment, would have no family in the city to guide and support her. Could she do this? Could she live her fairy tale and leave her sister all alone?

"No," Maren forced the word out. "I'll see her when I get back. Love you both."

She ended the call and stared at the ceiling. Chirping birds zipped past the window, and laughter drifted off the sidewalk, seeping through the curtains. Maren moved into the sun, hoping it'd lift her spirits. Nope. Her skin was frozen, her heart hollow—how could it hurt so badly and still be beating?

Two minutes. She had two minutes to wallow before moving on. This was just another dashed dream. Shouldn't she be used to those by now? She wiped away the tears with a piece of toilet paper, and pinched her cheeks to give them some color. That's better.

Pointing at her reflection, Maren said, "You're fine."

Her brain repeated the words as she flattened the duvet and fluffed the pillows. You're fine, you're fine, you're fine. She scooped her clothes off the floor and flung them into her suitcase. Cade's t-shirt was crumpled on the carpet, and she approached it like a beached shark—carefully. She pinched the edge of the fabric and carried it to the armchair. There. That wasn't so bad. No crying spells, no nuzzling his clothes. She could do this.

Footsteps approached the door, and Cade stepped inside. "Hope you're hungry. I brought donuts."

Holy shit, she couldn't do this.

Her knees turning to rubber, Maren clutched the windowsill. Sincere, thoughtful, he was unlike any man she'd ever known—and she was going to break his heart.

"Hey," he said. "Everything okay?"

"Yep. Is this breakfast? Yum." She swiped the bag of donuts and turned away. Sucked a deep breath. "I wanted to talk to you about something."

"What's up?" He asked, grabbing a water bottle from the mini fridge.

"I called my mom today."

"That's fantastic. How'd it go?"

"Great. Anyway, I—" Her foot caught on the bedpost, and she toppled to the floor, wrenching her ankle. "Dammit!"

He kneeled and reached for her leg. "Let me have a look."

"No. It's fine."

"I don't mind. You fell pretty hard, I'll—"

"I said, it's fine!" She batted his hands away, ignoring the hurt look in his eyes. Gripping the mattress, she hobbled to her feet. "I didn't mean to blow up like that. Sorry."

"All good." His pocket vibrated. Cade pulled out his phone and grinned. "Harlowe's on his way to the station. You ready?"

"Uh-huh." Maren bit the inside of her lip. She didn't want to lead him on, but she could postpone the break-up for a day. Or two.

In the lobby, he shot her a concerned glance. "You're limping."

"I'll live." Her ankle had swelled, and her sock was cutting off circulation, but she didn't want to stop now. Not when they were so close to getting answers. "Let's just keep going."

She stumbled, and he grabbed her arm. "Stop."

"Cade, I'm fine."

"You're obviously not. Your ankle is the size of a turnip and you can barely walk." He bent, motioning for her to climb on his back. "Get on."

Reluctantly, she hoisted herself up.

"You're heavier than you look." He laughed as she wiggled to get off. "I'm kidding. You're good, stop."

"This was your idea. Don't blame me if you've got sore muscles tomorrow."

"I won't. It's a quick trip."

Sweat beaded on her forehead, and her hair clung to her temples. Following his gaze across the street, she froze. "Cade, we don't have to. We can visit the pharmacy or grocery store."

"This is faster."

"Have you been back since ..."

"I don't even drive by."

"You sure you're ready?"

"I'm ready." He squeezed her legs tighter to his hips, and crossed to the building still bearing a shadow of his name.

Pride throttled her. After everything he'd endured, Cade still found the strength to duel his demons. Because of her? No. She couldn't let herself believe she'd played a part in this. That would only make leaving harder.

She rested her cheek on his hair. "As long as we don't have to break in."

He gave her a coy smile. "Where's the fun in that?"

His handsome laughter danced in the breeze, and with a blink, she captured the moment.

A memory to cherish after she'd gone.

Thirty

Cade teetered toward the back door, pushing through the overgrowth. He set Maren on the stoop, upturned a terracotta pot, and removed the spare key.

This was the ultimate test. Closing his business had been like leaping from an airplane. He'd hurtled through the air for six months, lost and helpless, suffocating in regret. Alice had opened his parachute, but it wasn't over yet. He had to face this place and heal his emotional wounds. He had to stick the landing.

On a deep breath, he pushed inside. Dust layered the floor, and staleness tinted the air as he helped Maren climb onto the examination table.

Legs dangling, she glanced around. "It's not what I expected."

"No?" He opened the storage closet and flicked the light on. Glass jars littered the shelves, holding cotton swabs and tongue depressors, and tubs of hand sanitizer sat beside bins of nitrile gloves. All these supplies, wasting away. Could've donated them, he supposed, but he hadn't wanted to deal with the emotions—or the memories.

With gauze in hand, he snatched a chair and crooked his finger at Maren. "Give me your foot."

She lifted her leg. "Did you have any staff?"

"I had a nurse and a receptionist."

"No other doctors? How'd you take time off?"

"What's time off?" He untied her sneaker and removed her sock. Smiled at those bubble-gum pink toes. Cupping her ankle, he asked, "Can you rotate this?"

She circled her foot. "See? I'm fit as a f"—she hissed as he pressed his thumb in—"uck!"

"Fit as a fuck? That's a new one." Smirking, he unrolled the gauze. Her ankle was swollen but had full mobility. At worst, a mild sprain.

Maren jostled him with her good leg. "Very professional, Doctor."

"I thought so." He finished dressing her ankle and pinned the gauze. "You'll want to stay off this for a couple days. There are crutches somewhere around here. I'll see if I can—What?"

"You're good at this. Doctoring."

"Then it was money well spent."

"I need the full picture." She pushed off the table and limped to the counter where a stethoscope was hanging above the backsplash. She snagged it off the hook and draped it around his neck. "There. Official."

"Just need the illegible handwriting and we're set." He removed the stethoscope and rubbed his thumb over the engraving.

It'd been a gift from Desdemona after his acceptance into medical school. Every family member had left their mark here. Peter had installed the shelves and painted the walls, and Greg had organized the grand opening while Lawrence had indulged in his favorite hobby: barking orders. His aunt, his butler, his cousins, all lost now.

Maren patted his chest, and the warmth of her palm zinged across his skin, waking every nerve. "We'd better go. Harlowe's probably waiting for us."

"Let him wait." He stepped toward her. "We need to discuss something first."

"We do?" She nibbled her lip. "What is it?"

"Your debt."

"My debt?"

He trailed a finger down her throat. "I provided a service. Yet here I stand, unpaid."

"My insurance will pay."

"That's it?" He leaned in and traced her ear with his tongue. "Not even going to thank me?" Her head fell back, and she made a delectable sound. A sexy, little whimper. "Can't hear you."

"Thank you." Her voice was hushed and breathy. Didn't she know that drove him wild? Cade grasped her nape and dipped his head to meet her awaiting lips. Their mouths melded, hands skimmed over fabric, feeling each other, learning each other. He pressed forward and trapped her against the countertop. Needed to consume her, to devour every inch. The room hummed, clothes rustling, zippers squeaking. Cade pulled down her shorts and—wait, why were her legs shaking?

The ankle. Shit. Horizontal would be best for this.

"Sorry." He kissed her nose, and his hands moved to her ass. "Wrap your legs around me."

Maren didn't protest. She looped her arms around his neck and clung to him. Could she feel it? The kicking of his pulse, the tumbling of his heart. All her fault.

Thunder and lightning, that's what they were. He and Maren had different goals to conquer, separate challenges to face, but they belonged together. Their emotional connection strengthened every day while their physical connection rocketed. Faster, hotter, brighter, until it exploded in a firework of lust and ecstasy. In that burst of color, Cade came alive.

He laid her on the table and kissed the dip of her ankle. Gliding his mouth up her calf, he nipped and tasted. Jesus, this flavor. Rich whiskey and salted caramel. Cade ran his tongue up her thighs, savoring the sensations. The ripples of stretch marks, the prickle of hair. Irresistible. She arched her back as he neared her heat. He smiled. She wouldn't escape so easily. He bypassed her underwear and kissed her navel. Maren jerked, moaning her protest.

"Not yet, baby." He dragged her blouse up and trailed his tongue along her abdomen. Her breaths grew ragged and by the time he reached her bra, she trembled. He drew a finger across the lace, smiling at the goosebumps, the shivers. He tore the cup down and encircled her nipple with his mouth as his hand ventured downward, slipping beneath the cotton. Slick and ready for him. Fuck, he loved that. He grumbled, rolling her nipple between gentle teeth.

"You've been waiting for this, haven't you?" he asked.

"Yes."

"Aching for my touch." He rubbed her wetness, his fingers pleasuring in slow circles. She closed her eyes, and he kissed the corners of her mouth. "I like knowing you think about this. Think about me." He increased the pace, pushing her to the edge, reeling her back. He wanted her weak, pleading. She dug her nails into his scalp, and Cade pushed two fingers inside her.

"Jesus." She panted, her knuckles whitening on the edge of the table.

"That's not my name."

Laughter simmered. Such a feminine, sexy sound that snapped his control. One-handed, he wrangled from his shorts and removed a condom from the pocket. When he tossed over the foiled package, she opened her eyes. Widened them.

"You bring those everywhere you go?"

"With you? Yeah." He curled his fingertips inside her, inciting a gasp. Nuzzling her ear, he whispered, "Because, truthfully, I think about this all the time too. Now open it."

He could've removed his fingers and opened the condom himself, but he didn't want to stop pleasuring her. Not until he was gray and frail. Maybe not even then.

While she ripped the foil, Cade brought her to the cliff again and this time, let her fall. She bucked and twisted, tightening around his fingers. And her moans—goddamn—he'd keep those on repeat.

"So pretty when you do that." Cade unrolled the condom and crawled on top of her. Their mouths met in a harsh, hungry kiss. He nipped at her bottom lip, rubbing himself against her wetness. "Do it again, pretty girl."

Her eyes flared. "Make me."

Yes, ma'am.

With a groan, he sunk inside her. She cradled him, wrapping her legs around his hips, urging him deeper. Warm, wet. Ripples of pleasure singed across his skin as she clenched around him. He flexed, and his vision fuzzed. So good, so good. Maren whispered his name, and he lost it. They climaxed together, a mix of rapid pulses and fleeting breaths. His limbs turned to gelatin, and he foundered beside her.

This place had weighed so heavily on his heart. Pain and regret fogged its rooms, its hallways. There was no haunting haze now. She'd brought back the sun.

"I'm cured," she declared, fishing her clothes off the floor and sliding into them.

He rolled to a sitting position. "I was hoping for some follow-up appointments."

"Not sure if my insurance will cover that."

"With the way you thank a man, you don't need insurance."

She furled her hair into a tail. "I didn't do much thanking."

"Ah, but you did. And I expect you'll do more before this trip is over."

"What sane woman wouldn't?" She stepped between his hanging legs and pecked his cheek. "This suits you."

"Sex? I'd hope so."

"No. This." Maren gestured to the examination room. "You're in your element here. Determined, focused—even when you're seducing your patient." She swiped a curl behind his ear. "You have no desire to come back?"

"I want to. Every day, I want to. But it's not that simple." He stood and grabbed his boxers. "This town worships me so much they ran out a grieving family. I can't risk that happening again."

"Why not practice somewhere else?"

"Because I like ..." With a hollow chuckle, he shook his head. "Funny. Was about to say I like being with my family. Guess that's not true anymore."

"This could be your new beginning," she said. "Your fresh start."

"Yeah. I might—" He looked at Maren, and his brain malfunctioned. He'd been to the Alps and the Eiffel Tower, had sipped wine on the beaches of Bali while sunset tinted the waves. But it was Maren's beauty that paused his world. She twinkled in the light, her eyes aflame and her skin aglow. Hell. She was his postcard picture, his Aphrodite reincarnated.

His fresh start.

She shifted. "Why're you staring at me like that?"

"Sorry." He coughed. Why did his tongue feel so big? Jesus, his eyes were watering.

"Are you all right?"

He nodded and pressed his fists against his eyes, waiting for the coughing to cease. What was he supposed to say? Stupid question, he knew exactly what he wanted to say. Had for a while now. But how would he say it without scaring her, without pressuring her? Greg's voice pummeled his ears like a damn battering ram: tell her, tell her, tell her.

"I care about you!" Cade winced. That was louder than intended, but at least it made the voices stop. "And I'm sorry if that complicates things, but you need to know."

She blanched. Backstepped.

Bad sign—he knew that. He also knew if he didn't confess everything, if she went home not knowing how strong his feelings were, he'd regret it for the rest of his life. His head no longer steered this ship. Now, his heart manned the helm.

"I've never met a woman like you. Always putting others before yourself. Kind, caring, and damn, if those burglar skills aren't admirable."

No smile or twitching lip. Maren remained rigid, her glimmer fading to matte.

He walked toward her. "You've turned my life upside down in the best possible way. Two months ago, I was drowning. No way forward, no way out. You saved me, and once we get this whole thing with Mom figured out, I feel I can finally—finally—move on." He grasped her hand, and the chill in her fingers sent his heart plummeting.

Smile, Maren. Or cry or laugh. Just do something, say something.

Goddammit, why wasn't she saying something?

"You mentioned new beginnings. Trouble is, I can't begin again unless I'm with you. Stay with me, Maren. I love—"

"Don't." Her finger shot to his lips. "Just ... don't." She stared at him, and her posture collapsed. "I can't."

"Can't what?"

"Be with you." She sidled past him. "I have to go home."

Her words were like an ax to his ribcage; his lungs compressed, and pain erupted in his chest.

A considerate man would've respected her answer and moved on, but Cade didn't want to be considerate; he wanted to be selfish. To sleep with her each night and wake up with her each morning, to share laughs and create memories. She wanted it too: her touches teemed with affection, her eyes with tenderness. One last time, he promised himself. One final push to get her to stay. If she refused again, he'd accept defeat—and let her go.

"Why go home?" She scoffed, and he said, "I'm serious. You hate where you live, and you work for a movie villain who we both know will fire you once Mona cancels our contract. Plus, there's no reason you couldn't support Minowa from here. What's holding you back?"

"I can't leave Min alone. Do you know how dangerous the city is?"

"If she's anything like you, I think she'll be fine." He crossed his arms. "What about your mom?"

"She's leaving again."

"Then I'll come to New York."

She narrowed her eyes. "You hate New York."

"I'd live in a cardboard box if it meant being with you."

"You'll be miserable there, Cade. I can't let that happen. I won't."

He threw up his hands. "Why can't you let yourself be happy?"

"Excuse me?"

"You're always bearing the burden. Giving up the career dreams and dealing with sleazy bosses, so you can shelter Minowa. Why're you forced to make the sacrifices?"

"I'm not forced to do anything." Her glare held fire. "I choose to sacrifice those things, I *want* to sacrifice those things."

"Bullshit." Cade crowded in, close enough to feel the heat radiating off her skin. Her expression softened, and her throat bobbed. "The way we touch each other, the way we look at each other. Don't tell me you can't feel it. This is what people spend their lives searching for." Holding both of her cheeks, he asked, "You're really going to throw it away?"

Say no. Please, say no.

"Yes." Maren twisted her neck. "I know what it's like feeling abandoned by your family. I can't do that to Minowa." Her voice broke. "I can't."

He dropped his arms. Stepped back. Odd, this bodily reaction. No prickle of anger. No tail-curling shame. Her rejection left only sadness. A deep, embedded sting even the finest surgeon couldn't extract.

"I guess that's it then." Cade grabbed the crutches from the adjoining examination room and handed them to Maren. "We should go before Harlowe gets impatient."

Her eyes glistened. "Cade? I'm sorry. I wish ... I wish things were different."

"Me too." He forced a smile. "Come on. Let's go."

They walked to the station without a word. People were gathered around patio tables, glasses clinking and beverages sloshing. The world buzzed with energy and joyful sounds. Meanwhile, his arms practically dragged on the pavement, and static hissed in his ears.

"How do you want to play this?" Maren asked. "We should call Maggie and see if she's got any news. Harlowe should know about her. Then we'll." She stopped and focused on something behind him.

He turned and all the blood drained from his face. That car outside the sheriff's station.

Desdemona's.

Thirty-One

"Cade, wait!" Maren's crutches clicked on the pavement like urgent Morse code. A pitiful pursuit. She made it four paces, and he'd already charged inside the sheriff's station. Dammit. Ignoring her burning armpits, she hurried after him. Clothing racks and chair legs threatened to topple her, but she managed to reach the station unharmed. Standing on the sidewalk, she swore.

Stairs. Why did it have to be stairs?

She grasped the railing and heaved her crutches to the top of the steps. Hopped, hopped. Sweat beaded on her temples, and her breaths were fast and ragged. Climbing six flights of stairs to her apartment was a breeze, but hauling herself up five steps on one foot? Goddamn Everest.

At the top, she rejoiced. Part of her wanted to fist pump like Rocky Balboa after his montage. Instead, she did the sane thing: she gathered her crutches and headed inside.

Wow. New Year's Eve in Times Square. Bodies bustled, phones shrilled, and officers yelled. Maren wrinkled her nose, pushing through the parade of collared shirts and coffee breath.

"Excuse me?" she asked, tapping on the reception desk. Three officers stood with their backs to her. Raising her voice, she called, "Can somebody help me, please?"

The shortest one turned. "Maren, right?"

The officer from yesterday. Glancing at his name tag, she said, "That's right. I'm looking for Cade. Have you seen him?"

The officer, Ronald, jerked his chin at her crutches. "You okay?"

"I'm fine. Do you know where Cade is?"

"He's with the sheriff. Not sure if they'd appreciate being disturbed."

"It's urgent. Please."

His lip twitched. "Take a seat. I'll go see about letting you in."

Maren found an empty chair. Her ankle throbbed, the skin tight and tender. She rubbed the area, keeping her focus glued to the gauze. She could feel people looking at her, and the stares made her itch. Was everybody wondering why she was there? It was a valid question—she'd been wondering the same.

Her presence served no purpose. The biography was canceled and, judging by the way he'd abandoned her outside, Cade no longer needed her help. Her fault, of course. His face flashed through her mind, stark with emotion, asking her to choose him. She'd snubbed the best man she'd ever known, and now, her heart ached so badly it made her sprain feel like a foot massage.

"Maren?" Ronald beckoned her forward. "Come with me."

She followed him around the corner, past offices and interview rooms. They stopped, and Ronald signaled for her to enter.

"She's lying!" Cade yelled, the conference table vibrating under his fist.

"Seemed genuine to me," Harlowe said.

Maren trod inside the conference room and lingered in the corner. Resting her crutches against a bookshelf, she waited for the conversation to die.

"I'm not surprised." Cade looked at the ceiling and shot an exhale. "She's had twenty years of practice."

Harlowe studied him. "Why're you so dead-set on Mona being involved?"

"Because there's no other explanation. She knew about the baby—Bryan's baby—and still let the investigation be shut down. Maybe her and Pepaw covered everything up, paid off the reporters. Your own deputy confirmed she's involved, we just don't know how deep yet."

The sheriff sighed and rubbed his eyes. "We'll sort this out. I sent my guys to pick up Bryan. In the meantime, I need you two"—he waved a finger between her and Cade—"to step back. From now on, we do this by the book. If what you've told me is true and someone really did poison Renee, then we need a professional investigation, not some amateur roadshow. Clear?"

They nodded.

"Now, I've got some questions."

She claimed a spot across from the men, and explained what they had uncovered. Harlowe stayed quiet, nodding occasionally and jotting down notes. With the story recounted, he tapped his pen on the pad and looked at her. "Could arrest you right now for breaking and entering."

She opened her mouth, but Cade spoke first. "You'd have a heck of a lawsuit on your hands, Sheriff."

"Hold your horses." Harlowe flashed his palm. "Was just statin' facts."

"How long has Desdemona been here? Did she tell you anything?" Maren asked.

"She's here on her own accord, and she wants Renee's case reopened."

"She does?" Cade knitted his brows.

"Indeed. Seems something you said last night must've gotten to her. Let me go check if Bryan's here. We'll get this straightened out. You guys stick around. Might need you later."

The door closed. Sun shone through the window, and dust danced in the light. Maren stirred in her seat. She wanted to hold his hand, comfort and console. But that privilege didn't belong to her, not anymore. A simple question was all she could offer right now.

"Are you okay?"

"On a scale of one to ten?" He threaded his fingers through his hair. "About a zero. Why would my aunt come here if she had something to hide? Maybe she isn't involved. Maybe Bryan lied."

She knew he wanted to believe that. Wanted to believe his family hadn't lied to him for two decades. But it wasn't possible for Bryan to orchestrate this alone. Every news outlet in the country had stopped reporting on Renee. No follow-up stories. No articles highlighting the twenty-year anniversary of her death. A small-town deputy didn't hold that kind of sway, but Maren wasn't about to reiterate that to Cade. She'd hurt him enough today.

"I'm sorry for putting you through this," she said.

"Not your fault."

"Some of it is." She twisted her hands in her lap. "My being here probably isn't helpful. If you want me to leave—

"You want to leave?"

"No."

He raised his head. Love brimmed in his eyes and threatened to whisk her to sea. Maren fought the tide. She inhaled deeply, corralling her galloping pulse and grounding her fluttering stomach. But the rope around her heart would take longer to sever. It pulled and pulled.

Breaking away from his intense look, she added, "At least, not now."

"Well, I'll keep you for as long as I can."

And pulled.

"Come on." He stood. "Let's grab something to eat. Got a feeling we'll be here a while."

In the hallway, Cade cleared a path, and she clunked behind him. Her ankle felt better; the throbbing had ceased. Now, it was only her heart that hurt—which appeared incurable. No matter how many times she tried to convince herself leaving was the right choice, it still hurt.

Pathetic. Maren set her jaw and pushed onward. She'd made her decision, and there was no point in second-guessing herself.

The reception area whizzed with whispers of Renee and the deputy. Maren was nearly at the exit when the door clattered open. Cade stopped, and she bumped into his stiff back.

"What's wrong?" she asked, peering around him.

"You son of a bitch!" Lawrence plowed through the crowd, his wild eyes trained on Cade. A few steps away, he cocked his fist.

Greg shot forward and grabbed his wrist. "Calm down."

"Fuck you." He struggled against his brother. "This asshole gets our mother arrested and you expect me to calm down?"

"You think clocking Cade is the best idea right now? Look around, man."

Every officer stared at Lawrence. Some wrinkled their foreheads in concern while others bent their knees, preparing to pounce. Maren white-knuckled her crutches. Drop the fist, please, drop the fist. After everything Cade had endured, the last thing he needed was a brawl with his cousin.

With a huff, Lawrence pocketed his hands.

"Smart move," Greg said. "Stop acting like a caveman and let's talk this through."

"Waste of time." Lawrence snarled at Cade. "You betrayed your family. I'm not listening to any of your excuses."

"Cade didn't do anything," Maren said. "Desdemona was already here when we arrived."

"You." Lawrence pivoted, and she swore she could see a fire blazing behind his irises. "This entire situation is your fault. Is it entertaining, ripping families apart?"

"Lay off, Lawrence."

"Don't touch me," he snapped, pushing his brother away. "Why the fuck would you do this to Ma? To us?"

"I'm surprised you don't know," Cade said. "You're basically Mona's second asshole. Did she not tell you Mom was pregnant when she died?"

Greg jerked back. "She was?"

"Bullshit." Lawrence adjusted his suit sleeves. "We would've known long before now."

"And what about the poison in her system?" Cade stepped forward. "Did you know about that?"

"Poison?"

"Don't believe a word he says, Greg. If this is all true, how come we didn't find out twenty years ago?"

Cade shrugged. "You'll have to ask your mother. She's the mastermind."

"She masterminded nothing. Speaking of which"—Lawrence glanced around—"where is she? If Harlowe thinks he can keep her here, he's got another thing coming."

Cade pointed a thumb over his shoulder. "They're in the interview room."

"Never thought I'd see the day you'd choose a woman over family." Lawrence looked at Maren and shook his head. "Hope she's worth it." With that, he stormed off.

"Sorry, Maren." Greg rubbed his neck. "He's not himself."

"I don't think this situation is easy for anyone."

"Got that right. I'd better go after him. Make sure he's not starting another skirmish."

"Cops can handle it." Cade looked to where an officer was escorting Lawrence to the interview room, then refocused on Greg. "You need to know what's going on."

His cousin nodded and headed for the chairs, walking like his spine was made of steel.

"For what it's worth, I don't think either of them knew," she whispered to Cade. "Greg was shocked. Lawrence, in denial."

"I noticed." He tugged on his earlobe. "I wonder how they'll handle the truth. Doubt any of us get through this unscathed."

Guilt needled low in her belly. She'd barreled into Thurstan Hall, revealing secrets and assigning blame. There'd been no fail-safes, no plans to exorcise the demons she'd summoned. Her life would return to normal soon, but Cade's would be unrecognizable. She'd fractured his family and shattered his heart. How could she have been so reckless?

Maren excused herself and plodded to the bathroom. She needed time alone to calm her mind and gather her thoughts. Her crutches clattered as she maneuvered inside the last stall, and her throat swelled. This was rock bottom, wasn't it? Huddled on a public toilet, crying over things she couldn't change. She wiped her cheeks and shuddered a breath. Pull it together. The sniffles subsided, and she was about to get up when the bathroom door creaked open. Footsteps sounded. Rapid, angry stomps.

"This isn't happening. This can't be happening." A woman's voice. Harmony's voice. "What am I gonna do?"

Maren groaned inwardly. Great, another life ruined. That's exactly what she needed right now. She wanted to take the cowardly way out—lift her legs and wait for Harmony to leave—but her crutches were visible beneath the stall. Apparently, the universe wanted her to face Harmony Coulter. Fuck you, universe. Swallowing hard, she exited the stall.

"Maren?" Harmony croaked.

"Yes." She gripped her crutches to stop her hands from shaking. "Is everything all right?"

"Far from it, cher. They've hauled in Bryan for questioning. My husband, the deputy of this town, is being questioned."

What was she supposed to say to that? Sorry about the infidelity, Harmony. Sorry, you built your life on a foundation of lies. Sorry, my actions revealed it all. That's rough, girl.

Terrible idea. She should stay quiet, let the woman vent.

"People are saying he hurt Renee. You think that's true?"

"I ... I don't know." She touched Harmony's shoulder. "But somebody hurt her, and your husband had a motive."

"Motive?" She whipped around. "What motive?"

Maren bit her tongue. Had she not devastated this woman enough?

"Please, cher." Harmony cradled her hand and gazed up, her eyes beseeching. "Tell me what's happening with my husband."

Where to start? She couldn't be the one to divulge it all; she had enough guilt to deal with.

"It should come from Bryan."

"He won't tell me anything. Never has. I know you two are talking." She squeezed Maren's hand harder, and choked out, "I'm beggin' you, please."

Maren escaped her grasp, and pried open the door, holding it with her good foot. Mustering her best empathetic look, she said, "I shouldn't talk about—"

"The affair?"

Her mouth dropped. "You knew?"

"Some things even Bryan can't hide." Harmony dabbed her eyes. "I had my suspicions. He didn't come home that night. Showered immediately once he did. Even in school, Renee had a hold on my Bryan."

"He never told you?"

"And shatter his 'perfect' marriage?" Harmony scoffed. "Never. Bryan values appearances too much."

"There was ..." She tipped her head back and blew out her breath. Might as well rip the bandage off. "There was a baby too."

Murmurs drifted through the air vents, and pipes clattered in the walls. The faucet leaked, haunting the bathroom with an incessant drip, drip, drip. Harmony stared at the hand dryer, her expression empty of emotion.

"Baby," she whispered. "How'd you find out about that?"

"It's a long story, and there's still so much we don't know."

"Is that the evidence they have against Bryan?"

"For now." Maren inclined her head. "But I won't stop investigating until I find out what happened that night. I promise."

Harmony's lips tightened, a flash of frustration that soon dissolved. Poor woman. The questions must be piling up. Support her husband or believe the allegations? Trust her heart or her brain? The storm of conflict would batter her, drown her in opposite emotions. Anger and sadness, relief and anxiety.

"Could you tell me what you know?" Harmony asked.

Maren wanted to hug her, to tell her that everything would be okay. But that was a lie. Her marriage was broken. Her husband, involved in a murder investigation.

Nothing would ever be okay again.

Thirty-Two

Greg sat with his hand covering his mouth. He'd said nothing for ten minutes. Greg Thurstan, the one always prepared with advice, had nothing to offer. No affectionate shoulder slap. No cheerful "hang in there, man," or "I'm here for you, man."

Jesus, was Cade really missing his cousin's counsel?

Not crazy, given the circumstances. Officers had shunned their deputy, a wife her husband, a nephew his aunt. Relationships were disintegrating and loyalties fading. It wasn't weak to desire normalcy while navigating this dystopia.

Swallowing the bubble of embarrassment, he looked at his cousin. They'd spent years crafting blanket forts and re-enacting their favorite wrestling moves. Surely, they had to share a telepathic connection by now, right? Their eyes locked, and Cade pleaded inwardly. Smile, buddy. Just one smile. One sign that this family isn't teetering on the cusp of a volcano.

His cousin turned away, and goosebumps crept down his body as the dread set in. The last time he'd felt this alone was right after Mom died. He needed something to latch onto, a light to guide him through this suffocating darkness. It wasn't Greg, and as much as he wished otherwise, it wasn't Maren either. The person spurring him forward was ... Mom. She'd made mistakes—like anyone—and died because of them. Was this some twisted version of atonement? Could Bryan be that cruel? Cade needed to find out. For his mother, for himself, and for the baby who was never born.

His cellphone rang. Blocked number.

"Hello?" he asked.

"I've got Ana booked into rehab."

Cade stepped to the window, searching for quiet. He'd been expecting the call from Dr. Garcia, and truth be told, it was a welcome distraction from pondering the destruction of his family. "Which place? I'll organize payment."

She named the facility. "It'll be a long road—for both of us—but this is a step in the right direction."

"I'm glad. How's everything else?"

"I've got an old colleague working on identifying where those toxins came from. Nothing yet. I did, however, get DNA results for the baby. Your sheriff will want to see this. You got any contact information?"

"I can get some." He walked to the front desk, and relayed the contact information back to Dr. Garcia. "Did the DNA match?"

"Yes. Bryan Coulter is the father."

Cade shut his eyes. Hearing the results directly from the doctor made it real somehow. This wasn't a bad dream. Mom had truly been carrying a married man's baby.

"Thanks, Doc," he said. "Call me when you've identified the source of the poison."

"Sure. I know it's not my place, but ... you don't sound too surprised by the DNA results."

"Truth be told, he already admitted to being the father. Officers are speaking with him now."

"They think he was involved?"

"It's an angle they're looking at."

"Interesting." She drew out the word, and he couldn't help but notice the skepticism in her voice.

"What's wrong?" he asked.

"It's probably nothing."

"Tell me anyway."

"Typically, when a man commits murder, he'll opt for something messy. Gun, knife. Those kinds of things. Poisoning is a clean crime."

"You ... you think a woman did this?"

"I think it's very possible. You see—Cade? Cade?"

Dr. Garcia was a whisper in his pocket as he rounded the reception desk and stomped down the hallway. Officers called after him, and he dodged their every attempt to stop him. What had Maren said before? A billion-dollar motive? There was only one woman in the world who had that—and Cade couldn't wait anymore. The ceiling shook as he barged into Desdemona's interview room.

Harlowe jumped to his feet. "What the hell? You can't be here."

Peter and Desdemona sat on the other side of the table while Lawrence leaned against the wall.

"You're not welcome," his cousin spat out.

"Come on now, Lawrence," Peter said. "I'm sure if we sat down and talked this—"

"Did you kill her?" Cade skewered his aunt with a glare. "Did you fucking kill her?" She didn't look up, and his vision flashed red. He stepped closer, but Peter and Harlowe intercepted him. He struggled, staring at Desdemona over their shoulders. "Look at me! Look at me and tell the truth for once!"

"Enough!" Harlowe yelled and turned to Desdemona. "I allowed Peter and Lawrence into the interview room as a favor to you, but I won't have brawling in my station. Cade, wait outside and I'll speak with you after I'm done talking to—"

"It's okay, Sheriff," Desdemona said. "I'd like to speak with Cade alone, if I may."

"You expect me to give you an interview room?"

"Is someone else going to be using it?"

"No, but it's only supposed to be used for official interviews."

"Was this an official interview? As far as I recall, I came in without legal counsel to speak with you about what my nephew told me last night. A conversation between friends. If that has changed ..."

"It hasn't, ma'am."

"Sensational." She swatted the air. "Gentlemen, kindly leave us."

Lawrence's eyes popped. "What? Did you hear what Cade sa—"

"I heard. Please, Lawrence. Leave."

"I'll be right outside," Harlowe said.

"Thank you." The door closed, and Desdemona gestured to the opposite chair. "Sit."

"I'm good."

"Must you be so stubborn?"

He shrugged. "It's hereditary."

She rubbed her arms. "You said some hurtful things."

"Doesn't make them untrue."

"You think I'd kill my sister?"

"I don't know what I think." He strode to the table but didn't sit. "Tell me the truth. Please. You knew Bryan was hiding the autopsy results. Why didn't you say anything?"

"There were other priorities."

"Other priorities?" He shook his head. "Your sister was murdered!"

"We don't know that."

"She was poisoned."

"Poisoned?" Her skin flushed. "That's impossible."

"The autopsy says otherwise."

"But how could he ..."

"Who?" Cade planted his hands on the tabletop. "Tell me what happened."

"You won't understand." Tears shimmered in her eyes.

"Try me."

"I... I..."

Desdemona, speechless? Under different circumstances, it would've shocked him. Today, it enraged him. His mother had lain in her crypt for twenty years without justice—she wasn't waiting another goddamn minute.

"Were you angry she stole the company? Needed revenge?"

"No." She wiped her cheeks. "That's not true."

"Did you get someone else to do your dirty work? Blackmail Bryan into keeping the coroner quiet?"

"You're wrong."

"Then correct me. Or are you afraid? Afraid to admit you killed your sister because of our fucking comp—"

"I never wanted the company!"

Never wanted it?

Cade pulled out the chair and waited for her sobs to stop. Watching Desdemona succumb to her emotion made his stomach roll; he'd never seen her like this. Pale, delicate. Broken. Was this the face of a cold-blooded killer?

"Is that why Pepaw didn't name you his successor?" he asked softly.

"I wanted to paint." She blew her nose into a handkerchief. "Daddy tried to entice me for years. Taking me to the office, introducing me to the board, but it wasn't for me. One day, he sat me down and said Renee would take over."

"That must've felt good."

"One of the happiest days of my life."

"What happened after that?" When she looked away, he reached across the table. "Look what these secrets have done. Our family has turned against each other. A murder has gone unsolved." His hand settled atop hers. "Help me end this."

Silence plagued the room, and for a moment, Cade thought she'd never answer. But finally, she squeezed his fingers. "Renee told me about the affair a few weeks before her birthday. She was so ashamed. To do that with a married man ..." She shook her head. "Sinful. I told her to forget him, and she wanted to. But she couldn't."

"Because of the baby."

"Yes. I was scared Daddy would alter his succession plan after finding out about the pregnancy, so I tried to help her. For weeks, Renee and I discussed options. She refused abortion and adoption; she loved the child. Wanted to keep it."

"Why not raise it on her own? It's not like money was an issue."

"Renee was about to inherit one of the biggest companies in America." Her face twisted as if she'd ingested earwax. "A woman at the reins, that was hard enough for the corporate suits to accept. Could you imagine the uproar if we added new mother to her resume?"

"That's disgusting."

"That's reality." Her smile was tight. Cautious. "Back then, anyway. I believe we've challenged those biases."

What an understatement! The company thrived under female leadership. Desdemona hadn't turn tail when Renee died, despite how badly she'd wanted to. She'd put in the hours and proved the naysayers wrong. This was a woman who never gave up, who protected her family with the ferocity of a mountain lion. This was a woman he needed in his life. The doubt that had been poisoning him crumbled. Cade didn't want to rage. He wanted to understand.

"What happened next?" he asked.

"Renee shared the news with Bryan. He was conflicted. Excited to help raise the baby, but didn't want to leave his wife. Though, as far as I know, their marriage was already on the rocks."

"Three miscarriages will do that."

"I suppose. Renee gave him some time to think everything over. She was planning on following up after her birthday. Never got the chance." Desdemona folded her handkerchief again and again until it was the size of a stamp. "I told Daddy about the baby afterward. It was him who insisted we hide the pregnancy. Said he didn't want to disgrace Renee." Her fingers brushed her chest. "In my heart, I knew the truth. He didn't want to tarnish our reputation. Didn't want scandal plummeting the stock price."

"Why didn't you do something?"

"What was I supposed to do, Cade? Everyone was depending on me to step up and run TIG: my parents, my children, my future grandchildren. Was I supposed to go against Daddy? Let down my entire family?"

"Mom was part of that family."

"She was gone. But you were still here. Lawrence and Greg were still here. If I spoke out against Daddy, it would've affected the business. The business which sustains our entire family. Sustains you. I couldn't change what happened to Renee, but I could still protect the other people I loved."

"What about Dr. Garcia?"

"We told Bryan to monitor her. We wanted to know who she was talking to and ensure we handled them delicately."

"Meaning?"

"We paid for their silence." Desdemona traced a circle on the table. "Bryan continued to keep an eye on the doctor. Made sure she wasn't gossiping about Renee or the baby. He was doing well up until recently."

"What happened?"

"When it became clear Maren wasn't going to drop the Renee business, I called Bryan to make sure he knew where the doctor was. I didn't want Maren finding out about the baby and broadcasting it to the world."

"You were the person on the phone."

"Sorry?"

"Maren was hiding in the office when Bryan took your phone call. She was already looking for the real autopsy report."

"And she found it, I gather."

"Yes."

Desdemona rolled her lips together. "What did it say?"

"You really never saw it?"

"Never." Her posture deflated on her exhale. "Daddy relayed information but never showed me the report. I didn't know about any poison."

"But he must've known. Why sweep that under the rug?"

"I'm not sure. He was raised in a small town where doors are left unlocked. Murder would've been the last thing on his mind." Desdemona fisted her hair. "He must've thought Renee committed suicide. Her mental health wouldn't have been stellar, what with the pregnancy and the stress of transitioning to CEO."

"If that's true, why wouldn't he share his suspicions?"

"He wasn't that kind of man. Always thought he could handle everything himself, carry all the burdens. I only knew about the pregnancy because Renee told me. If it were up to Daddy, I wouldn't have known about that either." She stared at her lap. "I would never hurt my sister, Cade. Never."

"I believe you. But why take down all her portraits?"

"I needed to show everyone that I could successfully replace Daddy. I couldn't focus with reminders of Renee around, so I put everything in storage. And the house staff wouldn't stop talking about her, so I had to let them go. All except Peter. He knew what I was going through. He knew not to talk about her." Desdemona wiped her eyes. "She meant so much to me, and to see her every day, hear about her every day ... I couldn't handle it. Still can't."

"This isn't a healthy way to cope, Auntie. You need to talk to someone and deal with your grief."

"I know. There are many things I would've done differently, knowing what I know now. All these years, Renee's murderer has gone unpunished. I'm so sorry, honey."

Cade walked to the other side of the table and wrapped her in his arms. "We'll make this right."

"I'll help however I can. Can I speak with Maren? I'd like to apologize."

"Sure."

"Cade?" He stopped at the door and glanced at her. "I love you, sweet boy."

The grin took up half his face. Bright, wide, and genuine. "I love you too."

Worry had weighed like sandbags on his body, but now his shoulders were high, his steps confident. He hadn't escaped the depths yet, but light was trickling through the surface. Glimmers of hope. He clung to that hope and walked to where Greg sat—alone.

"Where's Maren?"

Greg glanced up. "Harmony couldn't stop crying, so Maren took her outside."

Of course she did. Woman didn't know the meaning of "take it easy on that ankle".

The streets were quiet as people finished up their shopping trips and loaded their cars. The air was damp and smelled like grease from the restaurants preparing for dinner service. Nobody was sitting on the benches or loitering on the sidewalk. He peered into a few storefronts and scratched his head. With Maren's injury, they couldn't have gone far. He headed to the back of the station, but the lot contained only a handful of police cars. No Maren. No Harmony.

Where the hell—

His phone rang, and Cade removed it from his pocket. "Hello?"

"Me again," Dr. Garcia said. "Is everything okay? I think our last call must've dropped."

"Everything's fine. What's up?"

"I think I've figured out what happened to your mother. Have you ever heard of Atropa belladonna?"

"Is that a drug?"

"It's a plant. Deadly nightshade."

A plant? He blinked, twice. "Are you sure?"

"I've got the results right here. Belladonna poisoning isn't pretty. Convulsions, hallucinations."

His muscles turned to stone. "How would it get in her system?"

"There was a party that night, right? Someone could've slipped it in her food or brewed it into tea. A few berries can kill a full-grown adult."

"Is it native to Louisiana?"

"No. That's the strange part. It's difficult to cultivate too. For someone to grow this, they'd need to be an expert gardener. Do you know anyone like that?"

Thirty-Three

"You missed the turn." Maren twisted in the passenger seat and looked out the window. They'd driven right past Main Street.

"Did I?" Harmony sighed. "My mind is a million miles away."

"I can't imagine what you're going through."

"It doesn't feel real. I had the perfect husband. The perfect life." She glared at the windshield. "All ruined."

Her chest tightened. Harmony had been inconsolable earlier, tears and snot rolling down her face. When they hadn't allowed her to see Bryan, she'd asked Maren to go for a drive and get some air. Maren had accepted; she'd wanted to escape the noise—and Lawrence's scornful stare—but now she was eager to get back and find out how Cade was holding up.

"Thanks for coming with me," Harmony said.

"Of course. You shouldn't be alone right now."

Her hands tightened on the wheel. "I'll have to get used to being alone if Bryan is convicted."

"Nonsense. You've got a lot of friends in this town. Don't be afraid to lean on them."

"Not sure they'll like me much anymore."

"Don't say that. None of this is your fault."

"I know." Her lips curled inward. "It's yours."

She'd expected this—blaming others was a natural reaction to heavy emotional turmoil—so instead of going on the defensive, she said, "We should probably get back." She gestured to the next side street. "Pull in there, and we can turn around." The car didn't slow, and she frowned. "Harmony, you missed the turn again."

"Silly me. We'll catch the next one."

"Okay." She side-eyed the woman. Where was the sagging body and quivering chin? Her sadness seemed to have molted into ... confidence? Something wasn't right.

"Bryan used to take me on this drive." Harmony opened her window and smiled. "I'd sneak out of my bedroom and he'd pick me up down the road, so my father didn't see the headlights."

"That's nice, but ... why're you telling me this?"

"You don't even care, do you?" Her jaw tensed. "Bryan is a good man. He doesn't deserve what you've done to him."

"Pull over here, and I'll call someone else for a ride. You won't have to worry."

"Won't have to worry?" The laugh made Maren's blood run cold. "I've got mortgage bills and business loans, and you've taken my husband away. Believe me, I've got plenty to worry about."

"And I've expressed my sympathy many times. What else do you want me to do?"

"I want you to leave—forever. Then everything goes back to normal."

"Let me out, and I'll be on the first flight to New York."

"I'm afraid I can't do that. You won't stop until the truth is revealed, remember?" The tires whirred louder. "The truth can't come out. Not after everything I've done."

"What have you done?" She glanced at where her purse sat in the backseat. Out of reach. There was no way to grab her cellphone. No way to call for help. She was on her own.

A smile slithered across her lips. "You'll see."

A sign indicated they were leaving Penngrove, and Maren's stomach plummeted. Missing those turnoffs hadn't been accidental; Harmony knew exactly where they were going.

And she was the only one who did.

"I'LL KILL HIM." CADE paced behind the one-way mirror, guzzling his third cup of coffee.

"Take it easy, son," Peter said.

"Take it easy? Maren is missing." He pointed to where Bryan sat in the interview room. "And he's in there with 'no idea' where his wife is. If anything happens—"

"Nothing will happen." He squeezed Cade's arm. "Harlowe's breaking the rules by letting us be in here, and losing control isn't helping anyone. We need you focused. She needs you focused, hear?"

Peter was right: getting angry wouldn't solve anything. Cade apologized to the narrow-eyed officer in the corner, and turned back to the interview.

"I can't help you, Reggie." Bryan leaned back, leveling his gaze on Harlowe. "I don't know where she is. Frankly, even if I did, I wouldn't tell you."

"Why's that?"

"You think I don't know what's going on?" He crossed his arms and jerked his chin at the mirror. "Thurstans need someone to blame and you wanna railroad Harmony."

"All our years working together and you think I'd do that?"

He shrugged. "Money changes people."

"Bribes? No. I just want the truth."

"I told you the damn truth! Yes, Renee was carrying my baby. But I didn't kill her. And neither did Harmony."

"Prove it. Let me bring her in."

Bryan snarled and looked away.

Harlowe neatened his papers. "You never told Harmony about the affair."

"Can you blame me? When Ian Thurstan says to shut up, you shut up. That's not a family you want to cross."

"That's not the only reason." The sheriff laced his fingers and asked calmly, "How was your marriage?"

"Terrific."

"Ain't what I heard. Rumor is you were fighting a lot after the miscarriages." Bryan said nothing, and Harlowe leaned forward. "Throw me a bone, Deputy. Give me something."

He sighed. "We'd lost three babies, and she wanted to keep trying. I didn't."

"Why?"

"She was crying all the time. Falling apart. I hated seeing her like that. If we lost another pregnancy, it'd shatter her, and I wasn't gonna put her through that pain again."

"What about your pain?"

"It was nothing compared to what she went through. I wanted kids, but Harmony needed them. She always wanted the perfect family—to make up for her childhood, I suppose—so losing those babies was like losing herself." He shook his head. "I just wanted her to be happy."

Cade suppressed his scoff. Husband wants his wife happy, yet he sleeps with another woman. That makes sense.

"Then years went by. The bakery was doing well, and I'd been promoted, and we were finally smiling again. It never made sense to tell her about Renee."

"You don't think she knew?"

Bryan rubbed his eyebrow. "How could she? It was one time. One stupid time."

"You know how gossip travels in this town."

"Impossible. I didn't tell anyone, and neither did Renee."

"She told Desdemona. Your secret wasn't airtight."

Bryan shook his head. "If Harmony knew, she would've said something."

"Really? Or would she stay quiet to keep that life you built together?"

"Arrest me." He threw his chair out. "Arrest me or I'm leaving."

Cade mirrored Bryan's movements and strode to the door. This wasn't over. Even if it meant following Bryan through hellfire, he was getting Maren back. He wouldn't lose another woman he loved.

Harlowe slammed his palm on the door, trapping Bryan. "If Harmony thought Renee was stealing you away, would she put a stop to it? Would she kill for you?"

"Get out of my way. Now."

"Will we find nightshade in her garden? Is she still growing it?"

"Harmony didn't kill anyone. You have any other questions, speak to my lawyer."

Cade stormed after Bryan, but the sheriff grabbed his arm.

"Let him go," Harlowe demanded, tightening his grip.

"I just want to talk."

"Sure you do. Settle down, take a walk, and let me do my job."

Cade dropped his head and focused on breathing. His limbs ached, his heart thundered, and he was too weak to move. A familiar paralysis. He'd felt the same twenty years ago when he'd traipsed into the bayou searching for his mother, and look how that had turned out.

He balled his fists. No, this time would be different.

This time, she'd be alive.

"For pity's sake, you're making me gray." Peter came up beside him. "What were you thinking, running after Bryan like—"

"You need to tell me everything you know about Harmony Coulter." Cade stared hard at his butler. Nobody had secrets in this town. Someone knew where she was—and he'd harass everyone to get her back.

Hang on, Maren. Hang on.

"Where are we?" Maren asked.

A side road? No, road was too generous. This was an unpaved strip of land moated by swamp water. Tree branches spanned the sky, creaking like rusty swings. She did a double-take at the dashboard clock. Late afternoon. Impossible. Judging by the darkness, it had to be midnight.

"This is where I grew up," Harmony said.

They rounded the bend, and a building came into view. Its roof sagged, and the walls were nothing but weathered plywood. The car stopped, and Maren moved for her crutches. She wormed between the front seats, the console stabbing into her ribs. She snuck her hand beneath the crutches and slipped it into her purse's front pocket. Her fingers touched the corner of her phone, but before she could grasp it, Harmony wrenched her away.

"You won't need those."

"I can't walk without them."

"They won't do any good out here. Ground's too soft. Come on. I've got something to show you."

Clawing at the door for support, Maren exited the car. Her soles sunk into the muck, and her legs burned as she limped along the footpath. "What're we doing here?"

"You ask too many questions."

"I'm only trying to help."

"Did I ask you to? Did anybody?" Harmony spun around. "It's not right what you've done. Poking your nose into my business, wrecking everything. I was doing fine until you came along."

"I'm sorry I've hurt you but—"

"You're not sorry. Yet." She pushed Maren toward the front door. "Inside. Now."

Enter an abandoned house with this crazed woman? Fat chance. She had to get out of here, but the property was full of pitfalls: thick tree roots and slick mud pits. It was impossible to navigate this terrain one-footed. And with no other houses around, screaming would be useless. Maren had no other choice. Her pulse pounding, she hobbled onto the porch.

A shabby place, with its grime coated windows. The living room was empty except for two upturned, wooden chairs. Even the kitchen had—

Oh my god.

Her vision went spotty, and sweat seeped beneath her waistband. Sitting on the counter, right beside Harmony, was a silver pistol. Adrenaline numbed her extremities. Every ache disappeared, and every thought disintegrated—except one. Get out. Maren dashed to the door, grasped the knob. And the gun blasted. She screamed as the bullet shredded the doorframe.

"Where are you going, huh?" Harmony wagged the weapon, gesturing for her to step away from the exit. "Sit down."

"Please." She squeezed her eyes shut. "You don't have to do this. You don't have to hurt me."

"You sound like me." Harmony tapped her knuckles against a closet. "My parents used to lock me in here for hours. No food. No water." She crossed the kitchen and pointed to the spattering of brown stains. Blood, had to be. "This is what begging got me. Lucky for you, I'm not that cruel."

"I don't understand. Why're you doing this?"

"Because you're trying to take him away!" She threw her arms out, and Maren winced. "Bryan saved me from this. For the first time in my life, I knew what love was and my future was bright. I had a wonderful life and a caring husband."

"He cheated on you."

"It was her fault." Her jaw hardened. "Jezebel."

"Renee?"

"She could've had any man she wanted, but she went after my Bryan. Then gave him the one thing I failed to." She glanced out the window, and Maren followed her gaze. Amid the overgrowth sat three little gravestones. "I used to cower in my room, cursing my parents, and dream of the day I'd have my own family. My children would never feel fear. Never question their mother's love." She pressed her nose against the glass. "That dream never came true. I buried my sweet babies out here, so Bryan wouldn't see me mourn. Seeing me cry always upset him, and I couldn't risk him being unhappy. He was all I had."

"I'm sorry. It must've really hurt that he'd betrayed you." Maren looked around, searching for a weapon or an escape. She'd listen, and she'd sympathize. Keep Harmony talking. Keep her distracted. "But there's no reason to be angry with me. I'm just the messenger."

"The messenger? No." Harmony scoffed. "That was Renee."

"Renee told you about the pregnancy?"

"Came right up and said she's carrying my husband's baby. Such a vile creature."

"Why would she tell you that?"

"Because she wanted me to leave Bryan. Everyone believed she was a good Christian. But good Christians don't seduce married men and have fatherless babies, do they? She needed a husband to uphold her sterling reputation. But she wasn't getting mine. I made sure of that."

She swallowed. "Did you ... did you kill Renee?"

The slow smile told her all she needed to know. All this time she'd blamed Bryan and Desdemona while the true killer puttered under the radar, doling out brownies and beignets. How could she have been so blind?

"She made it so easy too." Harmony chuckled. "A bit of nightshade juice in her soda and poof. She was gone."

"How'd she end up in the pond?"

"I took her for a walk. Wanted to 'smooth things over'. By the time we got out there she was tripping over herself. All it took was a good, solid push. Nobody even noticed we'd been gone."

"That simple, huh? You took away a mother, an aunt, a friend." Rage bubbled in Maren's belly. "And you don't feel a damn thing, do you?"

"She had everything," Harmony spat out. "Money, success, beauty. I grew up with nothing, and finally I had something. I was the deputy's wife. She wasn't going to take that from me." She examined the gun. "And neither will you."

"You think killing me solves anything?" She reached back and grasped the chair, her palms leaking icy sweat onto the wood. "They'll still arrest Bryan even if I'm dead."

"They don't have enough evidence for an arrest. Without you, nobody will follow up." Harmony jabbed the barrel against Maren's temple, accenting every word. "You're the one who pushed this. You're the one who kept asking questions. Everything will die with you."

The woman truly believed it would be over once Maren died. Ridiculous, but she couldn't reason with someone this far gone. She had to take action.

Maren didn't think. She squeezed the chair and threw it over her shoulder. The wood collided with Harmony's head, and the gun skittered across the floor. Maren lunged toward it, voices ringing in her ears. Mom and Minowa cheered her on, and Cade's low whispers propelled her forward. She'd see her loved ones again. She wouldn't die here.

Pain exploded in her leg as Harmony captured her ankle and yanked her down. Maren screamed, and her chin ricocheted off the floor. Harmony slithered toward the pistol, smashing her elbow into Maren's nose. Blood poured into her mouth, and sweat stung her eyes. She had to keep going. Had to keep fighting. Head pounding with adrenaline, she launched at Harmony. Punched her side, desperately trying to drag her back. Amongst the grunts and shrieks, sirens wailed.

Cade. He found her. Holy shit, he found her.

"Police." Maren laughed and loosened her grip. "They're here. It's over."

"No! It's never over." Harmony catapulted forward and snatched the gun. "I won't live without him."

"Stop, don't!" Tears burned as she shielded her face. This couldn't be the end. There was so much she needed to do, so much she needed to say. Squeezing her eyes shut, she recited every word.

Minowa, I forgive you.

Mom, I missed you.

Cade, I love you.

The gun fired.

And the words stopped.

Thirty-Four

SIRENS BELLOWED IN THE distance as Cade stomped on the gas pedal and barreled down the driveway. Branches slapped his mirrors and gravel peppered his windshield. Once they'd learned Harmony's location, the sheriff had ordered him to stay put. His response? Sprinting to the parking lot. Fuck obeying orders. They could arrest him later. He'd serve a dozen life sentences if it meant finding Maren unharmed.

He crested a hump in the road, and the shack appeared, overgrown and rundown—with Harmony's car sitting out front. Thank goodness they were still here. He slammed on the brakes and darted outside, his ribs aching around his thrashing heart. Please be alive. Please be—

The first gunshot stole his breath.

The second shattered his soul.

"No!" He rocketed over the porch and thrust inside. Blood. Everywhere. Pooled on the floor. Spattered on the cupboards. Dripping from her hair. "Maren."

She was kneeling on the floor, her chest rising. His body nearly buckled from relief. Alive. His love, his everything, was alive.

He fell down beside her. "Tell me what happened. Where are you hurt?"

She shuddered. "Sh-she put the gun to her ... and she ... oh my god, she ..."

While Maren choked out sobs, he ran his hands over her body. Cuts and bruises, nothing serious. His tunnel vision waning, he moved to Harmony. Her arms were limp, and her eyes glassy. He pressed two fingers into her carotid. No pulse. Blood matted her hair and oozed from her crown. Suicide. And Maren had witnessed it.

"Are you okay?" He removed his shirt. Cleaned her face, wiped her hands.

"She wanted to kill me." The haunted look in Maren's eyes made his lungs constrict. "And your mother. Jesus, she killed ..."

"I know, baby, I know. Shh." He cradled her, his throat thickening. "You're safe now, hear me? You're safe."

"You found me. I can't believe you found me."

"Damn right, I found you." He held her head against his chest. "And I'm never losing you again."

WAITING-ROOM CHAIRS MADE TERRIBLE beds. Cade yawned, massaging the stiffness in his neck. The darkness outside said he hadn't slept long, and the wall clock confirmed it. Good. They'd admitted Maren hours ago, and he wanted to be there when she awakened.

"Hello." Desdemona approached, skittish as a traumatized antelope. "I hope you don't mind me being here." She suffocated her purse strap. "How is she?"

"Bruised and exhausted." He gestured to the seat opposite, and his aunt sat down. "She'll be on bed rest until her ankle heals, but she's alive."

"Thank God." Looking at the ceiling, she blew a breath. "I can't believe this happened."

"Me neither."

"I hope … I hope you know how sorry I am." She pursed her lips. "Had I been honest from the start, we wouldn't be in this predicament."

"You don't know that."

"I do. I said such awful things. Ripped this family apart." Her voice trembled. "Can you ever forgive me?"

"We never would've found Maren without you. You saved her life, Auntie."

"I-I did?"

"You did. If you hadn't remembered Harmony's old house, we never would've found Maren in time." He looked into her tearful eyes. "As far as I'm concerned, that makes up for all past misgivings."

"Thank you." She patted his cheek. "Oh, I almost forgot. I brought you something." From her purse, she removed his favorite shirt.

He smiled. "How'd you know?"

"Mothers know everything. Besides, I wasn't about to let you meet Maren's family in those bloody clothes."

"Thanks, I didn't"—his head popped through the neck hole—"Wait. How did you know *that*?"

"Peter might've shared his itinerary for this evening. Your mama would be proud." Desdemona framed his face. "You've taken good care of Maren."

"I'm in love with her."

"I know." She kissed his nose and sat back down.

He smiled as Desdemona twisted her lipstick. "What're you going to do about TIG?"

"Pardon?"

"Come on, Auntie. You said yourself running the company was someone else's dream. Isn't it time to pursue yours?"

"Mine?" Her eyes glittered, and dulled one second later. "I couldn't. There's too much to do. The charity gala is coming up and the shareholders wouldn't—"

"There will always be a million reasons to say no." He grasped her hands. "As much as it pains me to admit, Lawrence is ready to take over."

"I'll think about it." Her attention shifted to something behind him. "You've got visitors."

Peter hurried past the vending machines. "Sorry we're late. The airport was insane."

Cade rose as the women neared. Rebecca held his gaze, and he wiped his hand, preparing to shake. But Minowa flew across the room, her blonde hair flailing, and the hug almost knocked him on his ass.

"You saved her life," she whispered into his chest. "Thank you."

"What a greeting," Cade said, patting her back. "I'm not sure what to say."

"You don't have to say anything. Just know you've got Minowa Sharpe's stamp of approval."

She angled away, and he saw Maren in those eyes. Her warmth. Her kindness. Looking into them brought immense comfort, like returning home after months abroad.

"For heaven's sake, Min." Rebecca laughed. "Let go before you strangle the man."

"Oops." Wincing, Minowa stepped back. "Sorry."

"No worries." He smiled and shook Rebecca's hand. "Happy to meet you."

"Likewise. I wish it were under better circumstances."

After introducing his aunt, he led the women to Maren's room, and they peeked inside. The blanket was snug against her chin, and her hair was flared on the pillow. Even when sleeping, the woman left him breathless.

Rebecca shifted. "Peter said her injuries weren't life-threatening."

He nodded and explained the details.

"We're lucky it isn't worse." Minowa stared at her sister. "Should probably let her rest, I guess."

He bumped her arm. "She'll wake up soon anyway. Go ahead. Sit with her."

"No, I'm not ... I'm not her favorite person right now."

"Nonsense. She'll be happy to see you." When Minowa hesitated, he added, "How about this? If she isn't, I'll give you fifty thousand dollars."

She snorted. "You're not serious."

"I'm dead serious."

"That's crazy."

"Then I guess I'm crazy."

"What if you win? I've got nothing to pay you."

"Seeing Maren smile will be payment enough." He tipped his head. "Deal?"

"Deal." She twisted her fingers and took a deep breath. "Okay. Here goes. You coming, Mom?"

"Right behind you." Rebecca paused on the threshold. "Thank you, Cade. For everything."

"My pleasure."

He watched as Minowa leaned into her mother, weeping silently. And he finally understood why Maren couldn't stay.

She was tethered to her sister. Their bond, forged by decades of hardship and interdependency, trumped everything—and everyone. Thurstan relationships were different. In his family, they didn't struggle to survive. But that didn't mean Maren needed a savior. She needed a partner. Someone who would sacrifice and compromise. Cade wanted that honor, to make her feel special, to put her first—and he knew exactly how to do it.

Maren cuddled deeper into the blankets. Her ankle throbbed, her knees stung, and her bones felt as weak as a virgin mojito. One more hour, then she'd get up. Maybe. The heart monitor beeped and footsteps scuttled down the hallway. She wriggled onto her side, inhaling deeply. Chemicals, medications, and ... gardenia? Her eyes sailed open. Minowa stood near the end of the bed, gripping the footrail while her mother sat beside her with one hell of a tan. Was she hallucinating?

"We're so glad you're okay." Mom. Talking. This was no hallucination.

"You're here." Maren rubbed her eyes. "You're actually here."

"Of course, sweetheart." She parked near the pillow. "We couldn't stay home with you in the hospital."

"How'd you know I was here?"

"Cade called. Bought our flights and everything."

Her throat closed. "I can't believe he did that."

"Me neither. Oh, my girl." Mom brushed her cheek. "It's great to see you."

Maren's lips trembled, and she opened her arms. She yearned for the comfort only a mother could provide. Mom dove in, and four years of bitterness evaporated like tears on a stovetop. God, she'd missed this woman.

Mom wiped her cheeks. "We've got lots to catch up on, but I know you two need time. Want anything from the vending machine?" After noting candy orders, their mother left the room.

"Hi." Minowa tucked her hair behind her ears. "How're you feeling?"

"Better."

"That's good." Her glistening eyes met Maren's. "I'm sorry for hurting you. For lying to you. If I'd known how unhappy you were—"

"Come here, Min." She propped up on her pillows and pulled her sister down for a hug. "The blame is on both of us. I should've let you know I wasn't okay. I should've communicated better, and I'll rectify that—starting now." Easing back, she smiled. "I'm glad you're here."

"That's such a relief." Minowa crawled onto the bed and snuggled in. "Even if it lost me fifty grand."

"What?"

She laughed. "Never mind. Cade seems nice."

"He is. We had dinner on a riverboat ..." Maren didn't usually kiss and tell, but for her sister, she did. She shared every swoony moment up until the conversation at Cade's practice.

"He asked you to stay with him? That's incredible."

Maren's heart sputtered. "I let him down easy."

"What?" Her sister sprung to her feet. "This man is an amazing kisser, treats you like a queen, saved you from a homicidal maniac. And you're gonna leave him with a pat on the back and an 'atta boy?"

"That's right."

"Why?"

"We hardly know each other."

"Maren."

She counted the threads in her blanket. "I don't want to leave you."

"You left me like a week ago."

"Must you always argue?"

"It's good practice." Perched on the edge of the bed, she touched Maren's knee. "Stay in Penngrove."

"And abandon you?"

"It's not abandonment." She wriggled closer. "You deserve happiness, Maren. You deserve love."

Who'd given this girl permission to grow up? Maren blinked hard. She'd vowed to raise her sister, to provide protection and support, and scrounge for kindling when she couldn't afford logs. Minowa had gathered those sticks, lit the tinder, and blazed into womanhood. She was strong, selfless, and shining like a solar fire.

Maren felt nothing but pride as she bathed in her sister's warm glow. "Promise you'll be okay without me."

"I'll thrive without your nagging."

"I don't nag," she said, tears streaming down her face.

"You do." Minowa kissed her forehead. "But I love you anyway. Now quit your blubbering and get up. If Cade sees your bedhead, he might change his mind."

"He's seen it." Grinning, she swung her legs off the bed.

"And he still loves you? That's a keeper." Her sister snuck under her arm, and they staggered to the bathroom.

Maren brushed her teeth and combed her hair. Looking somewhat presentable, she faced her sister. "Well?"

"Beautiful. Who doesn't adore hospital chic?" Minowa jumped back and rubbed her hands together. "Now, if you'll excuse me, I'm off to find my future brother-in-law."

"We're not getting marr—" The door shut, and Maren shook her head and eyed her reflection. She could do this. Confess her feelings, broadcast her vulnerability, violate her instincts. Easy peasy.

Feet thumped the floor, and she tensed.

"Maren?" Cade's voice.

"In here." She swallowed.

"You're supposed to be resting."

"I had to pee." She grasped his offered arm. "But I feel great, thanks for asking."

"Wow. Defying death makes you sassy."

Snarling playfully, she climbed onto the sheets. "Have you slept?"

"Some. The chairs here suck." His hair shimmered with grease, and his eyes carried shadows.

"You didn't go home?"

"No," he said quietly. "I didn't want to leave you."

"After our talk, I thought ..."

"I'd stop loving you?" He shook his head. "I'm afraid it doesn't work like that."

Wonderful. Cade hadn't lost his affections, so there was nothing to fear. Stop stalling and tell him. "I'm happy you're here."

"Yeah?"

She nodded. "I wanted ... Well, I was hoping we could talk about ... stuff, y'know? And things."

"Stuff and things?" He raised an eyebrow. "Are you sure you're okay? You didn't hit your head, did you?"

Wimp. She groaned inwardly. "Just tired."

"Any nightmares?"

"None."

"Don't be ashamed if they happen. They're normal after such a traumatic experience."

"I know. Have you spoken to Bryan?"

"Harlowe did."

"I hope he's all right."

"Unbelievable. Still thinking of others after all you've been through." Cade touched her cheek. "You're amazing, you know that?"

"You're not too bad yourself." She leaned in, savoring his warmth, his scent.

"I can't let you go."

"Sorry?"

"I can't let you go, Maren." He inched away and looked at her. "I tried respecting your decision, to accept that you'd never be mine. But you're in every part of me, like this beautiful disease I can't cure."

"Did you just call me a disease?"

"A *beautiful* disease."

"Damn. Look at me swooning." She fanned her face, and he clasped her hand. "You don't have—"

"I love your devotion to family, and I'll never ask you to choose between me or Minowa. But I can't be apart from you, so ..." He inhaled, rubbing his thumb along her knuckles. "I'm moving to New York. I just talked to Mona, and they'll start looking for my replacement at TIG. You, my dear, don't get to say no this time."

She grinned. "I wouldn't dream of it."

This man—this extraordinary man—wanted to leave everything behind for her. Maren's heart fractured her ribs. Cade Thurstan was her first prize, her pot of gold after years of chasing rainbows.

She grabbed his shirt with both hands and pulled. He tumbled on top of her and opened his mouth, but the kiss silenced him. It was urgent and tender, fire and ice. She hungered for his skin, and her hands explored, cupping his nape, petting his face, feeling his stubble. Everything about him, so damn perfect—and he was hers.

Cade retreated. "Not sure the nurses will appreciate our dry humping."

"Coward." She pouted. "Why do I love you again?"

"Wait." His eyes shone like a dog's when the leash comes out. "What'd you say?"

"I love you."

"I love you, too." He kissed her again, soft and slow. "New York. Milan. London. I'd be happy anywhere as long as I'm with you."

"Let's stay in Penngrove."

"Are you sure?"

"Positive." She nuzzled his neck. "Do you know where my phone is?"

"I could find out. Why?"

"I'd like to give Primrose a piece of my mind."

He grinned, tugging her close. "About damn time."

Thirty-Five

MAREN SHUT ONE EYE and made a frame with her fingers. "The banner's crooked."

"Or maybe you are," Cade replied, straightening her head. "Better?"

"No. Can you grab the ladder?"

He groaned. "Again?"

"Third time's the charm." She poked his side and skipped across the street.

It was a lovely day for renovating. The sun was cheerful, the humidity light. Wind chimes jangled and orange leaves fluttered past storefronts. Tourist season had ended, so locals strode the sidewalks. Maren waved to them. Her town, so friendly and colorful, had become her personal paradise.

"You need a hand?" Maren asked Peter as he wrung out a sponge.

"About finished, actually. How do they look?"

"Wonderful." The windows shone like polished pearls. "Did the plywood leave any damage?"

"No, ma'am. We were careful." He leaned back on his heels. "It felt real good pulling that down. How's Cade?"

"Anxiously excited."

"I'm proud of that boy. Never thought he'd find the strength to reopen this place."

A delivery truck rumbled through their side alley, and Maren followed it to the back door. The driver dropped down and headed toward her with a clipboard under his arm.

"Maren Sharpe? Sign here, please."

She completed the paperwork and showed him where to unload the furniture. Couches and tables, bookshelves and office chairs. The place almost looked like a doctor's office now.

"Found the ladder." Cade announced, his sneakers smacking the hardwood behind her. "What're you doing?"

"Admiring our hard work." Sighing, she looped her arm through his. "It's finally coming together."

"We should celebrate."

"How?"

"Great question." Heat blossomed in her neck as Cade gripped her hips. He leaned in, and stubble grazed her cheek. "I'd start by taking off your shirt." He slid his hands upward, his thumbs tickling her ribs. "Then your bra. You wearing one, baby?"

Shit, that voice. Hot and seductive, stemming from deep within the chest. It made her abdomen clench. But they couldn't do this. Not now.

She glanced at the windows. "Your family is—"

"Hush," he demanded, corralling her into the darkened exam room and claiming her mouth. His tongue was fervent, coaxing her open as his fingers skimmed over her bra. "You want to know what comes next?" His lips moved to her jawline, and she tipped her head back. He hovered, exhaling a hot breath. "Answer me."

"Yes." She arched and pressed against his arousal. "God, yes."

"I'd run my tongue up your stomach. Between your breasts." He coiled her hair around his fist. Tugged. "Take one of your pretty nipples into my mouth. Lick you. Tease you." Cade's teeth sunk into her shoulder.

Static growled in Maren's ear. Her pulse and his words, the only sounds breaking the barrier.

"These would come next." A finger crooked in her waistband. Nails scraped denim. Lips scorched skin. "Slip my hand between your legs. Feel you, aching to be fucked." His thigh inched forward and urged her open. Enticing her to play his game, tightening that knot of desire low in her belly. "You'd be ready. Wet. Panting."

She gasped. Closer. Had to be closer. Maren nestled beneath his jaw, her arms lacing his neck. Heat radiated from his body, and she fastened to him. The man who filled her heart, livened her spirit—and made her tremble with desire.

"I'd test you first." The promise captivated her ear, and he captured her lobe in his mouth. "Slide one finger in. Maybe two. But you'd want more, wouldn't you?"

"Yes." She moved her palms down his back, so smooth and muscular. She touched the button of his shorts, but he snatched her wrists and trapped them behind her.

"So desperate." Cade tsked, pinning her with those lustful eyes. "Be patient, my love. By the time I'm done, you'll be on your knees, begging me to fuck you."

"Hey, get out here!" A voice called, but her brain was too mushy to decipher whose it was.

"Coming." He backstepped. Smirked. "Looks like story time is over."

"Wait." On wobbly legs, Maren stomped in pursuit. "Seriously?" He vanished outside, and she gaped at the doorknob. That man was a goddamn sadist.

After cleaning herself off, she went outside and grinned at the car pulling up. "What happened to the board meeting?"

"Canceled it," Lawrence said, climbing from the car and removing his suit jacket. "I wouldn't miss today."

"What's so special about today?"

"Oh. Nothing." He scratched his throat and looked away. "Isn't your family leaving?"

"You'd never cancel a meeting for that. What's going—"

"Speak of the devil." He shot his arms out. "Minowa, Rebecca. How the heck are ya?"

"We're good," Minowa said slowly, cocking her head. "Are you okay?"

"Me? I'm fantastic. Running a business, you know how it is. Busy, busy, busy." His chuckle sounded forced. "Think I'll go see where Cade's hiding. Bye, ladies."

"Goodbye." Mom stared after him. "Don't think I've ever seen him nervous before."

"It's like seeing a two-headed cobra. Intriguing, yet deeply unsettling." Maren helped her family with the shopping bags, and escorted them back to the practice. "Find anything good?"

"You should see the portraits we got. They'll go perfect in your reception area." Minowa gazed onto Main Street. "I wish I could stay longer. We never went thrifting, Maren."

"We can go in December."

"But you're starting on Monday. What'll you wear?"

"I don't know. This?" Maren thanked Peter, who held the door open for them.

"*That?*"

She laughed. "I'm assisting the museum head. Not Louis Vuitton." Piling the bags on the front desk, Maren smiled. Furniture, check. Décor, check. Doctor—she looked through the windows—uncheck. Where had Cade gone?

"SHE KNOWS. THEY ALL do." Lawrence paced, his hair crackling as he thrust his fingers through it.

Cade rolled his eyes. "Calm down."

"I was subtle. But that Maren, she's a human lie detector." He wiped his forehead. "And Minowa's like a truth vulture."

"Hey, I'm supposed to be the nervous one."

"I'm not nervous." He corrected his posture and twisted his cuff links. "I'd just despise myself if I bungled your proposal."

"Why?"

"With that hullabaloo last summer ... I don't want to disappoint you again."

"I wasn't disappointed. Pissed, sure." He squeezed Lawrence's shoulder. "You were protecting your ma. I understood that. Still do."

A sedan rolled into the parking lot, and Greg climbed out.

Lawrence gave a slow clap. "Look who finally showed up."

"Fuck off."

Cade tilted his head. "What put the bee in your bonnet?"

"Sorry." Greg winced. "The flight was delayed and traffic moved slower than a hungover sloth. I'm not the Thurstan chauffeur, y'know."

"Would you rather be installing baseboards and washing windows?" Cade asked.

"Honestly—"

The rear door whipped open, and Desdemona flew out, throwing her arms around Cade. "Hello, my dear! We're not too late, are we?"

"You're right on time. How was Tahiti?"

"Sensational." His aunt looked up, barefaced. "Lovely retreat. Great grief counselors. Those two months on the beach were like salve on my soul. But I missed my boys." Her sneakers squeaked as she kissed Lawrence's cheek. "Where's my future daughter-in-law?"

"At the practice. I didn't want her seeing you because she'd know something was up."

Desdemona bounced on her toes. "I'm over the moon for you two. Shall we?"

"Sure." Cade inhaled, fiddling with the ring box in his pocket. "Why don't we—"

"Hold on." She withdrew something from the car. "There. Ready."

He stared at the flower vase. "You ... you brought magnolias?"

"I wanted her with me for this." Closing her eyes, Desdemona tipped her nose to the sky. "Miss you, Renee."

"Miss you, Mom."

Sunshine warmed his face, and birds chirped on the branches. There she was: mom, wrapping him in light, cheering him on, always present.

Lawrence patted Cade's back. "Peter's probably ripping his hair out trying to keep Maren occupied. You ready?"

"Yeah."

Greg hooted. "Let's get you hitched!"

"Cade and Lawrence—two men who have never set foot in a supermarket—went grocery shopping." Maren tapped her foot. "That's the story you're going with?"

Peter dunked his sponge into the bucket. "Yes."

"Aren't groceries your job?"

"I'm getting old." He straightened and stuck out his belly, feigning a back injury. "Can't do manual labor anymore."

She gestured to the cleaning supplies. "You're doing it right now."

"What can I say? My bosses are drill sergeants."

"Relax, Maren," Mom said. "Come eat."

"Fine." She headed to the grassy patch where Minowa and her mother sat on a picnic blanket, and reached for the takeout bag. "How's the food?"

"Amazing." Minowa bit into her pasta. "For a small town, Penngrove has decent food options."

"Have to keep the tourists happy. And the locals." Maren was pleased to see people trickling into the restaurant next door—the building had lain vacant for months after Bryan left town.

She was sweeping the crumbs off her shirt when Cade walked toward her. Hopping up, she asked, "Where were you?"

"We were, y'know ..."

"Grocery shopping," Peter called.

Cade kissed her head. "Grocery shopping, exactly."

"You're lying."

"No, I'm not. Hey, did you know the banner's crooked?"

"Are you—" She snorted. "I've been trying to fix that for twenty minutes."

"You should've said something." He waved toward the ladder. "Peter, can you...?"

"Why can't you go?" Maren nudged him with her elbow. "Afraid of heights?"

"He needs the exercise."

"Sure, he does." She turned away from Cade and focused on Peter. "Higher on the left ... little more ... Perfect."

Everything had led to this moment. The renovation delays and supply issues, the nights spent collecting assurances from townsfolk to never harass fellow patients—it'd worked wonders in convincing Cade to reopen. After everything he'd done for her in the last year, the man deserved to do what he loved: helping others.

Maren read the banner—Thurstan Family Medical. Opening Soon!—and her heart somersaulted. It was really happening; Cade was finally resurrecting his dream.

"Do you like it?" She spun around. Froze.

Everyone stared. Lawrence, Greg, Minowa, even Peter had scurried over. And was Desdemona standing next to him? When did she get back? Smiles balled their cheeks, and their expressions brimmed with anticipation as if she was a magician rummaging through her top hat.

"What's going on?" she asked Cade.

"Sorry about the audience. They'd promised to stay away until afterward"—he fired them a glare—"but stubbornness runs in both our families, I guess."

"But why ..."

Cade drew out a small box and opened it. The ring sparkled with simple elegance. She stumbled backward and flung her hand to her chest. He claimed the other and squeezed.

"I was frozen when I met you. Immobilized by guilt and regret, but you thawed me. With your kindness. Your humor. I love you, Maren. And I'd like to spend the rest of my life loving you." He rubbed his thumb over her knuckles. "Will you marry me?"

"Yes!" She latched onto him, happy tears staining her cheeks.

He encircled her waist and lifted her off the ground while their families cheered and congratulated them. She burrowed into his shoulder and closed her eyes. The fight was over; at last, she had everything she needed.

A belly full of food. A soul full of hope.

And a heart full of love.

WEDDING BELLS ARE RINGING in Penngrove, and you're on the guest list! Would you like to see Cade and Maren exchange vows? By signing up to my newsletter, you'll gain access to this exclusive bonus scene, and be the first to know about upcoming releases and giveaways. I'd love to have you! To take advantage of this offer, please visit: www.kaileesaunders.com/bonuschapter

ACKNOWLEDGEMENTS

I'll be honest, part of me still doesn't believe I'm writing this section. The acknowledgements. The end of the book. The end of a journey, really. Because that's what Bitter Bayou was: a journey. Writing this novel filled me with so many emotions. Good, bad, and everything in between. Without my unwavering support system, I never would've crossed this finish line.

Grandma Edie. You put that first romance novel in my hands and introduced me to a genre that has brought an intangible amount of joy to my life. Such a crazy grandma move, to give her teenage granddaughter a book full of sex, but I'm so grateful you did. Love you always.

Maaam. Are there any words? You'd crawl through hot coals for your children, and I can't begin to thank you for all the sacrifices you've made. Even if I'm thousands of kilometers away, I know you're always in my corner. The word "mother" elicits such warm feelings for me, and that's because of you.

Daddio. Well, I finally finished this damn thing! No matter what adventure I pursue, you're always there to hype me up. Moving to Toronto? I'll give you the tour. Writing a book? Let me know when it's done so I can shout it from the rooftops. Your strength and kindness never fails to amaze me.

Mami, you were my first reader, and you loved Bitter Bayou even when it was terrible. I'm so thankful for all your encouragement and kind words.

Tati, you're always available to offer a smile and a laugh. Thank you for cheering me on even when I felt like giving up.

Rebecka, my amazing editor. You never gave up on me and always pushed me to be better. Thank you for sharing your knowledge—and your patience!

Bianca, for taking my cover design ideas and turning them into something wonderful!

To my Vlad. For always lifting me up and believing I could fly. You are everything to me, and I love you more than anything in the world.

And lastly, to you! By reading this book, you're making my dreams come true, and that means so much to me. Thank you for taking a chance on a new author!

Growing up, Kailee wasn't the artistic one. In fact, her macaroni portraits consistently received failing grades (but the way her mother treasured them you'd think they were crafted by Van Gogh). She couldn't dance, sing, or paint. But write?

Oh, how she loved to write.

And when she received her first romantic suspense novel from her grandmother, Kailee's world changed. Because in those pages, between the sexual tension and adorable banter, she discovered her muse.

Today, she inhabits the snowy plains of Eastern Canada, living her own happily ever after with a man who puts all her fictional heroes to shame. With her word processor forever within arm's reach, she's building her author dreams one book at a time.

To keep up with all her latest releases, sign up for her newsletter or follow her on social media! All links can be found on her website: www.kaileesaunders.com